the A U T O B I O G R A P H Y *of* G O D

the AUTOBIOGRAPHY of GOD

❧

a novel by Julius Lester

🦁 ST. MARTIN'S GRIFFIN ⋈ NEW YORK

www.stmartins.com

Book design by Jonathan Bennett

Library of Congress Cataloging-in-Publication Data

Lester, Julius.
    The autobiography of God : a novel / Julius Lester.
        p. cm.
    ISBN 0-312-28820-4 (hc)
    ISBN 0-312-34848-7 (pbk)
    EAN 978-0-312-34848-9
    1. Jewish women—Fiction. 2. Holocaust, Jewish (1939–1945)—Fiction.
3. Counseling in higher education—Fiction. 4. Jews—Poland—Fiction.
5. Torah scrolls—Fiction. 6. Women rabbis—Fiction. 7. Vermont—Fiction.
I. Title.

PS3562.E853A97 2004
813'.54—dc22   2004046820

10 9 8 7 6 5 4 3 2

In memory of my relatives who died during the Holocaust

Julius Weil, Concentration Camp, Gurs, France
Siegfried and Sonial Weil, Auschwitz
Else Wolfsheimer and family, Sobibor

and

For my wife, Milan,
who sustains me

the AUTOBIOGRAPHY *of* GOD

ONE

❧

It had arrived.

Rebecca placed the receiver in the cradle of the phone as if returning a keenly honed sword to its velvet-lined case. She slumped back in the office chair and stared at the computer screen but her eyes did not see the words of the case file flickering there.

It had arrived.

When she got home, it would be lying on the front room floor in the early darkness of naked autumn. On any other day she would have come in, placed whatever she was carrying—books from the college library, groceries, the *New York Times*, the mail—on the long black mahogany table, taken off her coat and laid it over the back of the black leather couch, sat in her rocking chair and gone through the mail. But tonight she would hurry along the hallway past the front room and the adjacent middle room and rush up the stairs.

That's what she had done last summer when she came home and saw a furry brown bat hanging upside down from the exposed beam in the front room. After a sleepless night of hearing the bat's wings slicing distress into the air, she got the stepladder and a frying pan.

There had been a problem, however. It was Saturday morning, Shabbat, an early summer Shabbat morning when the air was so soft and gently warm she felt awash in holiness. "*Uvtuvo m'chadeish b'chol*

1

yom tamid maaseih v'reisheet," she said to herself, quoting from one of the Shabbat morning prayers—"In Your goodness, day after day, You renew creation."

Could she kill a bat on Shabbat? Somewhere in the Talmud one of those crazy Galilean rabbis had to have asked, *Is it permissible to kill a bat on Shabbat?* Unfortunately, her set of Talmud was in the front room—with the bat. Then she wondered: was a frying pan kosher after you killed a bat with it? A good Orthodox Jew would've resolved the questions before acting. Being a Reform Jew (and a good one) she balanced herself on the stepladder (her left foot on the lower step), hit the bat with enough force to smash an atom, and threw it and the frying pan into a large black garbage bag, the kind with a drawstring, which she pulled tight and dropped into the green trash barrel in the garage.

The problem *it* posed could not be resolved so directly, especially since she did not know why she thought a problem existed. But she would let it lie there, which is what it had been doing for more than fifty years anyway. What would another day matter?

She supposed she should call Saul and Patric and tell them it had arrived. More than anyone, they had pressed her to send away for the Torah scroll. That had been five years ago. There was no need for it now, though Saul and Patric might try and convince her otherwise.

Saul Greenberg was an enormous man, a reputed computer genius who taught at the college. He had grown up on Long Island where, on Sunday mornings and Tuesday and Thursday afternoons, his parents and a hundred others deposited their children at temple for Hebrew school to learn the rudiments of Hebrew and something about Judaism and Jewish history. Rebecca didn't know what had happened or when, but something had transformed Saul into a Jew who prayed the requisite three times a day, seven days a week, his body bending rapidly back and forth as if he were the victim of uncontrollable spasms. Despite such pious earnestness, he told her once that his soul was as parched after prayer as it had been before. Rebecca was afraid Saul would see the scroll's unexpected arrival as a sign from God. Whatever the scroll's arrival might mean, Rebecca knew it wasn't that.

She had no idea how Patric would interpret its coming. She had not seen him after what happened at his house on New Year's. She missed him. He had been the first faculty member to befriend her when she had come to work as a therapist at John Brown College five years ago. Rebecca had been flattered that one of the country's leading authorities on religion would want to be friends with her, a failed rabbi, but he seemed to enjoying talking with her, especially about religion, something she knew little about besides Judaism. He was a devout Episcopalian, though she wasn't sure what that was exactly. She had never understood the differences between the various Christian sects nor why there were so many of them. They all believed Jesus was the son of God who died and rose from the dead to save everybody from sin. What was left to disagree about? Having grown up in the Williamsburg section of Brooklyn and attended yeshiva until she went to Columbia, Rebecca had never had a reason to think much about Christianity. She had not had to confront one of the religions Judaism had birthed until she became rabbi of Temple Sinai in suburban Pine Grove, New Jersey (which was devoid of pines and groves), and found herself invited to participate in interfaith services and have lunch with ministers eager to display their Christian liberalism by eating with her at Hunan Israel, the kosher Chinese restaurant in the next town.

Perhaps the five years of hearing her ministerial colleagues piously refer to what they called the "Judeo-Christian tradition" led her to say more than she intended that October afternoon of her first year when she and Patric were chatting in a booth at The HangOut, the café on the lower level of the Student Activities Building.

He made some reference to the "Judeo-Christian tradition" and gave her an unctuous smile like the ones Jim Swisher, one of the ministers in Pine Grove, used to bestow on her, as if he were making her an honorary Christian. Sitting there opposite Patric and feeling herself getting angry, she realized for the first time how stressful it had been to maintain clerical cordiality with her Christian counterparts.

"Did I say something wrong?" Patric asked, forcing Rebecca to bring her mind back from Pine Grove.

She looked across the table at him. He returned her gaze, bewildered by the anger he saw in her eyes. His face, covered with a neatly trimmed white beard and mustache, was lean as he was. The full head of dark hair was streaked with enough gray to make him look like a very distinguished sixty-three-year-old. Most striking was the softness in his dark eyes. What had he done in his life that God had rewarded him with eyes that gleamed so fiercely with kindness?

"You happened to touch one of my pet peeves."

"Which is?"

"I don't think there is such a thing as the 'Judeo-Christian' tradition," she answered.

"And why is that?"

"Well, it implies that Jews and Christians believe in the same things, and we don't."

"We share a common scripture," Patric put in.

"Not really. Christians appropriated Jewish scriptures as their own. The Christian Bible is primarily Jewish scriptures, which you call the Old Testament. The Jewish Bible does not contain your so-called New Testament."

The kindly eyes narrowed but Rebecca was back at Hunan Israel telling Jim Swisher all the things she had been too young and shy to say six years ago.

"And then there's Jesus," she continued. "In ancient Israel each year at Yom Kippur, Jews symbolically put all their sins on Azazel—a goat—and sent him into the wilderness, taking our sins with him. I've always thought it arrogant and presumptuous for a man to proclaim himself scapegoat for the world."

Rebecca stopped, having been far more blunt than she had intended. She waited tensely for Patric to refute her petulant assertions with a litany of scholarly references. Instead he smiled wryly, shook his head, and chuckled softly.

"You know, I'm supposed to be an authority on religion and yet, with a few simple sentences, you made me realize that I know nothing about Judaism. I've spent months at Zen monasteries in Japan, with Hindu holy men, with the Dalai Lama. I've been to the Wailing Wall in Jerusalem but I've never taken the time to study in a yeshiva. I've appeared on panels with rabbis but can't recall ever having a conversation of any length with one—until now. I've always assumed that Jews and Christians had so much in common there was no need for me to examine Judaism closely."

A few days later he called and asked if she would consider leading Shabbat services at her home a couple of times a month to help an ignorant Gentile educate himself. He added that he had spoken with some Jewish faculty members who said they would be interested in coming. She doubted that the few Jews at the college or the ones scattered through the mountains of northern Vermont near the Canadian border were really interested. Jews only moved to the most remote part of one of the most rural states because he (and she) wanted to get as far away from other Jews as possible.

She had no desire or intention of being a rabbi ever again, but she couldn't say no to Patric, flattered that he thought she had something to teach him, he whose books and tapes on religion were very popular. He had also hosted a popular fourteen-week series on religion for a cable network during that awful spring when she and her husband were separating and she was deciding to leave her congregation before they fired her.

But flattered as she was, Rebecca's first impulse had been to say no so loudly it would've been heard in Montreal. She didn't want to spoil a perfectly good Shabbat with services. Having spent the week counseling students, staff members and even an occasional professor, she looked forward to being alone on Shabbat. But once she began considering the idea she found herself fantasizing about her home becoming a place where Jews came to worship and study and, in so doing, redeemed her failure as a congregational rabbi. In nervous anticipation of that first service she duplicated ten copies of the opening prayers, psalms and morning service from a siddur, and that week's Torah portion and translation from a Chumash. She was surprised when twelve men and three women crowded into the front and middle rooms of her house.

She led the service singing the prayers in Hebrew in her beautiful soprano voice, gratified that many sang along with her. With the completion of the morning service, it would have been the time in a synagogue to take the Torah from the ark and read from it, but she had no Torah scroll. Instead she led a discussion on the Torah portion which that week was Noach, the story of Noah and the flood, among other things. The excited conversation extended well into the afternoon.

Rebecca dared hope her redemption was at hand, but as autumn meandered toward winter, the group's interest in talking about the week's Torah portion, God and holiness was not as compelling as sharing their adolescent memories of the rebbetzin's greasy cholent, the sweetness of the lokshen kugel made by this one's grandmother, the tenderness of the brisket made by that one's mother, and how another could not hear the Kol Nidre without remembering how he felt as a little boy standing next to his grandfather, enveloped by the huge *tallis* draped over the old man's shoulders. Their Jewishness consisted of little more than shtetl nostalgia, something American Jews from deracinated suburbs were prone to since they did not speak Yiddish or Hebrew and thought they were being good Jews when they ate bagels, lox and cream cheese on Sunday morning.

Many of them had moved to Vermont in the late sixties and early seventies to pursue a back-to-the-land fantasy, though most had been New Yorkers whose walking on the land until then had consisted of the grass in Central or Prospect parks. But they had learned to walk not only on grass but on snowshoes to care for livestock when the temperature was twenty below and in heavy boots through the viscous mud of spring thaws. It had not taken long for them to realize that there was no romance in the vagaries of farming and raising livestock and some discovered a talent for making pottery or cutting boards, wooden spoons, salad bowls and lamps to sell to vacationing New Yorkers who projected a nostalgia for Eden onto Vermont. One had discovered he had a talent for making dowsing rods while another had made a small fortune by pressing and sealing Vermont's famous autumn leaves into hard plastic cases and selling them. (Native

Vermonters did not understand how the state had come to embody the American ideal of pastoral virginity, but they did what they could to profit from the projection.)

Married to non-Jews, they had settled into contented non-Jewish lives on Vermont's steep back roads, had children and, the next thing they knew, twenty years had passed and one day dim ancestral memories were awakened when they heard that a rabbi had moved to the area and Saturday morning services were being held at her house and one Saturday morning they told their families they were going out, just out, no place specific enough that a spouse or one of the kids would ask to come along, and they came to the services, some with wary curiosity, others with the nervous enthusiasm of puppies. They were surprised when they walked in and saw someone they had known for fifteen years but neither had known the other was Jewish. There was even one couple whose wife learned for the first time that her husband was a Jew and she wondered what else he had hid from her but she would always be afraid to ask.

One Saturday morning before the group's appetite for nostalgia had been sated, Saul had asked Rebecca how they could acquire a Torah scroll for their nascent congregation. The others became excited. Rebecca didn't want to squelch their enthusiasm, but even a small scroll cost upward of twenty thousand dollars.

"But you can't have a Jewish community without a Torah scroll," Patric had put in.

That wasn't true, Rebecca corrected him. "The first thing Jews do when they want to start a community is acquire land for a cemetery. You can have a community without a Torah scroll. You can't have one without a cemetery."

At the next service two weeks later Saul announced he had

information about a place in England where Torah scrolls stolen by the Nazis had been deposited after the war and the scrolls were sent out on permanent loan to any congregation that requested one.

"But we aren't a congregation," Rebecca argued.

"But we will be," Saul insisted. "We will be."

Everyone present pleaded and begged her to write a letter to the repository and request a scroll. Against her better judgment, she did. Ironically, only seven people came to the next service. There had been snow that Saturday morning but many people, including her, had four-wheel-drive vehicles, and snowfalls of six inches or less did not stop Vermonters from going wherever they wanted to. But attendance continued to decline until the Saturday morning in late February when only Saul and Patric came.

What had happened in New Jersey had happened again, only this time she did not have to watch it taking place over five long years. If she had been a good rabbi, that is, if people had felt she had something to offer, they would have continued coming. Two Saturdays a month. How onerous a commitment was that?

A synagogue's membership increased when the rabbi spoke words that caused beauty to flower in the soul. The membership at Temple Sinai had dwindled steadily during each of her five years, and so what if members had been moving to the next town where there were trees, even groves of them. The synagogue board had wanted to move the synagogue, too, and they finally voted to do so over her protestations. After such a rejection of her leadership she'd had no choice but to resign. She'd heard the new temple's membership had increased by almost half. Maybe that was because her successor wanted people to call him Bob and he didn't mind playing golf on Saturday afternoons at the country club with the Catholic priest.

Maybe that had been her problem. The congregation had wanted a friend, not someone who insisted on being addressed as Rabbi, someone responsible for a two-thousand-year-old tradition whose focus was how to meld holiness into daily life. If people addressed her as Rabbi, she had thought, they would be acknowledging that tradition and possibly begin living in closer relationship to it, something not possible if they addressed her as Rebecca.

But that wasn't it, she concluded. She hadn't spoken to their needs. If she had, they would have driven the fifteen miles back to the synagogue each Shabbat to hear her, to be with her. This wasn't unreasonable because, every year at Rosh Hashanah, thousands and thousands of Bratslaver Hasidim flew from Israel and the United States to Uman in the Ukraine to begin the new year at the grave of their founder, Rebbe Nachman of Bratslav, who died in 1810. Dead, he inspired more Jews than she ever had, even though, through some accident of fate, she carried the same surname.

Patric tried to convince her that the weather was responsible for the drop in attendance. Saul wondered if some of the non-Jewish spouses were feeling threatened by this sudden interest in Judaism on the part of their husbands. After all, for the past twenty or more years these were families that had gone to church together, celebrated Christmas, bought new clothes for the kids at Easter and hidden dyed eggs around the house for them to find.

Rebecca remained convinced that people had stopped coming because she didn't know how to communicate the beauty of Judaism in a way that would have made them realize they were being given a handful of diamonds, each one of such dancing brilliance that, like God, they could not be looked on directly.

Patric and Saul would probably still be coming. She understood the spiritual emptiness of Saul's life. Jews like him had wandered into her office at the synagogue thinking God was found in ecstasy. She supposed that was true for Hasidic Jews, but she, like most Jews, distrusted an excess of emotion where God was concerned. Feelings came and went like thundershowers in August. If God resided anywhere, she told Saul the one time she had made the mistake of going out with him, it was in despair and hopelessness. She knew.

Rebecca understood the emptiness in Saul. He was looking for God in his emotions instead of being still and letting God find him. But she was baffled by the void she perceived in Patric. How could a man who knew as much as he did about religion look at her as if she had something he needed? More than once during services she had seen him staring at her, his eyes pleading like those of a cocker spaniel wanting to be let into the house. She was sorry now that she had not been able to imagine what Patric thought she could give him. If she had, she would not now have to live with the painful memory of New Year's Day.

She had put an end to the services one Friday afternoon in March after meeting with a female student with a pierced lip, tongue and nose whose hair was orange on one side and purple on the other and listening to her talk for an hour, without inflection in her voice or expression on her face, about being abused by her alcoholic mother. When the student finally left, Rebecca sat at her desk, unable to move. She wasn't sure why that girl's story hurt her more than all the other stories she'd heard. That's what rabbis and therapists did; they listened to the horrors people endured in the belief that the mere listening was healing.

Perhaps it was the accumulation of all the stories, or perhaps it was her fear that talking about wounds merely inflamed them. Perhaps some wounds never healed and you had no alternative but to live with

11

the pain as best you could. All Rebecca knew that Friday afternoon was that if she had to open the siddur the next morning and read anything about God's goodness and how much He cared (*Ad heinah ahzahrunu rachamecha, v'lo ahzahvunu chasadecha*—To this day Your compassion has helped us, Your kindness has not forsaken us) she would either burst into tears, explode in a tirade of profanity or throw the siddur through the window. She called Patric and Saul and told them that Temple Beth Rebecca was closing its doors forever and hung up.

At the time she had thought of writing the repository in England and withdrawing the request for a Torah scroll, but she assumed they would investigate and discover there was no synagogue in Brett, Vermont, and that would be that. In the intervening four and a half years, she had forgotten about it until Mr. Applewhite, the postmaster, had called a few minutes ago.

"A crate from England is here for you."

He was the town storekeeper and postmaster. Within a month after she moved to Brett, Mr. Applewhite knew that a Brooklyn postmark was her parents, while New Jersey would be a former congregant, and Israel, friends. He had called her at her office shortly before Rosh Hashanah that first year to tell her she'd gotten a postcard from her mother, who was flying in to Burlington at four and "she's expecting you to meet her. Seeing that would be about the time you get your mail out of your box, and it's an hour's drive, she'd be worrying a while. I hope you don't think I'm being nosy or anything like that. In a town our size we tend to look out for each other."

Rebecca's mother had never entirely left Auschwitz. If she had been afraid to travel from Brooklyn to New Jersey to see "my daughter-the-Rabbi" lead services at her very own congregation, she wasn't coming to Vermont. Every year right before Rosh Hashanah, Hannah sent postcards to her cousin in Israel, another cousin in England, and friends who were also survivors, announcing arrivals everyone knew not to expect. The postcards were her way of making the visits.

The next morning Rebecca had taken Mr. Applewhite a jar of grape jelly she'd made just the week before from the Concord grapes she had seen hiding under enormous leaves of vines twining around a poplar tree just beyond the place where the road came to an abrupt end. When he asked if her mother had gotten in all right, she told him her mother had spent a year in Auschwitz and seldom left the house except to go to the hairdresser's and Bloomingdale's. She said it as casually as if she had commented on how beautiful the foliage was, and just as she did not feel responsible for the orange-red leaves of sugar maple trees, she felt no responsibility for her mother's inability to have a life outside or even inside the small, dark apartment she shared with Rebecca's father. Indeed, Rebecca had concluded that she did not like her mother, which was all right. How could you be expected to love or even like someone whom you'd had no choice about knowing? The Torah didn't say you had to love or even like your parents. Honor your father and mother. That was reasonable.

Rebecca assumed Mr. Applewhite had repeated the little story about her mother to his wife who repeated it to someone else's wife, or maybe her grape jelly had been better than she thought because after that morning people tapped their horns and waved when they saw her driving down the rutted hill called Pulpit Road, past the Gentrys' place, onto county road number 323 and into the center of Brett, where it intersected State Road 5 and created the corner where APPLEWHITE'S GENERAL STORE AND U.S. POST OFFICE stood next to the Texaco station that still displayed a round sign with a winged red horse on it. On the hill, above the intersection, the old Brett mansion, abandoned now, watched the town with the bitterness of frustrated hopes and rotted dreams. She turned right onto State Road 5, and twenty narrow and winding miles later she arrived at John Brown College, having tapped her horn and waved back to almost every car that had come toward her, sometimes tapping and waving first, always wondering to whom.

The civilities of dailiness were being extended to the Jew in their midst who received magazines and newspapers printed in the strangest language they'd ever seen. They were relieved when Father Lear told them it was Hebrew, not Russian. They had always known there were a few Communists teaching up there at that college and just because the wall over there in Germany had been taken down a few years ago and you could get a Big Mac in Moscow now didn't mean that Communism was a thing of the past because that Castro was as Communist as he was hairy and the Chinese still saluted a red star and if Father Lear hadn't told them that she was a rabbi they would have wondered why a young, single, educated woman would want to live in a little place like Brett if she wasn't a Communist, but then again, as Mr. Applewhite pointed out, what was in Brett that would interest the Communists, and Father Lear reminded them that Our Lord and Savior had been a Jew, which just proved once again that God moved in mysterious ways. Patrick Lear noticed that on the rare occasions when he happened to see the rabbi at Applewhite's, she was friendly but did not use his title when addressing him. Being of the new generation of Catholic clergy who encouraged their parishioners to call them by name, something the older members had difficulty with, he wanted to tell her she could call him Pat, but it didn't seem that she wanted to talk with him or anyone. Even though she was the most stylish dresser anyone had ever seen in Brett, sorrow wrapped itself around her like a beautiful and warm shawl knitted from the finest wool since Jacob made Joseph's coat. Larry Gentry, who lived a half-mile down from her on Pulpit Road and plowed her out in the winter and wouldn't accept a dime for doing it, said it was nice to know someone was living in the ol' Simpson place and, to tell the truth, he felt sorry for a woman as pretty as she was who had a limp which was how come she had that handicapped license plate on her four-wheel-drive Jeep wagon, but that showed she had common sense and would do all right in winters as cold and icy as the hairs on a polar bear's ass, beg pardon, and spring thaws that turned Pulpit Road into river bottom mud.

If Rebecca had known what they said about her those first months she would have told them that after being a congregational rabbi, six months of snow and ice and wind and subzero cold followed by rain and mud sounded like a spa vacation.

"Looks to me like the crate would probably fit in your Jeep with the backseat down, but it's too heavy for you to get in your house without help. When Larry Gentry comes in, I'll see if him and one of his boys can't take it up to your place in his pickup. Where do you want it?"

"You can leave it in the front room. And thanks a lot, Mr. Applewhite. As always, I appreciate your thoughtfulness."

"Don't mention it, Rabbi."

Rebecca sighed.

TWO

When she came home that evening she walked quickly along the hallway past the front room where the Torah scroll lay in the coffin-like crate and hurried up the stairs. She knew it was foolish to be afraid of an inanimate object, but she was.

She sat in her rocking chair and looked across the length of the valley to High Mountain. (She was convinced it was really Chai Mountain. Who would name a mountain High? No one had ever named a river Wet. The mountain's real name was *Chai,* Life, and the gentiles, not knowing how to hear Hebrew, heard "High." And she had found the proof in the house.)

The mountain was a succession of peaks, each taller than the previous one until there was a startling and sheer rise, as if Nature had gotten impatient with Earth's methodical and careful ascent and slapped her, suddenly and without premeditation, and in fear? anger? terror? Earth thrust upward to 3,800 feet, where, exhausted, it stopped and sat now, resentful and hurt, judging everyone and everything below, and its decree would never, no, not ever, be weakened by mercy.

Rebecca recognized she was projecting a guilt of some kind onto High/Chai (hi!) Mountain. But what she knew could not counterbalance who she was. And who she was was afraid. Having a Torah scroll in her house was like, well, like having God there. That was ridiculous, she told herself, but the fear that had settled in her abdomen with the heaviness of unending grief was not dislodged by calling it "ridiculous."

So she sat and rocked, glad now she had transformed the second floor of her house into a space no one had ever come to except her, a space where she could be alone with her memories, her dreams, her fears and all the emotions she was afraid to name.

Five years ago when she was considering buying the house, she had thought she would create a large open space downstairs by having the sliding doors between the front and middle rooms taken out and leaving the second floor as it was—four tiny, dark bedrooms, caves into which you went to sleep, off a narrow hallway. She would use one as an office, one for a bedroom, and the others for storage, and hope a coat or two of white paint would brighten everything.

One morning she got the key from the real estate agent and came out to the house by herself, which was fine with the agent though he knew it was against rules to let anyone go into a house alone, but "if you have a chance to sell the unsalable you bend the rules or ignore them especially in this part of the state which was depressed before the Depression and that house which was a depressing place when it was built back in my great-grandfather's time by somebody who obviously wanted to be left alone since there wasn't even a road going up that way then and wasn't nobody up there now except the Gentrys, the old man and his two boys, though how you could call forty-year-old twins 'boys' is beyond me because them two wasn't boys when they were boys, not after their mother got in the truck one fall afternoon when them boys wasn't more than three years old said she was going into Saint Albans to do some shopping and nobody has seen or heard of her since, not that old man Gentry went looking for her which is why some folks claim he killed her and buried her some place on the other side of High Mountain and some of the real old-timers say they never saw foxes looking as fat and sleek as they did the spring after Violet Gentry disappeared, so you damn right I let her have the key to spend as much time out at the ol' Simpson place as she wanted." Rebecca walked through the downstairs of the house that morning imagining chairs, sofas, paintings, sculpted pieces, lamps, indirect lights, and when she stood in one of the tiny rooms on the second floor she happened to see the mountain through an unwashed window. (She hadn't known its name then.) She went into the other rooms and looked through the windows, and afterward, standing in the darkened hallway, a single forty-watt bulb hanging, naked, from a fraying cord, Rebecca had a vision of what the second floor would look like if all the interior walls were removed to create a loftlike space and the ceiling to the attic above opened up and a skylight put in the roof. The 360-degree view of the valley and the surrounding mountains would be spectacular. She saw floors sanded and resanded until they were smooth to the touch and then finished and refinished until the wood gleamed with an inner radiance. She would not fill the space with much furniture—a futon for a bed, a couple of low bookshelves, a small desk, a rocking chair of course, and that would be enough. She would live encircled by the seasons and the light, by the darkness and the stars. She bought the house that afternoon using for the down payment some of the reparations money the German government had sent her parents all these years, money her father had invested and which had paid for her education at Columbia and her year getting her masters of social work. Now she would have to thank Hitler not only for her existence and education but her house.

Contrary to what she had first thought, the architecture of the

downstairs remained unchanged but the walls were stripped of accretions of awful wallpaper, as if each family who had lived there
had had to externalize its neuroses in patterns of flowers, or sailboats,
or stripes, and who had lived with the repeated pattern of a tree beside a stream coming from and going nowhere, when High Mountain sat in your backyard saying, "You want eternity? Here's Eternity!"
The woodwork had been stripped of layers of paint, the floors
cleaned and scraped of rug over linoleum over paint over dark finish
and as each generation of household occupants was revealed, she
wondered how someone thought he or she could live in a house and
cover over those who had been there before. Some days as she watched
the workmen, she could almost see the spirits of a family leaving as its
layer of wallpaperpaintruglinoleumdustdirt came off.

Finally, there came the late afternoon of a spring day when she
stood in the house and saw it as the original builder had. William
Fine. That was the first name on the abstract and she had been immediately suspicious. Fein? Feinstein? Feinberg? Why had a Jew built a
house in such a remote place? Was he escaping memories of pogroms
and thought he would be safe if he lived far from other Jews, isolated
and alone where no one would come unless they were coming to see
you, and wasn't that why she had bought it, the house no one wanted,
the house that had sat alone and vacant since the Simpsons had moved
more than a year before and although no one said so directly, she sus-
pected that local legend called the house haunted because the asking
price had been cheap enough to arouse suspicion, but that could have
also been because one had to love loneliness to live so far from people
and so close to the mountains.

The house was virgin fresh again, stripped to the wood William
FineFeinFeinbergFeinstein had measured and sawed and carefully

nailed into place, board by board. "Whoever built this place cared," Luke, the painter's daughter, said to Rebecca that afternoon, washing her hands of dust and oils and sucking blood from a finger where she had cut herself. After Luke dried her hands and sucked her finger again, she took Rebecca through the house pointing out how tightly boards fit at corners of the floor, showing her all the little things only someone saw who knew and loved houses as if they were alive.

Rebecca saw little of what Luke showed her and understood even less of what she said, but she felt Luke's love for the builder of the house. Perhaps that was why she stayed and looked around again after Luke, as tall and thin as her father, Edward, left, he to get in his Chevy truck and she to rev up her motorcycle which she rode winter and summer until she and Death would meet on a warm April afternoon the following year on a curve where a pothole, as deep and wide as dreams of love, had appeared overnight. Everybody said that a girl who rode a motorcycle was trying to make Death her husband anyway, so Luke had her wedding. Rebecca would go to the funeral to silently thank Luke for teaching her to see that a house could be a prayer as much as the words in a siddur.

On that spring afternoon after Luke and Edward had left Rebecca stood in the downstairs of her house that had been restored to what it had been when William Fine had built it and she wondered if he had lived there alone as she would, or had there been a wife and children? She was certain there had not been.

She pulled the sliding doors shut between the front and middle rooms, listening to how quietly the doors rolled on the tracks (and Luke had marveled at how securely the tracks had been put into the floor and the doorframe above). Then, there, by her hands she saw something, faint but definite, carved into the wood. One half was on the left side of the door, the other half on the right. She stooped and gently, tenderly, her fingers counted the six points of the star carved into the wood and in the center, on the right side of the door, the Hebrew letter *chet* and on the left side, the Hebrew letter *yud*. Together the two spelled *chai*—life.

And she cried not only a wetness from the eyes and on the cheeks and off the end of the nose but tears that break in the voice, tiny and hard like granules of sand, uncontrollable wracking sobs, tears that are from you but not of you, tears that were once lush grapes but having hung from the soul and remained unpicked through pogrom and the terror of black-suited priest and cross-crowned steeple resting in the horizon like a patient buzzard, unpicked through forced conversion and Shabbat candles lighted in windowless cellars, unpicked in the glare of five chimneys sending Jewish fat to Him and eventually the tears dry up and harden but one day love surprises you because it has come in an unexpected way and in the least expected place, one day when love has softened you without your knowing that you have been made soft, the hardened and dried grapes drop and there you are, stretched on the floor of an empty house, redeemed.

Today there was no feeling of a life about to be renewed, only dread, as she got up from the rocking chair, slowly went down the stairs, into the front room, and stared at the oblong crate. After a moment she got a crowbar from the garage and, kneeling beside the crate, slowly pried up the tightly nailed cover.

She took out the newspapers and straw stuffed on top of, under, and around the scroll and stared at the blue velvet mantle covering it. She slipped her fingers beneath the cover to feel the parchment of the scroll.

Kelaf.

She could hear the Rosh Yeshiva saying it. When he spoke Hebrew, Yiddish, or the Aramaic of the Talmud, she could hear the Jew. It was as if a different person came into him and he was not speaking but being spoken. When he spoke English it was only words. Unlike her parents, who had transferred the "oy" sound of Yiddish into the new tongue so that it was sometimes difficult to know which language they were speaking, with him there was no doubt. His English was almost without accent, and that was why it was just words. She was first-generation American, but English was not her native language. Neither was Yiddish nor Polish. She grew up hearing and speaking all of them and began learning Hebrew when she was three and Aramaic at eight. Her English was not like her ex-husband's, Dennis's, or Saul's. Whenever she had heard Dennis greet someone with a "How ya doing?," she saw cowboys driving five thousand head of cattle along the Santa Fe trail, wheat farmers in Kansas riding tractors, and apples shining like hearts in upstate New York orchards. When she heard his grandparents speak in their Boston accents she saw sunlight sparkling on the ocean and the white canvas of sailboats filled with wind, and heard croquet balls striking each other as ice cubes clinked gently against the sides of glasses filled with English teas. When Saul asked her in his New York Jewish accent, "Did you see the piece in the *New York Times* about . . . ?"—and it never mattered what—she had visions of men burrowing beneath rivers to make tunnels and walking the beams of skeletal skyscrapers sixty-five floors above the East River with as much ease as those below walked the pavement. In the voices of real Americans she heard jet planes breaking the sound barrier and jackhammers splitting boulders to make interstate highways. She loved listening to the unquestioned and unquestionable confidence in Patric's voice. No anxiety lurked at the edges of Americans' sentences. Was that why

Jewish sentences often ended with a question mark even if no question was being asked? Others heard the stridency and brashness and rudeness in Jewish voices, but not the existential fear beneath which lay the certainty that sooner or later someone would make you feel you didn't belong, someone would try to expel you, someone would try to kill you. Americans spoke as if they owned eternity. Jews were afraid even eternity was provisional.

Kelaf.

Why, after the accident, had her father taken her out of the yeshiva in Brooklyn and brought her to him? She would learn—accidentally—that her mother had known him before Time stopped moving in her life and her father had known him in the kingdom of fire, smoke and ashes. Why had her father entrusted her to him and why had she never been curious before now?

But why should she have been? The young accept the extraordinary as normal because they do not compare their lives with those of others when everyone is like them. In her neighborhood everyone's parents had numbers on their arms. Everyone's parents spoke Yiddish, Polish, and English with an accent. Only after the Rosh Yeshiva's death, only after his tombstone was the only witness to her words of thanks and tears of gratitude did she understand that the normal could be as extraordinary as the parting of the Red Sea.

"The best are always of *kelaf*. That is the part of the animal's hide closest to the hairy surface."

Outside it looked like any other brownstone between West End Avenue and Riverside Drive in the eighties. There was no sign indicating that it was a yeshiva, a religious school, a house of study, a synagogue, a remnant of a world that was no more and would never be again. On the ground floor was his office and the beit midrash, a long room where the men davened and studied from the large tomes of the Talmud. On the second floor was the boys' school taught by Reb Avrom Spivack, a tall, beardless young man who seemed in danger of being swallowed whole by his shyness. On the floor above was the girls' school taught by the Rosh Yeshiva. And, on the top floor, he lived— alone.

Why had he taught the girls? Why didn't he, the head of the school, a man whom they all knew was a lamed vavnik—one of the hidden thirty-six Righteous Men on whose account the world survived—teach the boys and leave the girls to Reb Avrom?

It was late afternoon the first time he took her into the beit midrash. The other children had left or been picked up by a parent. She was brought from Brooklyn each morning by her father, who then took the subway back downtown to the delicatessen near the Brooklyn Bridge where he worked, and then, when he finished, came back uptown to get her. That, too, was extraordinary, she realized for the first time, and she had never thanked her father for doing it.

The Rosh Yeshiva took a small Torah scroll from the ark and laid it on the table. He undressed it—removed the mantle—untied it, and rolled it open. As young as she was—and how old was she then? ten? certainly no older—she felt a tense stillness from the two men with long white beards who sat at a table in the back of the room studying Talmud together. Girls were not supposed to touch the Torah scroll. She did not know then that the Rosh Yeshiva was not recreating an old world but making one even he would not have conceived of if all had not perished at Auschwitz. He ignored the white beards and after a few days they ignored him and her, pretended that what was happening at the front of the room was not.

"Ze eili v'anveihu—This is my God and I will glorify him." She sat on a high stool so she could see the scroll, could hold the parchment between her fingers and feel kelaf and the softness of the red Torah mantle. "The rabbis of the Talmud translate that phrase differently. Instead of 'glorify Him,' they translate it 'adorn Him.' Not adore. Adorn."

She gasped audibly and he looked at her and she saw that he loved her and loved her understanding. "Adorn Him!" she exclaimed and then she laughed with delight as she tried to imagine dressing God.

The Rosh Yeshiva understood her laughter as what it was—ahavat HaShem—love of God. He walked over to a shelf and came back with a large volume of the Talmud. She remembered it even now—Tractate Shabbat 133b.

> Make a beautiful sukkah in His honour, a beautiful lulav, a beautiful shofar, beautiful fringes, and a beautiful scroll of the Law, and write it with fine ink, a fine reed, and a skilled penman, and wrap it about with beautiful silk.

When she was older and had established an almost sexual intimacy with Saks and Bloomingdale's, she thought a woman rabbi, at least, was supposed to be God's Calvin Klein or Carolina Herrera. That was what Dennis had not understood. Was it not also adorning God when she adorned herself? Despite her limp, and the nose that was a little too large, the hair just a bit too curly, the eyes that were a little too round, the lips that were a little too full, and yes, the breasts that seemed ready to burst with too much milk (though that would never happen), she took the time to take what God had given her and transform it into a vessel of beauty. Was that any different than taking wheat and transforming it into flour and the flour into challah braided like the hair of the Sabbath Queen?

For eight years, four days a week, she had stayed after school and studied Torah and Talmud with the Rosh Yeshiva. The last year was the most frightening one of her life to that time because it marked the end. She was going to have to leave the only world she had ever known; she was going to have to leave him. Often, the human animal dresses terror in rage, and expresses both in a way unlike either.

One morning she arrived at the yeshiva and locked herself in the bathroom. Fifteen minutes later she emerged with her lips painted the brightest and most garish red ever placed in a cheap lipstick tube. Her cheeks were smeared with a rouge of comparable frightfulness while her eyes were almost closed from the weight of purple eye shadow and mascara.

Morning prayers were just ending when she walked in. The Rosh Yeshiva glanced toward her but said nothing. When the other girls looked at her they reacted as if they had seen the witch of Endor and they waited for him to expel her as he had Shira Rifkin when she had come to school in a sleeveless blouse and miniskirt.

But it was as if he had suddenly lost his sight. When he called on her to recite, it was in his usual flat tone of voice. Morning became afternoon and the secular studies teacher, Reb Mordechai, came in. He, too, looked at Rebecca but said nothing. As the school day came to a close she was ready to throw herself on the floor at the Rosh Yeshiva's feet and beg his (His?) forgiveness.

Just as Reb Mordechai was getting ready to dismiss the class, the Rosh Yeshiva came in, a rare smile on his dark face.

"A story to end the day," he began. All the girls turned and glanced at her, knowing that now she was finally going to get it!

"In Taanit 7b are these words: 'Rav said: A man is forbidden to say: How beautiful is this alien woman!'" He paused and looked around, enjoying their attentiveness. "Now, you might say this is obvious. The pious Jewish male does not look at a woman. And to look at an alien woman, a woman who is not a Jew? Oy gevalt! What pious Jewish man would look at an alien woman? Rivka!"

He used her Hebrew name which he did most often when they studied together. She did not know why he had chosen that quote from the Talmud and where he was going with it but addressing her as Rivka called her into a space and time of holiness in which Rivka was the wife of Isaac and the mother of Esau and Jacob who protected the spiritual heritage, a time when Rivka was the daughter of Shmuel and the mother of Binyamin who became the father of Rivka who gave birth to Shmuel who gave birth to Rivka which was her so that she was not just Rivka herself but she was all the Rivkas and herself, too, because a Jew was never a solitary individual. Never.

"Rivka? What Jewish man would look at an alien woman?"

She forgot the makeup on her face, most of which had faded as the day and her anxiety progressed until her lips and cheeks were now suffused with a pale rosiness and her eyes seemed to carry the dark circles of a romantic weariness. She did not know how beautiful she looked.

Even if she had known, she would not have cared because the Rosh Yeshiva had asked her a seemingly innocent question. But such did not exist. At least, not in Talmud.

"What pious Jewish man would look at an alien woman?" he repeated softly.

She smiled and looked at him. "Many. If there had not been many doing it, Rav would not have forbidden the act."

He nodded. "Nachon!" He turned to the class. "Obviously, many pious Jewish men were looking at the non-Jewish women and enjoying what their eyes saw. So, Rav says, 'A man is forbidden to say: How beautiful is this alien woman!'

"This makes sense, does it not?" It was a rhetorical question and everyone knew he was going to tell them that it did not, which he did.

"The Talmud does not stop there, however. It continues and says: 'An objection was taken.' Once Rabban Simeon ben Gamaliel was standing on a step of the mountain of the Temple and saw an alien woman who was exceptionally beautiful. He said, 'How manifold are thy works, O Lord!' quoting Psalm 104:24. The Talmud continues and says, 'Rabban Simeon was merely giving thanks to God. For a master said: He who sees goodly creatures says' "—he stopped and looked deliberately at Rebecca and then, continuing—" 'Blessed is He in whose world are such creatures as these!' "

He waved an arm in a gesture of dismissal and the room emptied quickly, leaving her alone in the room with him, mascara-tinged tears making a sooty trail down her face. On her way to the subway that evening she bought her first copy of *Vogue*.

The Jews of Czechowa had certainly adorned their God. The mantle covering the Torah was a sheath of light blue velvet. Unlike many other mantles she'd seen, this one did not have embroidered onto it the names of those who had given it or in whose honor it had been given. Some religious genius had known to leave it to shimmer like the color of sky against which the silver breastplate smoldered like a distant sun. *Ze eili v'anveihu.*

She lifted the scroll from the crate and, holding it in her arms, she rocked it, back and forth, to comfort those whose sobs she thought she heard. How was she supposed to live in her own house with weeping that could never end? But the blue mantle of the scroll seemed to speak only of joys, past and future.

"Some might think we Jews are crazy. There are millions of printed Hebrew Bibles in the world. Why do we still insist on reading from a scroll in the synagogue, a scroll that takes a year to prepare and costs thousands and thousands of dollars? Even Reform Jews have not gotten rid of Torah scrolls in their synagogues.

"Why go to all the work to write a Torah scroll when the same words are already in a book? And the words in the book have the vowel markings which makes it easier to read.

"Let us imagine, Rivka, all the difficulties entailed in making a sefer Torah. Can you walk into a stationery store and buy kelaf?"

She had smiled at the obvious silliness of the question. "And if you could, some rabbi would find something in the Talmud to say you couldn't," she answered.

The Rosh Yeshiva had smiled at her as if he could not believe who she was, and even now she wished she could see whom he had seen when he looked at her because if she could, she felt she would know herself.

"You are quite right, Rivka. But imagine that you are walking through the woods and come across a deer which died from natural causes or was killed by wolves or some other animal. Can its hide be used for a Torah scroll?"

"Yes," she answered immediately.

"Yes," he agreed. "Rabbi Joshua said that the deaths of such animals were an act of HaShem." Then he stopped and looked at her. She knew he was waiting for her to ask a question.

She thought for a moment and then remembered. "But the meat of an animal found dead in the woods from natural causes or after being killed by another animal is not considered a gift from HaShem for eating. Such meat is strictly forbidden. Why is nonkosher meat good enough for the word of HaShem but not good enough for your stomach? Shouldn't it be the other way around?"

"Excellent, Rivka."

He seldom answered her questions and he did not this one. In Judaism the object of learning was not to build a better mousetrap but to ask a better question. The questions you asked indicated just how closely you were attending to Him.

"Kosher or not kosher," the Rosh Yeshiva continued, "it goes without saying that a gentile cannot transform the hide of this dead deer into the parchment of a Torah scroll. Why? Because the one doing the preparation must do so with the constant thought that it is going to be used to receive the mystical letters of the holy tongue of the God of the Jews."

The part of Rebecca which Columbia had taught to believe in the humanistic ideals of Western civilization was not comfortable excluding the overwhelming majority of humanity, but the part in which she was Rivka then and now would always stand apart from the rest of humanity, and the scroll she was holding was a symbol of that, the Jewish way of saying that yes, the Christians came and took our scriptures and claimed them as their own and by the fourth century of the Common Era (or Anno Domini—in the Year of Our Lord— as the Christians so arrogantly put it), Jew and Christian read scripture from codexes and the Jews said no, and it was ruled that Torahs had to be on parchment, not papyrus as were codices, written on one side rather than both, as were codices, and in scroll form rather than flat like codices. The very physicality of the scroll was a statement of separation and distinctiveness: I am a Jew, despite what you say about me, despite what you do to me. I am a Jew!

She continued rocking, holding the Torah scroll tightly to her breast, her eyes closed. This was all that remained of the Jews of Czechowa. They were scarcely memories any longer because only a few old gentiles even remembered that there had been Jews in Czechowa but they wouldn't remember as Jews remembered. The gentiles of Czechowa didn't remember Hanukah candles and *charoset* and when Mendl ran away to join the Baal Shem Tov and the time Hadassah stood up in the women's section to say Kaddish for her dead little brother and was forbidden to ever come in the shul again and they certainly didn't remember Sinai because they weren't there. This Torah scroll was memory and burial ground. The Jews of Czechowa now lived in her house.

Rebecca laid the scroll gently on the long table. She slid the mantle halfway off, then stopped. She gasped as she saw that the scroll was tied in a knot. Tears came into her eyes and began trickling down her face as she finished removing the mantle. She then picked up the scroll and, clasping it to her breast again, sank to the floor and began rocking furiously back and forth.

Eventually her eyes had no more tears. Getting up, she laid the scroll on the table again and looked down at it as if into the face of a baby that had been nursed and now slept. She looked again at the piece of cloth tied around the scroll. She had expected it to be the same blue color as the mantle. But it was a wide piece of white cloth. Handwritten in black ink and in Yiddish was the name, Avram ben Moshe—Abraham son of Moses. Next to it, a date, 6 Elul 5691.

She knew the custom in Eastern Europe had been for a mother to save the wimple, the cloth used at a son's bris, and on his first birthday, she would take her son to synagogue and the Torah scroll would be tied with his cloth. The next time the scroll would be so tied was on the day he became bar mitzvah.

She went to the bookshelves for a volume that gave the Julian and Hebrew calendars from 1900 to 2100 and discovered that 5691 corresponded to the secular calendar year of 1931, which meant that Avram ben Moshe was thirteen in 1944. Her hunch was confirmed. The Jews of Czechowa had just completed Avram ben Moshe's bar mitzvah when they and their Torah were taken away.

The Nazis had waited, deliberately, purposefully, until Shabbat morning, until Avram ben Moshe and his family and the entire community were gathered in shul to wish him a good marriage, many years of learning in Torah and *ma'asim tovim*—good deeds—and then they marched in. The knot in the wimple told her it had to have happened that way because it was forbidden to tie a knot on Shabbat. If the Nazis had come in before the reading of the Torah, the wimple would have been tied in a bow, because one could tie and untie a bow on the Sabbath. If they had come in after the reading of the Torah had been concluded, it would have been tied not with the wimple but with its regular tie, a piece of cloth the same blue color as the mantle. The Nazis had come in after the Torah had been opened and someone— the Torah Reader, the gabbai, or even Avram ben Moshe himself— had rolled the Torah closed and retied it with the wimple in a knot. That explained the letter from the Repository indicating that the kosher status of the scroll had not been determined. No one had wanted to undo that knot, the last "words" of the Jews of Czechowa.

"This Torah scroll," the letter read, "belonged to Beit Tefillah— House of Prayer—in Czechowa, Poland. It was a small community of two hundred Jewish families who had lived in the area for almost five hundred years. It was liquidated by the Nazis in 1944. This Torah scroll was taken by the Nazis to its repository of Jewish ritual objects where it was found by the British army after the war. The

Holocaust Memorial Repository was organized for the sole purpose of distributing these Torah scrolls from liquidated communities to synagogues throughout Jewry. We are pleased to present this scroll to you and your community on a permanent loan basis. Please be aware that it has not been determined if this scroll is kosher for use during synagogue services."

Rebecca slipped the mantle back over the scroll, then went upstairs and searched through her closets until she found a large shawl of lamb's wool. Returning to the front room, she wrapped the shawl around the Torah as if needing to say to the Jews of Czechowa, all those whose hands and eyes had read, carried, raised and gazed on this *sefer Torah,* all those who were the smoke in the raindrops now, that they were, at long last, safe from the long winters.

She went back upstairs to pray. The Jewish day began at the frontier between day and night as if light were a border separating distinct kingdoms. Sitting in her rocking chair in the middle of the room, she looked through the windows. Day's end was more than the sun setting in bands of orange that rested on the mountains like a *tallis* on the shoulders of an old Jew. The earth was turning away from the light and toward darkness. She did not like the illusion of the sun being the actor. What was important was the deliberateness of earth's turning away from the light. That was in the nature of things—away and toward, away and toward—the two motions creating the whole.

Even her parents did not understand. She would have thought they could. Before moving into the house (and for some months after), her mother especially had recited all the things that could happen to a woman living alone in an isolated house on a dirt road. Rebecca wondered, how could they have survived Auschwitz and still be afraid?

What could someone do to them that God hadn't done already? That was what she had concluded after God crippled her, after she lay in the hospital bed for months, after she learned how to walk again. Who could possibly hurt her more than God had?

The Rosh Yeshiva accepted the aloneness of knowing something that could not be communicated to another, accepted that he would be forever and always alone because of what he knew about God. She and the Rosh Yeshiva had chosen to see His evil. Her parents had not. They tried to pretend they were no different than others—but how could they when they had lived, night and day, smelling the flesh of Jews burningburningburning? God had decreed that their lives were to be otherwise; they had refused the offer (offering?). She and the Rosh Yeshiva had accepted. But to what end? She did not know. The Rosh Yeshiva, at least, had had her. She had no one and no purpose.

Since the accident all those many years ago, she felt most herself at night. The night nurses had not tried to cheer her up or amuse her or delude her into believing that being a cripple made her "just as good as any other girl or boy." Anyone who believed that didn't know how enamored children were of cruelty. Even when the nurses heard her quiet sobbing, even when they knew she stayed awake late into the night, they seemed to trust that she was doing what she needed to do to heal herself, and she was, though she could not have known it. What she had done each night was relive the accident, over and over, every detail, every emotional remnant and that was how she learned prayer was not the polite recitation of platitudes but rage and recrimination, defiance, obstinance, and a hatred of God's will.

Years later, after Dennis had left, she remembered and she prayed again each night before the gate at day's ending and day's beginning, prayed aloud, sometimes cursing, sometimes crying, sometimes pleading, and her only concern was to "break [her] heart before the Lord always," paraphrasing Rebbe Nachman, who had used the masculine pronoun, not believing a woman should or even could pray in such a way.

When she prayed, the words did not come easily or readily. How could they when addressing Him? Often she did not even know what needed saying, but tonight was not one of those nights.

"I am afraid," she said and immediately, almost as if she had conjured it, came the image of the Torah scroll lying on the table adored and adorned, tied with Avram ben Moshe's swaddling cloth, covered by a pale blue mantle and wrapped in her shawl.

What did she fear, she who knew God's evil, she who had grown up in the shadow of the crematoria, she for whom the dead had been more alive than the living? The first time Dennis had taken her to his home, she was stunned to meet his grandparents as well as his parents. There were actually people who had living grandparents, and not only that, but living aunts and uncles and cousins! She did not know how she would have acted toward a living aunt or uncle of her own, or even how she would have distinguished a living one from a dead one. Had she never actually met Leibl, her father's oldest brother, the *hazzan* with the voice so sweet that when he sang, HaShem would ask the angels to stop singing His praises because he wanted to listen to Reb Leibl? Had she never actually heard him sing Kol Nidre, his voice breaking, every word and every note sounding as if they had been marinated in the brine of Jewish tears? Had she never walked the streets of Vilna? Of course she had. Shimshon, the kosher butcher, had his shop diagonally across the street from that of Shimshon the tailor. His son, Aharon, had left to walk to Palestine

36

and was never heard from. Some thought he had made it. Most sa
he didn't. And no one could convince her that she had not tasted the
challah of Feigele, her mother's baby sister, challah as yellow and soft
as spring wildflowers, challah so fresh that the Sabbath Queen came
personally to smell it, or that she had not known Devorah, the aunt
who went to every funeral, whether she knew the deceased or not,
and sat in the women's section and cried, and when people asked her
why, she was as baffled as they were but after a while it was accepted
that where there was death, there was Devorah. "Devorah, I didn't
know one person could have so many tears," Rebecca's mother had
told her once in a rare moment of talking about the past. "Devorah
said all the tears weren't hers. She died at Auschwitz," Rebecca's
mother continued the story. "Different ones that have gone back to
visit—why they would go back to that place, I don't know and now I
understand people go there to visit like they're visiting an amusement
park. What's to see? Do they think they'll know what it was like for
us there? You can't know. I don't know who smelled worse, the ones
who were going up through the chimneys or we who didn't have paper to wipe our tushes. Thank God I know you would never go to
that place. If you want to go somewhere, go to Paris, someplace that's
beautiful. You hear me? Now, as I was saying: Different ones that
have gone back have said they thought they heard Devorah crying. It
wouldn't surprise me. I suppose somebody has to cry for those souls."

There were times, many times, when Rebecca had been almost
overwhelmed by the burden of remembering what she had not experienced with her flesh. If most of her memories belonged to others,
how much of her life did, also? Afraid that her tenuous self would be
devoured by centuries of Jews demanding allegiance, she sought sal-
vation at Columbia by falling in love her junior year with an Irish

hough he was the first boy to ever ask her out, the
in't seem to notice that she walked with a limp, she
ntention of marrying him, even when he started at-
es with her and was always asking her questions about
Judaism. ا ing the last semester of their senior year, he asked her to
marry him and she told him she couldn't because he wasn't Jewish.
He smiled and said, "But I am—now." For more than a year he had
been studying for conversion with the Rosh Yeshiva and neither had
told her.

Rebecca shook her head and, with difficulty, pulled herself from
the abyss of memory, a place in which she knew she spent far too
much time, but when the present was as nondescript as hers, the past
was like a large tapestry in which one could wander among the threads
and find details only those who had sewn the tapestry knew were
there. But if you were Jewish, living in the past was also to live in the
present.

THREE

❧

Rebecca looked at the calendar on her office desk. Her only appointment for the day was at four but that would change soon. It was almost that time in the semester when the stresses of college life worked their way to the soft places in the psyche where the wounds called mother and father pulsated quietly. Several students had come in that morning without appointments but their complaints could be resolved by getting enough sleep, which she encouraged them to do. Allison Manchester was a different story.

Rebecca looked at the file on her computer screen.

```
ALLISON MANCHESTER
Nineteen
Sophomore
New York City


11/5 – Came in without an appointment. Small, blond, very beau-
tiful. Large blue eyes. Something fragile about her. Signs of
nervousness and anxiety. Talked rapidly. Eyes moved rapidly
around room. Unable to maintain eye contact. Lots of nervous
laughter when nothing funny had been said. Wanted to talk about
```

a "friend" who had a problem but decided that everything would
be all right.

11/7 – Second visit without an appointment. Silent. Obviously depressed. Stared at her hands in her lap. "Aren't you going to ask
me what's wrong?" Said angrily, defensively. "I figure you'll tell
me when you're ready." "Suppose I'm never ready." "Then, that's
how it is." "I don't want you to get the impression that there's
anything wrong with me. I'm not crazy, you know. I just thought
it'd be a good idea to come by and check this place out." "And
what do you think?" She shrugged. "I'd heard that you were cool.
That you didn't pry or tell people how to live their lives."
"And?" Long silence, then tears, then the first real eye contact.
"I guess I wish you'd pry and tell me how to live my life."

"I had an abortion this summer," she said finally. "My parents
don't know. I'm Catholic and I didn't think I believed anything
the Church taught but I feel like I killed my baby. I killed my
baby." And she cried.

Rebecca had talked with her about the need to grieve and had offered to work with her in creating a ritual in which she could mourn
the dead fetus. That was what they were going to talk about today. Rebecca was looking forward to doing something creative with a client.
Perhaps the only part of being a synagogue rabbi she missed was the
rituals she had helped women create who had suffered abortions and
miscarriages, and there had been one voluptuous woman who'd lost
both breasts to cancer (and her mammary-fixated husband to a woman
with 36D breasts).

40

Closing the file, Rebecca exited the program, then the computer, and, after the machine finished making noises as if digesting something disagreeable, turned itself off.

Every afternoon from two to four, Rebecca sat in the back booth of The HangOut and did the *New York Times* crossword puzzle. Her first week on campus she had gone there and sat, having decided she wasn't going to wait for the problems to come to her. Within minutes, a girl with a headful of blond hair in braids like small snakes was sitting across from her talking about English lace. Few ever talked directly at first about what was bothering them. People used the language available to them, and sometimes English lace was English lace and sometimes it was the intricate and delicate pattern of a life. That girl actually collected English lace, however.

Getting up from her desk, Rebecca took the lamb suede jacket from the coat tree by the door and flung it over her shoulders. On a campus where blue jeans, sweat shirts and sneakers created an atmosphere of universal and disconcerting androgyny, Rebecca asserted her femaleness as if fulfilling a responsibility to the future of civilization. Dressing well was as much a mitzvah as *kashrut*.

Near the end Dennis had called her a JAP—Jewish-American Princess. He apologized immediately but that hadn't prevented him from telling her a few weeks later that she dressed more like a mannequin in Bergdorf's window than a rabbi. She hadn't realized until then that his love for her had not been as great as his pity. Sadly, he had been no different than most who thought the function of the handicapped, stray dogs and children was to be recipients of self-centered benevolence. But when she limped by in a lamb suede jacket, matching suede skirt and wine-dark silk blouse, what were they supposed to do with their pity? How could they warm themselves in the superiority of physical wholeness if she was expert with mascara, eye shadow, blush and lip gloss, if they looked at her and saw, not a cripple, but a woman whose full breasts were obvious behind blouses unbuttoned provocatively to reveal the lacy edges of a bra or teddy, whose round hips and firm thighs were outlined within tight skirts? They wanted to pour out pity like warm milk, but she wouldn't cooperate.

Her limp was not that severe and she could have had her left shoe adjusted, either with a raised sole or an insert. She and Dennis had argued about that, too. But she had never explained, not to him or anyone, about that eight-year-old girl who had come into Manhattan with her father on a Sunday afternoon, walking along Fifth Avenue, her father pulling her away from Bergdorf's window or they would miss the beginning of the concert and as they walked west on Fifty-seventh Street toward Carnegie Hall she ran ahead to look in the windows of the art galleries and boutiques stores and did not see the cab when it went out of control. An eight-year-old girl is small, scarcely larger than a fire hydrant, so small that an automobile should have no problem avoiding her, especially with so many larger objects around, but the cab missed the cars parked and double-parked and only scraped the fire hydrant and, as if it had a will and mind of its own, as if it had left its garage that morning with only one mission, it came toward her, its grille grinning wickedly as if its wish and intent was to embrace her, but it could not and she went through the air and through the window of a delicatessen (at least it was kosher), the cab following lustfully until it came to rest on her left thigh and hip.

She did not lose consciousness at once because she heard the glass shattering with sounds like wind chimes caressed by the gentlest wind; she heard the silence that followed, a silence so overwhelming that she wanted to cover her ears against it, and then came her father's screams and that released her into pain and just before the pain and shock and fear clubbed her into unconsciousness, there came the certain knowledge: God had done it on purpose.

As she walked down the steps to The HangOut, students coming up smiled and greeted her: "What's up, Rabbi?" (Rebecca was aware of how ironic it was that when she had wanted people to address her as Rabbi, they had done so resentfully. Now, when she did not want the title, it was offered openly and enthusiastically.) The young were offensive in many ways, beginning with the fact that they were young and she was not anymore. Thirty-eight was not old, especially if you looked twenty-eight. Genes. Her mother survived Auschwitz and looked as if her worst ordeal had been standing in line at the Exchange Desk at Bloomingdale's (which proved how illusory appearances were). Rebecca appreciated inheriting such genes, but working on a college campus where each September the most recent models of the young were unloaded, gleaming like automobiles coming off a transport carrier, she hated knowing she was no longer young and all the promise she had been was now regret. Rebecca's sole consolation was knowing that coiled within the body of the young, secure in the righteousness of untested youth, there awaited the moment they, too, would be wounded by the ineluctability of aging and its concomitant yearnings, regrets and sorrows for all that could not be undone and all that would never be done and, above all, a raging dread of the odor of one's mortality.

Rebecca continued along the hallway whose walls were covered with bulletin boards onto which were tacked posters and notices about campus events. She still could not believe that a campus so small could engender so much life, if that was what the notices indicated. The Ski Club was holding its fall organizational meeting; the Yoga Society met every Sunday morning and ALL ARE WELCOME; Black Students United were meeting Friday night; there were also notices for the Chess Club, the Science Fiction and Fantasy Club, Student Government, French Club, German Club, Astrology Club, History Club, and Marijuana for the Masses Society. Within the month there were going to be public lectures and panel discussions on the environment, the coming nuclear holocaust (she hated how that word had been appropriated to designate any event in which a great number of people had been killed or might be), reproductive technology, Palestinian rights, John Dryden (she might go to that one just to see who thought seventeenth-century poetry was worth sacrificing an evening for), DNA, Science as a Vocation, The Natural Superiority of WOMEN and The Oppression of the Transgendered.

She turned and continued to the end of the hallway and through the double doors into The HangOut. It was almost deserted as it usually was at two when most students were in classes or labs. The few students sitting at tables or in booths were either studying or talking quietly. In an hour, though, when most classes ended for the day, the place filled up quickly.

"Rebecca!"

She recognized the soft voice even before she turned to see Patric Marsh sitting in the booth she had just passed.

"Patric," she said, forcing herself to sound as if she was glad to see him.

What little social life Rebecca had—or did until last New Year's Day—was because Patric had been kind enough to invite her to dinner parties. He even bought frozen kosher entrees on his trips to

Montreal and kept them in his freezer so she could eat more than salad at his house.

"How're things?" he asked, motioning her to sit opposite him.

"Good. And you?" she replied, sliding reluctantly into the booth.

He shrugged, indicating the stack of papers in front of him. "I think I'm losing the battle to instill a sense of values in the young but, besides that, I'm fine."

He had been instrumental in the founding of John Brown College, but she still didn't understand why he had never accepted any of the lucrative offers he received from the University of Chicago School of Religion, or Harvard or Yale Divinity, among others. In his brown tweed jacket, button-down blue Brooks Brothers shirt (Rebecca recognized those kinds of things), and wide-twill corduroy pants (even though his pants were hidden beneath the table, Rebecca didn't have to see them to know that was what he was wearing), he looked like he should at least be dean of the chapel at some elite school where religion was a decorous undertaking designed to comfort the comfortable.

"What're you teaching this fall?" Rebecca asked, not knowing what else to say.

"My usual. Introduction to World Religions and the seminar on good and evil. I assume you still won't come and speak to either."

Patric's invitations to speak to his classes was a joke between them since he knew in advance what she would say. "Not this year. Maybe next."

"I really wish you would give teaching some serious thought. We need somebody to teach a course on Judaism. It's embarrassing that we don't offer anything. You should be on the faculty, not in Psych Services. Say the word and I'll talk to the president and have your appointment changed for next semester, and with a sizeable raise.

I know a very wealthy man who would like nothing more than to endow a chair in Jewish studies at John Brown College."

"You're serious, aren't you?"

"Very much so. You're a rabbi and you're the child of survivors. You have a lot to offer. There's no way I can convince you to at least talk about the Holocaust to my good and evil seminar?"

She shook her head. "You know I don't talk about that."

He nodded. "Yes. I know, but I've never understood why."

Rebecca tried to smile. "Maybe I don't have as much to offer as you think."

"Well, let's see. First-generation American, child of Holocaust survivors; fluency in Yiddish, Polish, Hebrew, Aramaic; ordained rabbi, therapist, and beneath it all, the soul of an editor at *Vogue*."

She smiled.

Patric smiled back. "Seriously. Why don't you want to share what you know?"

"What's to know? I'm no different than anybody else who owes their life to Hitler. I mean, if not for him, my Ukrainian father and Polish mother would not have been in Auschwitz and thus would have never met and I wouldn't exist. Every year at my birthday instead of singing 'Happy Birthday' I give a *Sieg Heil* and say, '*Danke schön, mein Führer.*'"

She noticed the look of shock on Patric's face. "Are you serious?" he wanted to know.

"You should spend a day around a group of Holocaust survivors' children. Best Holocaust jokes you'd ever want to hear." She moved to slide from the booth.

"Rebecca?"

She stopped, dreading what she knew was coming next.

"Isn't there anything I can do to make up for New Year's?" he asked, almost plaintively. "You indicated that you had forgiven me."

"I have."

"Then I don't understand."

Though Rebecca didn't want to talk about it she swung her legs back beneath the table and looked at him. "Perhaps we understand forgiveness differently."

"What do you mean?"

"In Judaism forgiveness does not mean a relationship can just return to what it was before. I have the impression that in Christianity to forgive someone means you forget what happened and everything is now OK. When you apologized and asked me to forgive you, I did, but that didn't mean I had stopped feeling hurt. I hadn't and I haven't. By saying I forgave you, I was simply saying that, out of my hurt, I wouldn't seek to hurt you. Sometimes things happen and friendships change and they can no longer be what they were. Eventually they become something else."

"Or not," he added somberly.

"Or not," she agreed quietly and eased herself from the booth.

FOUR

☙

As Patric watched Rebecca walk away, he wondered if she would have slept with him, maybe even married him, if he had been Jewish. He still wanted to think so.

Five years ago, when he and Rebecca had their first conversations in that very booth, he had made occasional references to an ex-wife and she to a former husband. But their relationship never reached that level of social intimacy where divorced people flirted by exchanging negative information about their previous spouses. By listing the defects of their exes, they were also describing what they wanted in a future spouse so the person they were talking to could know if he or she qualified. But beyond mentioning that she had been married, Rebecca did not respond when Patric talked about Jennifer.

At the short-lived Saturday morning services he had been surprised at how animated Rebecca was when talking with Saul Greenberg or any of the other Jews, and how reserved she was when talking with him. He doubted that she was aware of it and he certainly didn't think she purposely excluded him from the laughing part of herself; this was simply how it was. He didn't need to be told: she would never marry a non-Jew. He was hurt that a person of her intelligence could have such a provincial attitude.

His resentment was an unsettling emotion he preferred not to look at, for fear his opinion of himself would have to be modified to the detriment of his ego. But unexamined emotions find ways to express themselves, often disguised as humor.

"I don't understand how you do it, Rebecca," he would say loudly, sitting at the head of a laden table. "Here is a plate of mushrooms wrapped in bacon and topped with the merest sprinkling of freshly grated pecorino cheese and you aren't even tempted. Next to it are succulent shrimp with a homemade spicy sauce to dip them in and at the center of the table, the pièce de résistance—beef tenderloin tips in a burgundy cream sauce I myself created. Yet you sit there with a plastic fork and knife eating something disgustingly gray off a paper plate."

His teasing had the appearance of an older brother's affection for a sister. Then came New Year's Day.

On the first day of the year Patric invited a small and select group of people to eat, drink and discuss a topic he announced on the engraved invitations sent to the lucky invitees. This year he had chosen holiness as the topic. He had done so with Rebecca in mind, hoping that, by evening's end, she would have said something that would enable him to at least understand her better, and in understanding, his quiet obsession with her would die peacefully.

He took more care than usual with the menu and served roasted quail, white asparagus, wild rice, snow peas in a lemon cream sauce, anadama bread he had kneaded and baked, all accompanied by a Washington State pinot noir ("which is far superior to overpriced California and French equivalents"). Dessert was pumpkin crème brûlée accompanied by a moscato d'Asti.

For a man who was as fine a cook as Patric, food was not merely food. It was an instrument of seduction, and, the aroma of fowls cooked on rotating spits in the fireplace, the light yellow smoothness of the lemon cream sauce, the delicate egg and nutmeg of the crème brûlée beneath the thin crust of browned sugar were supposed to dissipate the inner reserve Rebecca maintained around him and release the sensual warmth Patric was convinced lay beneath. He did not understand how she could not be open to other ways of living and being. Did she honestly think God would strike her dead if, for one night, she ate a quail? In that New Year's Day meal Patric thought he made his desire for her as obvious as if he had walked in without clothes, his penis erect.

Patric had opened the discussion on holiness with an overview of how the subject was viewed in various religions around the globe. He purposely omitted any mention of Judaism, hoping Rebecca would notice and join. However, whenever he looked at her, he saw her gazing at the tablecloth, a blank stare on her face. Finally, annoyed, he asked, "What do you think, Rabbi?"

"What do I think about what?" she asked, blushing with embarrassment.

Patric threw up his arms in mock despair. "You are not only oblivious to incredible food but you ignore the brilliant and scintillating conversation that has been taking place in range of your hearing. Is the conversation of gentiles also not kosher?"

The four others at the table laughed politely, except Rebecca and Saul, who was sitting next to her.

Patric noticed the startled look on Rebecca's face and wondered if he had gone too far.

"I suppose it depends on the nature of the conversation," she responded, keeping her tone light.

"That is true," Martin Abbey offered. He taught the history of Christianity in Patric's English Department, but prided himself on his knowledge of Judaism. "Negative remarks about another are not kosher. Isn't that true, Rabbi?"

"Yes, it is, Professor Abbey," Rebecca responded, smiling at Martin, who beamed.

"Well, my dear rabbi and respected colleague. We are safe! No one at this table would ever say anything negative about a colleague or indulge in gossip." Everyone laughed loudly. When the laughter died, Patric continued. "Now that the words of our mouths have been given the rabbinic seal of approval, I will ask Professor Crawford to recount our discussion to this point and at the conclusion I think we would all be interested in your response, Rabbi, if you have one."

Roger Crawford was chair of the English Department. In his early forties, with thick, wavy dark hair, dark eyes, and a smile for everyone, he was boyishly handsome. There was at least one like him on every campus in America, male professors who seemed like the kid brother who would never grow up. They would never be accused of sexual harassment because they were so skilled at the craft of seduction that female students pulled them onto their young, full breasts without realizing that was precisely what they had been seduced into doing. However, Patric knew that Roger had become obsessed with a female student in his Love in Western Literature class and that he had been seeing Rebecca professionally, at Patric's suggestion.

"Well, to recap for the rabbi," he began in his soft, deep voice, "we have quickly dispensed with all those things commonly associated with holiness—churches, rituals, clergypeople, and the like. None of us consider any of these to be holy in and of themselves, not even our host, who knows more about such matters than most. For us holiness seems to reside in beauty. We feel closest to something we would designate as holy when we walk in nature, witness a sunset or dawn whose colors defy description. We also agreed that when we are in the presence of art, say a statue of Aphrodite or Michelangelo's *David* or a painting by Rembrandt, an etching by Dürer, Weston's photograph of a green pepper, Bach's *Art of Fugue*. At such moments we are in the presence of such beauty that we feel ourselves to be in the presence of the holy. It occurred to us, however, what if one were in the presence of a beautiful woman or, I should add, a handsome man? Certainly, there are men and women in the world whose beauty evokes some of the same emotions we experience in nature, emotions of overwhelming awe, emotions we do not hesitate to describe as religious. So, the question is: Can a beautiful man or woman evoke an experience of holiness?"

"What do the Jews say about this?" Patric asked, a little too forcefully. "I've read that Jews believe that their Talmud contains all knowledge. Well, surely there must be something in it about how one is supposed to respond to a beautiful woman or man, though I think I know what your Talmud says."

"And what do you think that is?" Saul asked, speaking for the first time.

"What else could it say but that one should not be around beautiful women?" Patric laughed. "Don't Orthodox Jews require women to cover their hair with wigs because women's hair is considered so seductive that it should only be seen by their husbands? And didn't I read somewhere that it is forbidden for a Jewish male to hear the voice of a woman singing? And in synagogues women must sit in balconies or behind screens so men will not be distracted from their prayers by a pretty face."

"But your question was about the Talmud, was it not?" Saul persisted.

"Yes, but why should that matter?"

"Well, because what the Talmud says is very different than what you have read. Do you mind, Rabbi, if I try to answer the question?" Saul asked Rebecca. "It would give me pleasure to show off a little of my Jewish learning."

Rebecca smiled. "Please. Be my guest."

"Thank you." Saul looked at Patric and then Roger. "In Tractate Tannit it says, and I quote: 'Rav said: A man is forbidden to say: How beautiful is this alien woman! Objection was taken: Once Rabban Simeon ben Gamaliel was standing on a step of the mountain of the Temple, and saw an alien woman who was exceptionally beautiful. He said: How manifold are thy works, O Lord!' quoting from Psalms one hundred and four, verse twenty-four. Rav then goes on and says: 'Rabban Simeon was merely giving thanks to God. For a master said: He who sees goodly creatures says: Blessed is He in whose world are such creatures as these!' "

Patric noticed that tears had come into Rebecca's eyes and wondered why.

Henri Fournier laughed and said in the heavy French accent he maintained assiduously though he had lived in America longer than in his native France, "What a wonderful response! Where do I sign up to become Jewish? Any religion that sanctions lust is the religion for me!"

Everyone laughed except Rebecca and Saul.

"But that is not what the passage says," Rebecca said quietly. "It is not lust that is sanctioned; it is God. 'Blessed is *He* in whose world are such creatures as these.' "

"So, lust for a beautiful woman is not holy," Crawford said, goading her.

"No," she replied.

"What a pity," Oliver Preston put in quietly. A promising violinist who had been stricken with arthritis before that promise was fulfilled, he always spoke with what seemed to be a sadness so deep one feared to get too close. "Rabbi, what if this woman's beauty makes everyone, male and female, feel more alive, feel more beautiful themselves? Is a beautiful woman holy? The ancient Greeks, if they had liked women, would have said so."

"Indeed!" Patric agreed. "Socrates said that love of the beautiful was a prerequisite, a necessary step toward the love of wisdom because wisdom is beautiful."

"And he also said," Roger added, "that what is beautiful and graceful deserves to be loved. So, if love of a beautiful woman is a necessary precursor to love of wisdom, then is not a beautiful woman holy?"

Rebecca responded softly. "Matthew Arnold wrote that for the Greeks what is beautiful is holy. For the Jews what is holy is beautiful."

"Let me see if I understand you correctly," Patric cut in sharply. "Am I to believe that the gray hunk of microwaved turkey breast you ate from a plastic tray with a plastic fork is beautiful because it is holy and that the golden-brown quail which Saul ate with gusto is unholy?"

Patric spoke with more vehemence than necessary in a meaningless intellectual discussion. But as he stared into Rebecca's eyes he could have sworn he saw in them a flicker of understanding, a realization that she had in that instant understood what she had been doing to him all these years by accepting his invitations to sit at his harvest table, that merely by coming every time he invited her she had encouraged him to persevere and hope that one day she would, at the least, come to his bed. How could he have been so naive not to have known from the beginning that she had no intention of ever being in an intimate relationship with him? He had been as big a fool about Rebecca as Roger was about the girl in his class.

"I envy you, Rabbi," he continued, not caring any longer how much he exposed himself. "I am sixty-three years old, a time when the cold shadow of mortality becomes thicker and darker. I have been looking back at my life and all I see is a man who spent his years reading books and to what end? So I could be quoted in the *New York Times* and be interviewed on television. I look back at my life and, try as I might, I can't see one good deed I've done in all these years."

Everyone at the table was shocked and a little embarrassed by this revelation. But rather than give him the confirmation he so desperately needed if he were to have any chance to redeem what had essentially been a wasted life, they were desperate to reaffirm the spirituality they had projected on him.

"You can't be serious," Henri offered.

"You are much too harsh with yourself," Martin added. "What about the thousands of people who are better because of your books, lectures and tapes?"

Patric waved the comments away as if they were annoying flies. "I had nothing to do with any of that. What I had to say just happened to converge with what many people needed to hear." Then he looked directly at Rebecca, sadness in his eyes now. "We should all envy you."

"And why is that?" Roger asked, his voice tinged with irony.

"Because simply by eating this and not eating that she does a— what do you call it?" He looked at Rebecca for help.

She lowered her head, as if not wanting to look at him.

"A mitzvah?" Martin offered.

"That's it. A mitzvah. A good deed."

"Not really," Saul corrected him quickly. "Mitzvah means

commandment. When I do a mitzvah, I am doing what I have been commanded to do by God."

"And that's not good?" Patric shot back. "Judaism makes it so easy to do good. Just do what God commands. You have no idea how much I envy you, my dear rabbi. I am ashamed to say this, and I've never said it aloud to anyone before and I probably wouldn't now if I'd not had too much to drink, but the sad truth of my life is that I have never had a direct experience of God. Can you believe that?" he asked, his eyes still on Rebecca. "I am a scholar of religion. I have studied the sacred scriptures in every religion, many of them in the original. I have lived in monasteries in this country, France and Japan. I have prayed, I have fasted, I have flagellated myself. I have begged God to reveal Himself to me, to allow me to feel *something* of His presence. The result? The older I become, the wider and deeper grows the emptiness at my center. Yet God is available to you every time you eat something kosher. In my cooking I offer you something of the essence of who I am. I don't understand. The food I cook with such love is not holy to you, but eating with a plastic fork food that must taste like cardboard and from a Styrofoam tray is holy. I don't understand. Please help me understand."

Patric made no attempt to hide the desperation in his voice and, by the hush that had descended on the table, it was as if everyone there knew this was no longer a conversation about food or holiness but about why she wouldn't sleep with him.

Rebecca had been looking down during Patric's outburst. In the silence the ticking of the pendulum clock on the fireplace mantel at the other end of the room seemed inordinately loud. Finally, Rebecca raised her head and looked directly at Patric. There was a coldness in her eyes he had never seen and he knew then that he had lost her, though he had never had her. But not having had her was different than knowing she was beyond him forever.

"I am not my taste buds," she said with quiet firmness.

"What does that mean?"

She shook her head as if she didn't want to talk anymore.

"What does that mean?" Patric repeated harshly. He was oblivious to everyone at the table except her.

Roger leaned forward, cleared his throat, and said in his honeyed voice, "Well, I'd much rather have an orgasm, which is certainly a lot more accessible than God." The laughter that started was stopped when Patric slammed his fist on the table so hard that the dishes and silverware rattled and a wineglass toppled over, staining the white tablecloth a deep purple as he yelled, "If experiencing God is not important, what is? If experiencing God in the very marrow of your being is not important, what is? And the Jews, the goddamn Jews, experience God simply by eating bad food!"

There was a stunned silence. No one moved. People watched the wine spread slowly along the center of the tablecloth until Henri Fournier took his cloth napkin and placed it in the wine's path. Patric had a look of horror on his face as he realized what he had said.

"Rebecca. I . . . I . . . I am so sorry," he stammered, reaching out and touching her hand.

"I think I should go," she said quietly, pulling her hand away and standing up.

"Me, too," Saul agreed.

"Rebecca?" Patric called out to her back as she went to get her coat from the bedroom where she had laid it across the bed with the other coats. He followed her, begging her forgiveness.

As she zipped up her jacket and put on her gloves, she looked at him and said calmly, "I'm sorry you have never experienced God, but that's not the fault of the goddamn Jews."

That night he wrote her a long letter of apology expressing his deep shame at his latent anti-Semitism. After several weeks he had received a brief note from her. She accepted his apology, she wrote, and added that any future invitations to his house would be refused. That was the last contact he had had with her until a moment ago.

FIVE

~

As Rebecca made her way to the booth in the farthest corner of The HangOut, she waved to Martha Stimpson behind the cafeteria counter. How odd that Patric, the person who she would have thought would have the least difficulty accepting her for who she was, had the most, and Martha, the one who'd had the most, now accepted her totally. And with each of them the issue had been food.

When she came to the college she had given Martha, who was manager of The HangOut, a list of kosher coffees, tuna fish, bread, and mayonnaise to order for her so she could eat there. Martha said it would be too much trouble to have separate food for one person. "What would we do if everybody started wanting their own food?" Rebecca went to Maurice Woodley, the president of the college. A tall, large man, but without a hint of fat, he commanded respect as much by physique and his direct gaze as charm and intellect. Though balding, his hair was brushed back tightly, which made the front of his head look prominent rather than merely bald and made him appear distinguished rather than aging. He said, "If the manager of The HangOut said it isn't feasible, then it isn't" and he had stood up from behind his large and shiny desk and extended a well-manicured hand to her, which she refused as she mentioned that the last thing she wanted to do was call the National Association against Anti-Semitism and have them put out a press release about a college's refusal to respect the religious practices of the only rabbi on its staff, which would mean her friend at the *New York Times* would be on the next plane eager to do an article on anti-Semitism at one of the most innovative colleges in the country (and even if her friend did work in advertising, she wanted to break into reporting) and Maurice Woodley pulled back his proffered hand and turned red beneath the tan he managed to keep twelve months of the year, blushing to the roots of his neatly brushed and graying hair and, though he spluttered that he didn't like being threatened, two hours later Martha's assistant called her office to say there would be no problem about her food requirements and, if there were ever any questions, she should not feel that the only way to resolve them was to go to the president. Rebecca's willingness to use power had angered Martha, but Rebecca met the older woman's sullenness with politeness.

One afternoon a few months later when Rebecca went to the door of the kitchen to get her tray from Martha, the older woman asked, "Are you a real rabbi?"

Rebecca wanted to laugh as Martha handed her a tray with a tuna fish sandwich on a paper plate and black coffee in a paper cup. "Yes, I am," she responded quietly.

"Well, you seem like a religious person. I mean, the way you carried on about the tuna fish didn't make sense to me, and having to have your coffee in a paper cup. Mind if I come and sit with you for a moment?" she asked rhetorically, leading the way to the booth in the back and sitting down. "My husband said that was your way of being religious just like making the sign of the cross is mine. My husband's always telling me that I don't accept nothing I can't understand and that's not always good. Maybe he's got a point. I don't know." She paused. Rebecca bit into her sandwich. "There's something troubling me that I don't understand and you being a rabbi, maybe you can help me. Why did my boy die in Vietnam?"

It was not a fair question to have to answer when you had tuna fish in your mouth, especially when the question was asked without the whine of self-pity.

Rebecca looked at Martha and saw not a thin woman in a white uniform (a dark brown handkerchief folded to a point and showing from the pocket over her left breast), saw not a woman whose eyes were as dead as stones, whose thin lips would always be locked in a hard line, but a girl, with long brown hair and eyes shining with the pride of creation, holding a baby. Rebecca saw her standing at the altar in her church for the baby's christening and saw the child grow to be an altar boy and what position had he played in Little League and what make and model was his first car? How do you bury the child you birthed? How do you watch the children of your neighbors getting their first jobs, marrying, and bringing grandchildren for visits on Sunday afternoons and you have only memories you don't know how to hold?

Rebecca saw that Martha had heard all the words of commiseration and sympathy and borne the stigma of the bereaved. Tears had flowed over her soul like creek water over stones until her soul was polished smooth, its graininess sparkling with the hardness of the summer sun. Only truth could withstand such anger.

"What did your priest tell you?" Rebecca asked.

Martha laughed bitterly. "He said it was God's will. You know what I said to him? I said what kind of God is He then if He wills the death of an eighteen-year-old boy? Father said that was blasphemy. I didn't care. I'm just a mother and I was asking a mother's question. He told me to have more faith, that God's ways could not be understood." She shook her head. "You would think that after all these years I would've reconciled myself to Kevin's death, but it's harder to live with now than it was then. They say time heals. That's not necessarily true. Sometimes time makes things worse and harder. One day I had a son. The next all I had was a question that can't ever be answered. It makes me so angry I could kill God! You're a man of the cloth, Rabbi, but I will not apologize!"

"Good," Rebecca said quietly.

"What did you say?"

"Maybe God owes you an apology."

"Is that the way Jews look at it?"

"Sometimes. Why shouldn't you be angry at God? Why is it that we're the ones who spend our lives trying to understand Him and His ways? Maybe it's time He tried to understand us. I'll tell you a true story: Several hundred years ago, the Jews of a certain town were massacred. A group of rabbis came together and put God on trial. Why had he permitted His people to be slaughtered, yet again? One rabbi spoke for the prosecution and gave arguments as to why God should be found guilty. Another rabbi spoke in God's defense. The other rabbis served as the jury."

"What did the jury decide?" Martha asked eagerly.

"They found God guilty."

Martha laughed. "I like that. But how do you carry out a sentence against God?"

"By being angry at Him, maybe. By letting Him know you won't say all the words of praise in the prayers and the hymns, by telling Him that He's wrong sometimes. Sometimes I get angry at God, too."

"If Father knew I was sitting here listening to words like that, he wouldn't let me receive communion."

"Have you ever washed the body of a dead child, Martha?"

Martha's eyes widened as she shook her head.

"In our religion, we don't embalm the dead. We prepare the bodies of our dead ourselves. There was a child, a girl, five years old, whose parents belonged to my synagogue. I had rejoiced with the parents when they told me they were expecting; I was at the hospital when she was born. I did the naming ceremony when she was given her Hebrew name, went to her birthday parties, and one day the phone rang in my office and the mother told me the child had fallen down the basement steps, steps she had gone up and down many times going to and from the rec room, but this time she tripped and she was lying at the bottom of the steps, dead, and would I please come over? I sat on the basement floor holding that life which had just ended, waiting for the police and the ambulance, and I refused to understand the God who permitted this. That night we washed her body and the next day we buried her and I had to say all the words a rabbi is supposed to say and I didn't believe any of them at that moment.

"So, my answer to your question, Martha, is I don't know. But don't you stop asking it. Maybe if we get angry enough at God, one of these days He'll have to give us an answer."

The next day Martha brought Rebecca's lunch to the booth and had done so ever since.

"How're you today, Rabbi?" Martha said, placing the tray with the sandwich and coffee in front of her.

"I'm all right, Martha. You?"

Martha shrugged. "I'm still working for a living, so something's wrong."

The two women laughed and Martha headed back to the kitchen.

Rebecca wondered, as she had many times before, how a momentary encounter with someone scarcely known could have such shocking intimacy, an inhaling and exhaling of the other as if, for an instant, you shared the same rhythmic heartbeat and the same breath as sweet as spring. How could you have such a moment with the guy filling your tank at the gas station, a moment in which the words exchanged were banal and clichéd, words that had been said by a million tongues ten million times. Maybe it was the very safety of the familiarity that circumcised the heart, removed the protective layers of flesh and laid bare the bloody, pulsating muscle and the wonder of it all—and so you laughed, the two of you, and entered intimacy.

"Hi, Rabbi!"

Rebecca looked up to see Allison smiling nervously down at her.

"I was hoping I would catch you here and save myself the walk to your office. May I sit down for a moment?"

Rebecca nodded, looking into the wide blue eyes scintillating with innocence, at the cheeks as naturally red as sin, at the long, straight blond hair, and she was offended that someone could be so naturally beautiful, and, as quickly, she was ashamed that she was offended.

"I wanted you to know that I'm feeling a lot better, you know, and everything's all right now. You know?"

Rebecca wanted to say, no, everything was not all right. Because you could smile did not mean the lips of the soul had turned upward. But she never forced others to look on their pain. That could be as fatal as looking at God face to face. Yet she was disappointed. She had gone to the basement last night and found the notebook in which she'd kept her notes on the women's rituals she had helped create and she'd been so looking forward to doing some meaningful work with a student rather than offering the psychological equivalent of a Band-Aid. "I'm glad," Rebecca managed to say.

"You aren't disappointed in me, or anything?" the girl wanted to know.

"Of course not," Rebecca lied.

"I mean, I know what I did was awful and all like that, but everything is fine now." She got up. "Thanks for all your help, Rabbi."

"You're welcome, Allison, but I didn't do very much."

"Oh, that's not true. You helped me a lot more than you know. Take it easy."

Rebecca wondered what had changed. Allison seemed happy, almost giddy, but wasn't adolescence defined by the ability to go from suicidal despair to ecstasy in the sweep of the second hand around the face of a watch? Her eyes idly followed Allison as she walked away and slid into the booth opposite Patric. She was only there for a moment before leaving. Patric's attention returned to the stack of papers before Allison disappeared through the door.

Rebecca was surprised at how angry she was with Allison. She should know better than to pin her hopes on an undergraduate giving meaning to her life. Disgusted with herself she opened the *Times* she had brought from the office, went immediately to the Arts and Entertainment section, found the crossword puzzle on the next to last page and, with her Montblanc pen, wrote ALP in answer to the 1-Across clue, "High in Switzerland."

S I X

❧

Rebecca was still angry when she got home that evening. Instead of hanging her lamb suede jacket in the hall closet as she did normally, she threw it onto the black leather sofa in the front room, then sat in the rocking chair next to the long table on which the Torah scroll rested and started rocking back and forth furiously.

Why didn't people want to receive what she had to offer? she wondered.

The self-pity in the question did not negate her need for an answer. All she wanted was to bring others into relationship with their souls as the Rosh Yeshiva had done for her. Was that so awful?

Perhaps it was because no one had ever *asked* her to do anything with their soul. But was that true? What about Saul and Patric? But no. They had wanted her soul for themselves. That was different than the Rosh Yeshiva making her soul as precious to him as his own.

When she had walked into his office with her father that first day he got up from behind his desk with its stacks of papers and books, walked around it and squatted in front of her so that she was looking directly into his face with its flourishing and untrimmed black beard and dark eyes as unforgiving and content as death. These were eyes that could understand her.

"So you have a wound, too," he said to her in Yiddish, not smiling.

After the accident, adults always smiled at her and their smiles made her angry. The Rosh Yeshiva didn't smile and she felt loved. "So do I," he continued. He unbuttoned the sleeve of his white shirt, pushed it and the sleeve of his dark coat up to reveal the numbers stenciled on his forearm, numbers like the ones on the forearms of her father and mother.

"There are some Jews with wounds like mine who have had operations to have the numbers removed from their arms." He rolled down his shirt and coat sleeves slowly as he talked. "Other Jews I know put Band-Aids over the numbers. And who am I to say that they should not? But you and I know something, don't we?" He stood and showed her the ritual fringes of the *tallit katan*—small prayer shawl—that showed beneath his vest. "The observant Jewish male is commanded to wear this so he will be reminded constantly that he is to love God. A wound is a reminder, too." He paused. Then he smiled but there was no happiness, joy or light on his face—only the warmth of never-ending suffering borne in the silence of cruel love. "We will become good friends. Yes?"

She nodded and returned his smile.

What did it mean to put a person in relationship to their soul? Maybe it was to help someone know that nothing mattered more than the quality of their living. That was what she had learned from the Rosh Yeshiva though she hadn't lived her life with such focused clarity. But at least she had known and still knew that was how she was supposed to live, how she wanted to live. How had the Rosh Yeshiva instilled that desire in her? Perhaps by living with his wound without flaunting it to draw attention to himself nor by letting it define him. It was and he was.

"But you and I know something, don't we? A wound is a reminder, too."

What had his wound reminded him of? And why had he thought
she, a child, knew what he knew? She had never asked, ashamed for
him to learn that she didn't know. But he had probably known that.

Rebecca slowed her rocking, sighed audibly, and released some of
the anger from her body. She got up, took her coat from the couch and
hung it on a wooden hanger in the hall closet. She loved the luxuriant
softness of the lambskin and ran her fingers lightly over the sleeve closest to her. She'd seen the coat in the window of a boutique on Madison
Avenue shortly after she'd returned from Israel the summer of her
move to Vermont, and even through the store window she had loved it
with a passion that probably bordered on idolatry. How could she love
something that could not return her love? The saleswoman had
helped her rationalize such an outrageously opulent and expensive
purchase by saying it would be perfect for Vermont's long winters,
which it had been.

She started to close the closet door, then stopped and opened it
again. Staring at the coat she saw it in a way she never had, saw it not
with that part of her which loved sensuous beauty but through her
mind which did not see the creamy softness of the beige leather nor the
white fleece of the lining but went beyond appearance to an implied
and prior reality. For the first time in the five years she'd owned the coat
Rebecca permitted herself conscious awareness of the lambs whose
lives had been taken in order to make her coat. She knew she was being
sentimental (and thinking about those lambs would not keep her
from wearing the coat and enjoying its warm sensuality). Yet she was
ashamed that she had not, until that moment, permitted herself the

ιe deaths of living beings—*nefesh chayah* they were
ιh—were integral to the pleasure she derived from the

ε reminders, too."

But only it you permitted yourself to be reminded, if you did not try to eradicate the wounds or cover them with bandages. Or wear a beautiful coat without wanting to know how such beauty came to be. And that was why she was so angry with Allison. She did not want to be reminded that she was wounded.

Closing the door of the closet she walked along the hallway, through the middle room and into the kitchen. She filled the electric kettle with cold water and plugged it in. As she looked through the large rack where she kept her teas, she found herself silently thanking Dennis for the ritual of tea, a drink she'd scarcely had until they married. She wondered if he ever silently thanked her for anything. She doubted it. What could she have given him that would have been worthy of his gratitude? Certainly not love. She supposed she had loved him as best as she knew how, but how much love had there been to give when she had married him because, well, because he was there and he didn't have a discernable limp of body or soul. She had loved his tallness, his blondness, the blue of his eyes, and the smile that was always in those eyes and on his lips. She married him thinking her wound would be healed by the beauty of his smile.

When the water in the kettle began boiling, she poured it into the white pot on whose bottom she had sprinkled a teaspoon of black tea leaves. She unplugged the kettle and took the pot and a small white tea bowl into the front room and sat down again in the rocking chair. She closed her eyes, rocked slowly back and forth and listened to the silence, a presence she knew more intimately than any that could be evoked with words. Silence was not the absence of sound but was itself a sound that could be loud or soft, soothing or disturbing, complex or simple. Dennis had never understood her silences and she hadn't tried to help him. To do so she would have had to talk and interrupt the very silence she had no desire to disturb.

She had grown up with silence. Many times she and her father would be studying Torah at the table in the kitchen when silence would descend in the middle of a sentence or the imperceptible pause between one syllable and another. Sometimes he would emerge from the silence to tell her a story from before the war or after the war but there was never a story about the war and that time summed up in one sibilant word—Auschwitz.

She knew when memory had thrust him back there because he sat at the table, the Chumash open before him, eyes staring at its pages but not seeing them, and the silence became heavier and heavier until eventually he got up and trudged slowly into the bedroom at the other end of the apartment. Sometimes she could hear faint whispers of conversation between him and her mother. Most of the times, however, the only sound was silence descending like the darkness created when the lid of a casket was closed.

So many times she begged him to tell her about that place, but he would only shake his head. Once, however, he looked at her with an almost sweet sadness and said, "Whatever I would say would be a lie. The words to tell the truth about that place will never be created."

Had that been her excuse for not telling Dennis what had caused her limp, why she had headaches so crushing and spells of vertigo so debilitating that there were days she could not get out of bed?

"How can I love you if I don't know what hurts you?" he asked once.

She knew he was referring to the story about the Hasidic rebbe who asked his followers if they loved him. With great fervor they told him they did. Then he asked if they knew what hurt him. When they said no, he responded, "How can you say you love me if you don't know what hurts me?"

Rebecca had felt guilty when Dennis reminded her of that story but not so guilty that she disturbed her silence. Now she wondered if there wasn't something very male about the story. Why did Dennis need to know *what* hurt her? Why had it not been enough for him to simply know that she hurt? She thought she knew the reason because she had seen the look on his face too many times, that look that said, "If I knew what was hurting you I know I could fix it." Men, or maybe it was just American men, were accustomed to fixing things as if that was their God-given duty. Rebecca resented the presumption that all wounds could be healed. They could not. Some wounds were reminders, if you allowed them to be.

The seed of a marriage's possible dissolution was planted at the same time and with the same care as the seed of its potential. Rebecca had been drawn to Dennis because he was not wounded, but the absence of an apparent wound had made it impossible for him to enter the silence where her soul resided.

During her years as a congregational rabbi she had counseled couples whose marriages were in crisis and she had always been surprised by how much anger some of them had toward each other. She envied the passion they lavished on each other even if the ultimate goal of that passion was mutual destruction. How shabby her own marriage seemed when compared with the extravagant emotions she had witnessed in other unions.

The only emotion her marriage evoked, then and now, was an affectionate indifference. She supposed she could have lived that way for decades, maybe a lifetime, convinced that a relationship of pecks on the cheek once or twice a day and pleasant conversation at dinner about matters of no consequence was preferable to loneliness. But one morning she awoke and was startled to see a man asleep next to her. There was something vaguely familiar about the straight blond hair and she knew, somehow, that the eyes beneath the closed lids were a cerulean blue. Then she recognized that it was Dennis, her husband, but recognition did not bring the relief of warm memory but only images as gray and wrinkled as old newspaper photographs without captions—there he was on the other side of the Ping-Pong table in his parent's basement, smashing the ball over the net and into her chest, laughing, and there he was, still as a mountain, hunched over a chessboard playing against a Jew in the Soviet Union, it sometimes taking a year to make six moves as the postcards went back and forth—and more and more images came but none of them elicited joy or sadness. She liked him; she respected him but he was absent from her emotional life.

She was ashamed. Her father's memories were so filled with emotion they could reach from long decades past and claim him body and soul, but she lay next to her husband and could not find even a smile in her memories of their marriage. That same evening she did the most honest thing she'd done in all their years together and told him she could not be married to him any longer. She did not explain and, worn down perhaps by having tried and failed to live with her silence, he did not ask for reasons. She had seen him only once since he gave her the get—religious divorce—before an Orthodox bet din in Brooklyn.

In downtown Jerusalem there was a small Yemenite kosher

restaurant on a short, narrow, cobblestoned street closed to automobiles. Bookstores, small galleries and arty shops lined both sides. Rebecca liked to sit outside beneath the restaurant's awning and eat mishmishiya—a lamb stew with apricots, ginger, cinnamon, and a lot of other spices she couldn't identify—and sip a glass of kosher red from a winery on the Golan Heights. She could sit as long as she wanted which she did in the heat of an afternoon, reading and watching the continual stream of people going past—beautiful Israeli girls in sundresses and sandals strolling casually, aware of but seemingly indifferent to the openly lustful male stares, college-aged American Jews on a year abroad studying at Hebrew University and wearing T-shirts emblazoned with the names of their American schools, young Israeli men and women in the crisp khaki of the Israeli Defense Forces, rifles slung casually over their shoulders, and Hasidic men in their black suits, hats, open-necked white shirts and full, unkempt beards walking hurriedly, eyes fixed in front of them to avoid even an inadvertent glance at a woman. It was June, a month before she learned she had more passion for a coat than she'd ever had for her husband, two months before she would be moving into her house in Vermont to begin her life again and so she had come to Israel for three weeks to immerse herself in Jewishness before going to a place where Jews were few.

Rebecca's first year in rabbinical school had been spent in Israel, and each year during her rabbinate, she had brought a group of congregants on a tour of the country she loved and hated almost equally. Israel was the place she felt least a Jew because as a woman she could not enter most synagogues and worship and pray as a Jew who believed God needed and wanted women's prayers in equal voice to men's. However, the antiquity of the land, the immediacy of the past in practically every stone, also made Israel the place she felt most a Jew.

That June afternoon as she sat in the shade ben. awning she was wondering how often she would once she was living in Vermont when she noticed far ι tall Hasid, with blond hair showing from beneath his striding quickly past. A blond Hasid stood out among the ι ι accustomed dark beards, and, as he came closer, Rebecca realized the man was Dennis. The scraggly yellow beard and the earlocks were unfamiliar to her, but the loping walk was not. It was Dennis. She was sure of it.

She started to call his name as he came abreast of where she sat but something made her pause. What if it wasn't him? But even more frightening, what if it was? What would she say? Was there anything to be said? She wondered what he was doing in Jerusalem and when he had become a Hasid and why, for God's sake. Why? Had he been in the process of becoming a Hasid when he insisted on giving her the get and had her appear with him before a bet din of black-hat rabbis? If she had felt anything beyond curiosity, she would have called out his name and seen if the man she thought was him would turn around. Instead she watched him turn a corner and disappear.

She poured tea into the small bowl and sipped quietly. How odd that she had a warmer affection for him in memory than she'd had when they were married. Perhaps some events achieved life only in memory. Perhaps that was how it was for her parents. Decades had to pass before they could experience the emotions which near-starvation, deprivation, terror and psychic numbness had not allowed them to experience then. How cruel memory could be that it held onto and preserved that which you did not want to remember and had no reason to remember and served it to you when you thought you had, at long last, escaped the past.

She looked at the shawl covering the Torah scroll. A knot was a memory, too, as she pictured the one tied around the scroll. But what happened to a memory when those to whom it belonged were no longer alive to receive it? That did not matter if you were a Jew. Jews took as their own memories they did not remember.

She got up and gently unwrapped the shawl from around the Torah, then lifted the scroll up from the table enough so she could slide the mantle off. The knot seemed to be staring up at her as if it wanted to tell her all it knew. It was the only surviving memory of that Shabbat morning when Avram ben Moshe became bar mitzvah in the town of Czechowa. But that knotted wimple contained other memories, too, memories of Moshe, the father of Avram, and Moshe's mother whose name was not, of course, recorded on the wimple. Rebecca decided to give her a name since memory did not record everything, did not record even everything that was important. She decided to call Avram's mother Leah for the despised wife of Jacob because Avram's mother had been despised by memory.

Rebecca's hand rested lightly on the wimple, and memories seemed to stream from it and into her as she saw the day Leah told Moshe he was going to be a father, of the day Avram was born, of his first words, his first steps, the first day he went to cheder and the *melamed* had written an alef on a slate and put a dollop of honey on it and told Avram to dip his finger in the honey and then lick it so he would know that learning was sweet and the stream of memory leaped from Avram's first day in cheder to that Shabbat morning in August of 1944 when Moshe and Leah went to shul with Avram, their eyes filled with proud tears as they anticipated seeing their son stand before the congregation and read from the Torah and, without meaning to, at least not consciously, Rebecca's fingers began untying the knot. Then, as if coming awake, she realized what she was doing and stopped. Who was she to untie such a knot as this? How dare she undo a history which had been allowed to speak its silent eloquence for almost fifty years? But as her fingers resumed working at the knot, it was as if they were responding to what the knot itself wanted, what the knot had been pleading for someone to do almost since that Shabbat morning in 1944. Rebecca didn't know where such a thought was coming from but, despite her misgivings, she felt powerless to stop her fingers from completing its task. Once the wimple was untied, it appeared to fall gently to the table of its own accord.

Rebecca stood staring down at the still tightly rolled scroll, wondering what to do next. Should she open it? Even as she asked the question she knew she would, knew that she wanted to see what Avram ben Moshe had been chanting when the Nazis came in.

She unrolled the scroll only wide enough to see one column and her eyes fell almost immediately upon the words *Tamim tihiyeh im Adonai Eloheicha*—You shall be wholehearted with the Lord your God.

And she heard, yet again, the voice of the Rosh Yeshivah: "Wounds are reminders, too." Could one be wholehearted with God if she did not remember her wounds?

Tears came to Rebecca's eyes as she slowly rolled the Torah scroll tightly and, taking the wimple, tied it around the scroll in a neat bow. She slid the mantle over the scroll, then rewrapped it in her shawl.

It was past time for her to have said the evening prayers. She didn't know if she could pray that evening. Prayer required focus, required paying attention. She supposed love and prayer were a lot alike: both required the wholehearted attentiveness and focus of one's being. She was poor at both but her lips began to move with the familiar Hebrew words and cadences of the evening prayers, prayers she'd known by memory since she was twelve, but on this evening she poured her heart like water into the words.

"Yisgadal v'yiskadash sh'may ra-boh."

Rebecca was instantly awake and alert, sitting up in bed, her body rigid. She had thought the voices were coming from her dream, but no. As difficult as it was for her to believe, there was no mistaking: the voices were coming from downstairs, from the front room where the Torah scroll was. The voices were muffled, low, but the words of the Mourner's Kaddish were unmistakable. The Yiddish accents and Ashkenazic pronunciation of the ancient prayer's Aramaic words spoke of an age before the rebirth of the nation of Israel.

The voices stopped. Rebecca wondered why there was the sudden silence. After a moment she realized they had stopped at the place in the prayer where those in the congregation who were not reciting the Kaddish would say *Amein*, so be it, as it was the responsibility of those not saying a prayer to ask that its wishes be fulfilled. Shivering in the darkness, Rebecca waited for the *Amein* to be said except they would pronounce it *Omein*. It did not come. The silence deepened. She waited. Then, slowly, the realization came. Oh, no! They were waiting for *her* to say *Omein*.

She didn't know what to do. Maybe if she waited long enough they would go on without her, or they would say *Omein* themselves but the silence grew louder and louder until finally, unable to withstand it any longer, Rebecca whispered, *"Omein,"* and immediately the voices continued—

"B'olmo deev'ro chirusay, v'yam-leech malchusay. B'chayaychon, uvyomaychon, uvchayay d'chol bays yisroayl, Baagolo uvis'man kareev, v'imru—"

"*Omein*," Rebecca said so softly that she barely heard her voice, but the chorus from downstairs resumed immediately, and without thinking, she joined them in the next line, always said by congregation and mourners together—

"*Y'hay sh'may ra-bo m'vorach, l'olam ulolmay olmayo yisborach.*"

They continued with the prayer and she responded with *Omein* at the appropriate places as a chill pierced her body and caused her to shiver violently. After she said her final "*Omein*," it was once again quiet.

Magnified and sanctified be the name of God throughout the world which He has created according to His will. May He establish His kingdom during the days of your life and during the life of all the house of Israel, speedily, yea, soon; and say, Amen.

May His great name be blessed for ever and ever.

Exalted and honored be the name of the Holy One, blessed be He, whose glory transcends, yea, is beyond all praises, hymns and blessings that man can render unto Him; and say ye, Amen.

May there be abundant peace from heaven, and life for us and for all Israel; and say ye, Amen.

May He who establishes peace in the heavens, grant peace unto us and unto all Israel, and let us say, Amen.

After that they came every morning at 3:00 a.m. *Yisgadal v'yiskadash.* So many voices. Men's. Women's. Children's. They prayed softly, liltingly, *shmay raboh*, bespeaking a music of the spirit which baffled her. Why would they be lyricists?

Omein, she responded.

How did they know when she had said it and when she had not? Sometimes, to test them, she only moved her lips but allowed no sound to escape. It did not matter. They heard. When you're only ashes you hear the unfolding of pale green leaves in the spring. When you're only ashes, you see the design of every snowflake wherever and whenever it falls. When you're only ashes, you hear the flesh of the living as it rots.

After her final *Omein* Rebecca would slide slowly back beneath the covers, pulling them tightly around her. It was silent except for the faint sound of flames licking flesh and lapping blood. She would lie in bed, awake, and wait for first light to release her. With the softest touch of gray against the white walls she fell asleep until her clock radio/CD player awakened her at six with the "Siciliana" from Bach's flute sonata, in E-flat.

Every morning when she went downstairs, she looked for them. There was not even a telltale speck of ash on the shawl in which she had wrapped the Torah scroll. Yet she knew they were there. Why wouldn't she? She was a Jew and Jews believed in a God who could not be seen and did not care, a God whose invisibility was surpassed only by His silence. To the Christians He had come in the form of His own son. To the Muslims He had come through the prophet Muhammad. Only with the Jews had he not assumed human guise. Only to the Jews did he remain outside the bond of intimate relationship: HaShem—The Name.

Believing in ghosts was simple compared to believing in such a God. But it was not a matter of belief or disbelief. Being a Jew meant being rational enough to trust her experience, whether it was of God or ghosts. "Belief " was too timid a word for such terror.

How could she listen to voices reciting the Mourner's Kaddish at 3:00 a.m. and seven hours later meet with Brian Moon, her boss, and talk about an anorexic student as if the student existed in the same dimensions of time and space as the dead Jews of Czechowa? How did she live with gentile notions of the normal and still be a Jew? Patric Marsh had not grown up in a world where *Oy vay* was not only a personal expression of dismay, shock, surprise, fear, apprehension, pain, regret, horror, joy, disapproval, lament but the very saying *OY vay oy VAY Oyyyy Oy vaaay Oy VAAAAY OY VAY* drew to itself the ancestral memories of speaker and hearer like matter into a black hole and it was not only your *Oy vay* but centuries of *OY* and *OY vay* resounding back through time until one heard God say, "Let there be light," and some anonymous angel responded, "*Oy vay.*" Martha, who still grieved for her son, had not grown up in a world where every bagel eaten was compared to the bagels in the Karcelik—the open market—in Warsaw or Kazimierz, the old Jewish quarter in Kraków, or those made by this one's *mamale*—mother—or that one's *tanteleh*—aunt. Gentiles could only have one kind of reputation among those who called the smoke *mamale, mamenyu, bruderel, shvesterel, tante, zeyde, tate, tateleh, tatenyu, bubbe,* and that was why she had been surprised when the Rosh Yeshiva told her to go to Columbia.

He had not explained and she had not asked. She supposed in their world hers appeared to be without freedom and choice because she had not visited colleges and decided which was right for her. She had let someone else make the decision, a decision which she accepted without question or protest. She had never understood why Americans thought they were capable of making all decisions for themselves. Why did they think they knew what was best for themselves when they were only eighteen?

Her obedience to the Rosh Yeshiva was an expression of love. How many Americans knew a love so complete that you did not hesitate to entrust your soul to that person? If the Rosh Yeshiva wanted her to go to Columbia, something was there which he thought was important for her to learn.

The learning began at once. She sat in her first class on returning to school after Rosh Hashanah. Before the professor came in, she listened to students talking about their roommates and what classes and professors they had, and the football game that past Saturday. Something was wrong and she did not know what until she realized that the sound of the shofar was not still beating at their souls

"TERUAH"
TATTATTATTATTATTATTATTATTAT

They didn't know it was now 5731. For them it was still 1971. For her it would never be entirely. For them time was only 1,971 years old. They did not know how young they were to her.

That first year she also learned that many Jews were also gentiles, living in 1971, unable to pray the prayers polished and repolished by millions of tongues for millions of days. Their tongues would never add a sparkle to a *baruch* here and an Avraham there. He wanted her to know the pain of such loss.

"How do you bear the disjuncture between inside and outside?" she asked him. "How do I live knowing that everything they think is me is not who or what I am? I mean, I suppose it is, but it is not what is important—that I'm bright, well read, quick with words and all those things that are so important to them. None of that matters to me and what matters is not something they can know."

He could only shrug. "It is not my problem. Jewry has now moved to America. My job was to be sure you knew the problems."

So, she learned the pain and confusion of hiding that which was most precious. She was accustomed to mixing Polish, Hebrew, Yiddish, Aramaic and English when she spoke, alluding to or quoting from Mishna, Gemara, Rambam, Chumash, Rashi, and the Shulchan in the most everyday of conversations. Almost everything had been Torah in her world.

At Columbia, nothing was. She did not know how to decipher a language and ways of being in which the holy was referred to only in oaths and curses, a language in which people used "Well," and "like, you know," or squeals or profanity, giving primitive expression to inchoate emotions because they did not know language had the power to raise the dead.

"To be a Jew is to be a people apart, a separate people," he told her. "We belong only to HaShem. To belong to anyone or anything else is idolatry—husband, wife, children, job, Israel. It does not matter. That is why there is anti-Semitism. That is why they have always sought to kill us—Muslims, Christians, it does not matter. We salute their flags and sing their anthems but something in us stands apart, and that part is the Jew. That is the part that does not ask them to accept us. That is the part that wants nothing and needs nothing from them, the part that is beyond their power, beyond their control, beyond their ability to know. That is why they hate us. That is why they kill us. And that is why we do not die."

But he had. This year was his tenth *yahrzeit* as well as the tenth anniversary of her ordination. Ten years.

Wasn't it only a week ago that she left her last class of the day at Columbia, or her last one of the day at rabbinical school and gone to the *beit midrash* to sit across from him at the table in the diminishing light of day reading the conversations of men who had lived almost two thousand years before, men who were related to her because they cared so deeply about God that they gave their lives trying to ascertain how He wanted them to live.

Judaism was the religion of relationships and feminists did not understand that it was not the maleness of God which distressed them; it was their own relationship to maleness that was distressing. Judaism insisted on relationship. Everything in Judaism was done within the context of family and/or community. Americans did not understand what it was like to sit across a desk from someone for nineteen years, six days a week, and study sacred texts together, to study texts that engaged them in conversation not only with each other but with the texts themselves, to argue with, laugh with, and exclaim about the wonders of holiness. Neither could Americans comprehend the relationship of trust existing between teacher and pupil, the intimacy of soul that joined them like wind to wing.

It was an intimacy that intensified when, near the end of her years at Columbia, she told him she wanted to be a rabbi. What else could she have been? Hadn't he been training her to that end all along? Didn't he realize what he had been doing? Her father was ready to declare her dead and sit shivah. A woman rabbi! Shmuel was prepared to do almost anything to make amends to the Rosh Yeshiva for a daughter who would bring such disgrace by becoming a rabbi. But can you sit across a table from someone for almost two decades, studying holiness, and not know that you're in a relationship in which you are guaranteed that no harm will come to you? Of course he had been training her to be a rabbi, he said. But why would he do that, he who had been trained in the strictest yeshivot of Lithuania.

He shrugged. "I do not understand the ways of HaShem. I looked into your soul and saw Rabbi written there. Mine is not to understand. Mine is merely to obey. I have done what HaShem asked of me. And yet, I still do not believe a woman should be a rabbi."

"Are you sorry you obeyed?" she needed to know.

He paused for a long time. She still marveled at how completely his face was covered with hair, hair that was now as much white as it was black, but the fierceness in his eyes was, mysteriously, becoming more luminously hard.

"Unlike others, your mother and father, for example, I lost no wife, no husband, no children on the other side."

She stopped him. "My parents had other families?"

"I have been indiscreet," he apologized. "I assumed they had told you."

"No," she said in a hoarse voice.

"Many of us are like that, Rivka. Many of us do not want to remember, even though we cannot help remembering. I am not different. I have not told you much of the other side, either, have I?"

She shook her head.

"Perhaps it does not matter. And after all, what is there to say? Nothing, except I know now of what evil I am capable. Most people look at us who have the numbers on our forearms and they wonder how we withstood such suffering. What they do not know is that the greatest suffering was in being exposed to so much evil. The greatest suffering is understanding that holiness requires all of our attention and that evil comes from inattention to holiness."

He stopped and gazed over her right shoulder with that same look her father had when that place claimed him. After a moment the Rosh Yeshiva's gaze returned to this time and place and her. "I think your parents want you to know what they cannot speak of. I do not think your father would have brought you to me if he had not hoped that I would tell you something of what I know of them."

He paused again and Rebecca held her breath, afraid he would change his mind but after a moment, he continued and she let her breath out in slow relief.

"Your mother was married to a rabbinical student, David Plishke. He would have been a brilliant posek. I have no doubt his responsa would've brought light to us all. He was caught on the streets by the Nazis. They tore out his beard with their bare hands. Of course, when skin came with the hair, they did not seem to mind. They marched him to the shul and told him to spit on the Torah scroll. He said, 'How much is it worth to you to have me spit on the Torah? I will tell you how much it is worth to me. If you will leave the Jews of this town alone, I will spit on the Torah. If you will spare the life of every Jew here, I will spit on the Torah. That is my price.' They shot him. I know. I was there, hiding in a closet in the back of the shul. I heard him. There was not a quaver in his voice. He spoke offhandedly, casually. I was the one who told your mother what happened to him.

"When we were resurrected from the other side, I had no wife, no child to grieve. Why had I not married before? I did not know. Why did I not marry after? I did not know. I went to the matchmakers and they tried. Perhaps the women saw the chimneys of Auschwitz shining in my eyes. I do not know. Then, one day, your father came into my office. I had not seen him since the other side. I did not know that he and your mother had found each other, married and had a child. And I looked at you and it was clear. To teach you was what I was born to do. If I had had a wife, if I had had children, either I would have neglected you for them or them for you. That is not how HaShem wanted it. Through you, I am blessed."

She had not known if he would come to her ordination. Sumerian pagans were higher in his esteem than Reform Jews. She saw him sitting alone in the back of the auditorium. The beard was all white now as was the full and tangled head of hair. The eyes still blazed from beneath the black hat. Afterward, she went to him first, letting her parents and Dennis wait a respectful distance away. How did she say thank you? How *could* she say thank you? Wouldn't the words be an insult? You don't thank someone for taking you into his soul. She looked at him and, shocked, she saw tears welled in his eyes. Then, he, who in all their years had never touched her even casually, grasped her right hand and, placing his left one over hers, said, "Rabbi."

That was June. He died in November, on the twenty-fifth of Chesvan. When he did not appear for Shacharit—the morning prayers—Reb Mordechai went to the apartment on the fourth floor. He was lying in bed, having died in his sleep. *Baruch HaShem.* Blessed be the Name. Only the *tzaddikim* were permitted to go from sleep to death. To die so was thought to be a kiss from HaShem.

Reb Mordechai had called her father, who called her, and she was there that afternoon, sitting on the other side of the *mechitza*—the divider separating the women's and men's sections—in the room where she had sat with him almost every afternoon since she was eight years old. It was as if his work was done now that she was a rabbi, because the yeshiva never reopened. He was buried in a small Jewish cemetery in Stimson, New Jersey, where his brother had been rabbi and was buried. She had not known he had a brother.

To be a Jew was to live close to one's dead, visiting their graves on the *yahrzeit,* the day before each New Moon, during the month of Elul, the Sunday before Rosh Hashanah, the ten days between Rosh Hashanah and Yom Kippur. On the Sunday before Rosh Hashanah, Jewish cemeteries around the world were crowded. Even the Jews of Temple Sinai came to the cemetery at noon on that Sunday.

Her first such Sunday as a rabbi was overcast and cool, the kind of afternoon one shrank from, not wanting to be reminded of summer's shocking swiftness. The members of her congregation walked casually among the tombstones, pointing to this one or that one and exchanging a rueful smile or even a chuckle as they gave in to the sweet painfulness of memory. There was Avi Weiss, seventy-five years old, short, bald, with bulging dark eyes and a tiny tremor in hands where there had been none last autumn, who had owned a shoe store in Newark until the riots of 1967 when *they* had burned him out, burned *themselves* out, because Avi Weiss, like Mordechai his father before him, had sold good shoes at a fair price and many times when the choice was between the profit margin and some colored kid not going to school because he didn't have any shoes, Avi Weiss never chose profit and what was the thanks he got? Burn Baby Burn and he and his father had stood in the street and looked at the charred, blackened timbers, then climbed inside and stood there looking up at the sunny sky through what had been the roof, stood there in fishing boots ankle deep in water that smelled of ash and wood and leather and paper, ruined shoes floating on the water around them and Avi knew his father had died just then because death came when the spirit left the body and sometimes that happened years before the body could follow but Mordecai's body followed within a week. "And sometimes, Rabbi," Avi always concluded the story, "I want to

drive to Newark and ask the coloreds if Jesse Jackson or that Far-
rakhan character have put as many shoes on their feet as did Mordecai and Avi Weiss."

Rebecca had spent her years of college and rabbinical school learning to listen, not just to the words because she did not think it was possible for English to express all a Jew had to say; it was not possible for
any one language to say what it was *really* like to live separate and apart
on spiraling coils going outward and inward simultaneously, so she did
not believe the racism she heard in Avi Weiss's tone of voice, did not
confuse the man's inadequacy with language with any defect in his
character, because she knew he did not know how to speak the aching
that remained in his heart, the pain of the loss which time soothed but
never healed, not entirely, not ever entirely, and she wished she knew
how to teach Avi Weiss that it was all right to be a seventy-five-year-old
little boy who wanted his father.

She limped along the cinder paths reading the names on the tombstones of these who were also her congregants. Neither the Rosh
Yeshiva nor her teachers at rabbinical school had told her that to be a
rabbi was to care for the dead too, that sometimes it was unclear if
the dead were ever really dead. Moving through the cemetery that
morning, having first one and then another take her gently by the el-
bow and point to the gravestone of "my husband, my wife, my father,
my mother, my son, my daughter, my sister, my brother" and the
love, my God, the love that remained—

"Hy, my husband, was such a nice man. You would've liked him,
Rabbi."

"This one here, Abe Horowitz, his father and my father grew up
together on the other side."

"Thirty years I've been a widower, Rabbi. And not a day in those

91

thirty years have I not missed my Frieda, have I not walked in the door and wondered why she wasn't there."

There was an end to weeping. Mourning, however, ebbed and surged but never ceased flowing.

Maybe his death was his final teaching because, as she gathered the congregants to stand beneath the old and broad branches of an elm tree as if huddled together beneath the wings of Death itself, and as she led them in reciting the Twenty-third Psalm, which was recited at funerals and yahrzeit services, she knew their grief because it was her grief and when she sang El Male Rachamim—O One filled with Mercy—the traditional melody bound them together, not only with each other, not only with their dead and each other's dead, not only with all Jews who mourned and remembered on that day, not only with all the dead of all the Jews, but the ancient melody, a suppressed sob in her throat, bound them also to their own deaths and to those who would one day stand in a cemetery and remember them.

Stimson was an hour from her synagogue and, after she finished at the cemetery, she went to his grave. The clouds were darker when she stopped at the local police station to ask for directions to the Jewish cemetery. The young man behind the desk didn't know anything about any Jew cemetery but the chief happened to come in just then and on being told the problem, looked at the young man behind the desk and asked him what did he think was out "on Cemetery Road where the Christians were buried on the west side and the Jews on the east though there weren't many Jews buried there because there'd never been many Jews in that part of New Jersey not like around Teaneck and Engleside and all that part of New Jersey which really should've been given to New York because that New Jersey and this New Jersey were like mismatched socks and that was something Jews understood

92

better than most because they kept to themselves ate their own food kept their own language" and he had had nothing but respect for "the Rabbi, never understood how he lived from hand to mouth and sometimes it looked like he had a hard time of it just him and some old Jews in long black coats and black hats and black beards and black eyes come right after the war '47, '48 at the latest bought a piece of land outside of town at least it was outside then but since 1970 it had been inside the town though still wasn't nothing out there except the dead and the wind nope there wasn't even a trace of the synagogue though don't see how you could call it that because it wasn't nothing but a house and after the Rabbi died oh my six, seven years ago the few old Jews remaining moved away to live with their children and somebody said the Rabbi's brother came and sold the house and that was the end of the Jews of Stimson though somebody said there was a burying out at the Jewish cemetery back last November believe it was but don't know who that could've been and why they'd want to be buried in an unused cemetery no that's a right off Main Street and hell, town ain't big enough to lose your way in right off Main four blocks to Pine make a left and the next right is a dirt road and that's Cemetery Road—"

And there in the car between the two cemeteries as the rain began to fall in drops as large as sorrow, she cried for the first time since the Rosh Yeshiva's death and now, each morning at 3:00 a.m., she was being forced to mourn an emptiness that would never be filled.

SEVEN

~

She called it the dead season, that time of the year after autumn ended but winter had not yet arrived, the time when color had drained from the leaves yet they clung to limbs and branches as if they did not know they were going to fall, must fall, and then one night it rained, a hard rain, a steady rain, an all-night rain, a rain that brought with it cold Canadian air and the next morning was so gray it seemed to be merely a continuation of the night before and the roads were covered with wet, dead leaves as slick as the ice patches of deep winter. Trees that had been outrageous in their luxuriant greens of summer and shockingly forward in their reds and oranges and yellows of autumn were now stripped to the blackness of limb and branch and bark and trunk. She could sense a depression settling over the entire region, a sorrow for the spring and summer now past and a dread of the winter to come, a depression that dissipated, however, with the first light snowfall.

As she started driving down Pulpit Road, the sky was as gray as death, the air still and cold. The trees were bare and black, and even the green of the pines and cedars looked dull. If it did not snow that day, it would soon. She turned on the car heater, and was about to tune into the Vermont public radio station when the soft voice of a woman said, in Yiddish with a Polish accent like Rebecca's mother, "So, you're a rabbi?"

Oddly, maybe even sadly, Rebecca was not surprised. A normal person would have been startled and the steering wheel of the car might have jerked in her hand and the car would have gone into a ditch. But Rebecca did not register any reaction. Why would she have? She belonged to a people whose history included tales of a burning bush that said I AM THAT I AM, a people whose first patriarch was willing to sacrifice his beloved son, a people whose third patriarch worked fourteen years for the love of a woman, and what about Sarah who gave her husband another woman to have a child by, and Rebecca's own mother who still awoke nights screaming, so why would Rebecca be surprised to find herself addressed in Yiddish by a dead Polish Jewish woman while driving to work?

"This is something we never heard of—a woman rabbi," the voice continued. "Would you believe that even after you're dead you have to keep learning and making adjustments? *Oy!* It's not easy being dead, you know. It's not what you think. When you're alive, you think death is like sleep. You should be so lucky!"

Rebecca looked in the rearview mirror but saw no one in the backseat. As if something would've been different if there had been?

"They sent me. 'Why me?' I asked. 'What do I know about whether a woman could be a rabbi? Send someone who is learned.' You should hear the debates that go on. *Oy vay.* Rabbi Akiva, Hillel, Shammai, Maimonides, Rashi, *oy, oy, oy.* Back and forth, back and forth. Hillel says yes, naturally, and Shammai says no, and Maimonides is perplexed, and what do I know? I'm a simple Jew. In Czechowa, we did not even have a rabbi because we could hardly support ourselves. How could we support a rabbi? Reuven had been to yeshiva a couple of years and whenever we needed something done or said, if he didn't know it, he knew where to look it up. In the end, we were probably better Jews than the ones at the Great Synagogue in Warsaw. We got tired of waiting for Hillel and Shammai and all the others to agree and make a ruling so we decided we would make our own decision about you becoming our rabbi."

"I beg your pardon," Rebecca said, speaking for the first time.

"It's not a big job," the old woman continued.

Had Moses felt a little mad when the bush called his name? Had Abraham felt a little mad as he raised the knife and prepared to plunge it into the heart of his son? Had they felt as mad as she felt being interviewed to be rabbi to a community of Jews that had been dead for fifty years?

"Mainly, we need answers to some questions that are too difficult for Reuven."

"What sort of questions?" Rebecca asked, hating herself for asking.

"Well, Asher was hidden during the war by a Catholic family. They took care of him, fed him, saved his life. He and the oldest girl of the family fell in love during all this. She was the one who brought food everyday to the hiding place. After the war, they got married. They had a son who was converted to be a Jew and raised as a Jew. The question is this: His mother wants to participate at his bar mitzvah by reading from the Torah. But she's not a Jew. Can a non-Jew read from the Torah?"

Rebecca's hands gripped the steering wheel so tightly they hurt. "What are you talking about?" she asked, her voice tight. "Why are you asking me this? If they had a son after the war, then he became bar mitzvah years ago. What are you talking about?"

"Of course you don't understand. My apology. This is my first time talking to someone on this side and I forgot that you don't know what I know. When Asher and Marie married, the people of the village were outraged that a Jew had been hidden there during the war. So, they came; they took Asher. They made Marie watch as they killed him, then they killed her. Their son is the child they would have had if they hadn't been murdered. On this side where we are, there are no years. Asher and Sophie just decided that they want the son they would have had to become bar mitzvah."

"I see," she said quietly, though she didn't. "A non-Jew is permitted to read from the Torah because no one can harm the Torah, not even a goy. Generally, however, Jewish custom finds the very idea of a goy reading from the Torah to be offensive, and sometimes, custom has the power of law."

"Rabbi, we're not learned people. Just give us a straight answer. Should Marie be permitted to read from the Torah at her son's bar mitzvah?"

"Given that Marie sheltered and cared for a Jew, loved him and was martyred because of her love for him, I am proud that she would want to read from the Torah at her son's bar mitzvah."

"Thank you," the voice said, and with that, the Jeep felt as it did on any other morning.

Rebecca blinked and as if coming awake, she was surprised to find herself driving, effortlessly, the curves of Route 5 as it wound its way up and into the mountains to the college.

"You look like you've just seen a ghost," Melanie greeted Rebecca as she limped slowly into the office.

Rebecca almost burst into laughter but caught herself. "Do I look that bad?"

"No, but I see you almost every day and you've been looking tired, like you haven't been sleeping well. What's up, if I may ask?" Melanie was the receptionist of Psych Services. A short, thin woman in her early fifties, she had short hair too blond to be natural. Her lipstick was too red for the sallowness of her skin and the mascara (purple today) was not only the wrong color but seemed to have been applied with a trowel. When Rebecca had first come to the college she had wanted to take Melanie to the makeup counter of a department store in Montreal or Burlington and teach her about the infinite world of color and cosmetics but had never figured out how to make the offer diplomatically. But as she came to value Melanie, Rebecca had concluded it was better to let Melanie be who she was, a woman with a garish persona who could look at someone and know how they were feeling. She had worked for Psych Services since the college opened. Married to the college's lawyer, she also had a law degree but had never practiced, having chosen instead to be full-time chauffeur for their two boys, who had skied and played hockey in the winter, soccer and baseball in the spring, and football in the autumn while somehow finding time to also take piano lessons, participate in the geography, debate, and math clubs at school. "It wasn't as bad as you might think," Melanie explained once. "I got a lot of reading done waiting around for them while they were doing their various things. And you'd be surprised how much parenting you can do driving your kids here and there seven days a week." The boys had chosen to go to college in Montreal and both had married Canadian girls and stayed in Canada, one in Montreal while the other moved all the way to Vancouver where his wife was from.

Rebecca shrugged. "I'm all right. Just feeling a little tired the past few days."

Melanie smiled. "I know you better than you think I do and you look like you could use a friend. If you want to talk, I'm here."

"Thanks, Melanie," Rebecca said, forcing herself to smile, and then continued down the hallway and let herself into her office. Setting her brown leather bag on the desk, she took off her coat and put it on the wooden coat tree in the corner behind the door, then made it to the chair at her desk and sat down wearily. Her hands were trembling slightly and tiny beads of perspiration dotted her forehead. She looked hurriedly through her bag until she found the plastic pillbox she always carried. Opening it, she took out one of the large oblong pills and, opening the plastic bottle of water she kept on her desk, swallowed the pill quickly.

She sat for a moment, her eyes closed. The vertigo always came without warning or premonition. She felt only light-headed and the Meclizine tablet she'd just taken would be enough. More severe were the attacks which affected her sense of balance and made it impossible to drive. Worst of all were the ones that made it impossible to get out of bed because she could not feel her body being held by gravity. Attacks like that did not come often. *Baruch HaShem*. However, saying Kaddish with a community of Jews murdered at Auschwitz and having what seemed at the time to be a perfectly normal conversation with a dead woman was proof of some kind of light-headedness on her part.

Melanie was right. Rebecca needed to talk to someone, but who? It was nice of Melanie to offer but Rebecca didn't need someone who would want to comfort her. She needed someone who could help her understand what was happening. Were the Jews of Czechowa an objective reality? Or had she lived by herself for so long she was filling the emptiness by creating her own family?

She supposed she should talk to Brian. As head of Psych Services, he had a right to know, but he would probably put her on sick leave and send her off to some psychiatrist in Burlington. She thought about calling Patric. Of all the people she knew, he had the most knowledge about religious experience. Maybe visitations from the dead were normal in other religions. Hadn't she seen an article in some magazine about one day every year when Mexicans took food and wine to the graves of their dead and had parties there? Once, when visiting her parents, she'd seen something on television about Buddhists keeping altars in their homes on which they put pictures of their dead. She'd also seen a review in a Jewish newspaper about a book by some rabbi who claimed that many converts to Judaism were really the reincarnated souls of Jews killed in the Holocaust. She had supervised the conversion of one such person, a very intense young woman with large, almost yellow eyes and skin so pale you could almost see through it. Rebecca had thought she might be a little unbalanced when she started talking about dreams she'd had for many years of corpses piled high like stacks of wood and smoke coming from chimneys so tall they touched the bottom of the sky and a voice in one of those dreams gave her a new name, Chanah bat Yitzchak v' Shoshana, and she had not understood until she learned that the name was Hebrew. Rebecca had had misgivings about supervising her conversion but remembered how Jacob had wrestled with an angel and been given a new name and no one had ever called him mentally unstable. Who was she to question someone's dreams? And why was she questioning what was happening to her?

As much as she wanted to talk with Patric she was afraid he would think she was inviting him back into her life and she wasn't ready for that and didn't know if she would ever be. Saul was the one person who would've understood in his emotions what it was like to say Kaddish with dead Jews and become their rabbi. But she didn't want to invite him into her inner life, either. Rebecca didn't know if she was completely romantically unavailable or just not available to them. Ultimately, the distinction didn't matter.

The phone on her desk rang. By the flashing light Rebecca knew it was Melanie.

"Yes, Melanie?" she answered it.

"Miller James is here. Says he has a nine o'clock appointment."

Rebecca opened the bottom right drawer of her desk where, each afternoon before she left, she placed the hanging folders of the next day's appointments. The first one was James's.

"Send him back in five minutes, Melanie."

The job of a college therapist was not to delve into people's souls but help them cope when they didn't know how or weren't sure they could. Part of receiving a college education was learning how to live with stress, and, when students came to see Rebecca, she wanted to know what they had been eating and how often and how much sleep they were getting. It was almost magical how quickly overwhelming problems became manageable with a good meal and a long night's sleep.

That afternoon after her last appointment Rebecca felt that she wanted to take the advice she had given students that day and go home and sleep. But she wasn't sure lack of sleep was her problem, though she hadn't been getting much. Whether something was a problem depended on what you considered the norm. For her it had been normal to see her father and other Jewish men beating their breasts and weeping in shul on Tisha B'Av because the temple in Jerusalem had been destroyed in the year 70 of the Common Era. Was there another people on the face of the earth who shed tears over something that had happened almost two thousand years before? If that was her norm, saying Kaddish with dead Jews was not necessarily a problem.

If only she knew why. Why had they come? Was it because of the scroll? But she'd had the scroll for several weeks before they started saying Kaddish. It was as if something had happened which had awakened them. But what?

She didn't know and she was too tired to care. She was even too tired to go sit in her booth at The HangOut and called Martha to tell her not to bother making her tuna fish sandwich. Rebecca was tired of tuna fish; she was tired of The HangOut, and she was getting tired of students' problems. That wasn't good, but after five years there wasn't much variety in the problems of late adolescence. Most nineteen-year-olds had simply not lived long enough to have lives of much variety or complexity and their problems were beginning to bore her. But she couldn't afford to get bored. What would she do if she quit and left the college? She had no idea. Rebecca was almost forty years old and if asked what she wanted to do with her life, she couldn't answer. How depressing to learn that she was no different than any of the nineteen-year-olds she talked to five days a week. Some of them, at least, had dreams.

EIGHT

❧

Rebecca had just finished saying Kaddish with the Jews of Czechowa when the phone rang. She answered it with dread. Calls that came when night was thick brought only sorrow. "Hello?"

"Rebecca?"

"Brian?" It was Brian-Moon, the head of Psych Services.

"Sorry to bother you in the middle of the night but I just got a call from the dean of students' office. One of our students has been found dead on a street in Boston."

"Baruch Ata Adonai Eloheinu Melech Ha-olam, Dayan Ha-Emet."

"What did you say?" Brian wanted to know.

" 'Blessed are You, Lord our God, King of the Universe, the true Judge.' It's Hebrew, something Jews, well, some Jews, say on hearing of a death. What happened? Who was it?"

"All I know is that one of our students was found dead in Boston. We may be needed for grief counseling today, so if you could get in a little early, that would be good."

"Of course."

"That's it. See you in a few hours."

As Rebecca hung up the phone and got out of bed, she wondered why good news waited for daylight, waited until you had brushed

105

your teeth, put on clean underwear and had a cup of coffee and a
bagel while bad news waited until darkness was so heavy it muffled
even the hoots of owls, waited until your breath was bad and your
hair was dotted with tiny knobs of lint from the blanket, and your
bladder was full but you didn't want to go to the bathroom because
you were afraid you might wake up and not get back to sleep even
though you were already half awake from trying to hold it in. Maybe
once, she thought, pulling off her peach-colored Dior nightgown
and turning on the shower, she would be awakened at 3:00 a.m. by a
complete stranger saying she had just had the most amazing orgasm
and had punched in some numbers at random because she had to tell
somebody and her parents just wouldn't understand.

After showering and dressing, Rebecca packed a small bag with toi-
letries, a change of clothes and underwear in case she had to stay
overnight in a dormitory as she'd done last year when a student hanged
himself. But tonight's death had happened far from campus. Unless it
was someone very popular, she doubted students would react with the
same grief, anger and confusion as they had to the suicide. Most of
them had thought about suicide, at least casually. What adolescent
hadn't? A few of the students she'd counseled had made attention-
getting attempts, but someone else's success at it created the possibility
that they could be successful, too, which was why she had stayed in the
dorm of one student she'd been especially worried about. But a death
from a car accident, which she assumed this was, was different. As the
bumper sticker said, "Shit Happens" and while it was sad, it was also
part of life.

Rebecca went downstairs and into the kitchen where she ground
Ethiopian beans and brewed a small pot of coffee, toasted a bagel and
spread it with a mixture of lox and cream cheese, then sat at the

kitchen table and looked out the back window toward Chai Mountain whose outlines were just becoming visible in the retreating darkness. She liked living where she did not see houses or any other signs of people. Her house and land abutted a state conservation area on three sides and except for occasional hikers in summer and a few cross-country skiers in winter, she never saw anyone. She watched the gray dawn lighten the sky to reveal snow like a prayer falling in specks of silent whiteness, each flake a letter in the vocabulary of silence.

However, an hour later when Rebecca backed her car out of the garage, the snow was flinging itself from the sky as if it had been waiting with eager impatience for the day when it could once again cling to the earth with anxious love. If not for the death of the student, Rebecca would have stayed home because the roads would have been impassable by eight o'clock, the time she usually left. But it was six-thirty and had not been snowing hard long. However, there was already an inch or so on the ground as she started down Pulpit Road. She doubted the snow had started accumulating yet on the main roads. She smiled with pride as she slowly but confidently made her way to the bottom of the hill and turned onto the asphalt of county road 323 which, as she had thought, was still only wet. In five years she had learned a lot about Vermont winters and how to drive during snowstorms, not that there was any big secret. Keep your windshield clear, drive slowly, and brake even more slowly.

She switched on the windshield wipers and the fan for the heat and was just about to turn on the radio when a voice from the front passenger seat said, "So, *nu*?"

It was the old woman. Rebecca was happy for the company.

"Something happened. I have to go to work early," Rebecca explained.

"I didn't know if I should've warned you," the woman said, sadness in her voice.

"Warned me about what?"

"About the girl."

Rebecca was startled. "What girl?"

"The one that died."

Despite herself, Rebecca turned to look at the seat beside her, even though she knew it was empty. "You know about her?"

"She didn't have anyone to meet her, so we did. She's not Jewish but whether you're Jewish, Christian or whatever, that's not so important on this side."

"Are you telling me that you know who the student is?"

"What do you think I've been telling you?"

"I'm sorry," Rebecca apologized. "This is all very new to me."

"I understand."

"Really?"

"It's new to us, also. You have no idea how hard it is to find people on this side who will say Kaddish with dead people. But when you untied the knot in the wimple, we thought you might be the one we'd been looking for."

"Is that what happened?" Rebecca didn't know whether to laugh or cry. Unwittingly, she had summoned the dead Jews of Czechowa.

"And after you said Kaddish with us as if it was the most natural thing in the world, we knew we could trust you. We couldn't believe it when you did. If we hadn't already been dead, the shock would have probably killed us."

There was a long silence. Rebecca didn't know if the old woman was waiting for her to say something but Rebecca had nothing to add to the conversation. Not that she didn't want to because she liked having someone with whom to share the solitude, even if she was dead.

"You packed your bag, like you might not be back tonight," the old woman said, breaking the silence.

"I may have to stay over in one of the dormitories."

"We'll miss you."

Rebecca couldn't remember the last time anyone had missed her. Even if the ones doing the missing were dead, it was still nice.

"Who was the girl that died?" Rebecca asked quietly.

"Poor thing. She's very upset. She doesn't even know what happened to her. Oy. One second she was alive and the next she wasn't. She doesn't understand yet that she's dead."

"Who was it?" Rebecca asked again.

The old woman was silent and then she started whispering and then was silent again as if she were listening to someone. Finally she said, "I'm sorry. I didn't know."

"Didn't know what?" Rebecca asked.

"It seems I've said too much. I have to go."

And suddenly the car was empty.

After a moment, Rebecca turned on the radio, wondering why the old woman had thought it important to tell her about the dead student and that her death had been so sudden she had not had time to know she was dying. Whoever it was, Rebecca felt sorry for her. She couldn't imagine a death more horrible than going from consciousness to oblivion without even a candle flicker of recognition that your life was ending. Lying in the window of the delicatessen that long-ago Sunday afternoon she had thought she might be dying but even now she remembered that the sound of the breaking glass had been a music more beautiful than any she had heard since. She hoped her death would leave at least a heartbeat of time for one last experience of beauty, be it dust motes floating in a shaft of light, or the touch of a hand, or the cascading tinkle of death descending like snow.

Rebecca wiped her feet on the mat inside the front door, then went to Brian's office at the end of the hallway. His door was open and she could hear him talking on the phone. When he looked up and saw her standing in the doorway, he waved her inside and pointed to the chair on the other side of his desk.

"Yes, sir. I understand. Yes, sir. Yes, sir. Good-bye."

Brian Moon was a short, stocky man from whom sorrow shone as if it had been rubbed, polished and burnished until your own woes were reflected back as something of beauty. For Brian, however, there had been no beauty for fifteen years. He remembered every detail of that day not as memory but as an experience that happened over and over again, every detail, every emotion more vivid now than then. It was the day he defended his dissertation, and with all the work for his doctorate completed, his position on the psych services staff at Ohio State was assured. He hurried home to celebrate with his wife, Rose. As he approached the house he heard the baby crying and rushed inside wondering where Rose was. Calling her name, loudly and re- peatedly, brought no response except the heightened screaming of the baby responding to the sound of a familiar voice. Brian hurried to her room where she lay in her crib, changed her wet diaper and as he went in the bathroom to dispose of it in the pail he saw Rose lying in the bathtub, the water a dark red, almost black with the blood from her body which had poured from the deep cuts she had made in the wrists of both arms with a single-edged razor blade which lay on the floor beside the tub. For days, weeks, months after Brian looked for a note, for something that would tell him why. There had been no sign—or had he been so involved in completing his dissertation and preparing for the defense that he hadn't noticed? He wanted to blame it on postpartum depression but she had been ecstatic since Agatha's birth. Then why? Why? Only when her parents sued for custody of Agatha did he see Rose's letters to them saying she had never been happy with him and had made a mistake marrying him, that he was sucking the life out of her and didn't know it and that she hated him. All his psychological learning, all the years of analysis afterward did not make a difference; his emotional life stopped when he read her letters. He had never been able to reconcile the laughter in her eyes when she looked at him, her passion in bed, her exclamations of undying love with the words in those letters. Had she been crazy or was it him?

The court ruled that Agatha should remain with him and he moved to Vermont because he'd heard that New Englanders, and especially those in Vermont, didn't ask a lot of questions and that was good because he didn't know what he would've said about who he was. But his transformation from a man filled with self-confidence into one who spoke so softly it was sometimes hard to hear him, into someone painfully shy and diffident, inspired trust in those who brought their problems to him. People opened their hearts to him as they never had to anyone and, because of the quality of his listening, people left his office feeling they could cope and that living was not as difficult and onerous as it might have seemed a mere hour before. His daughter grew up to be tall like her mother with the same green eyes and long blond hair and Brian adored her.

He put down the receiver and said to Rebecca, "That was President Woodley." He smiled. "Obviously. Saying 'sir' is not something

I do on a daily basis. He wanted to bring me up to date on what happened."

"And what did happen?"

Brian shook his head. "The body of a female student was found lying in a westbound lane of Storrow Drive in Boston. She'd been murdered."

"I beg your pardon," Rebecca responded, shocked. "Did you say, 'murdered'?"

"Unfortunately. And I think she was someone you saw." Brian picked up the notepad on his desk and looked at it. "Allison Manchester? Didn't I see her name on your list of student contacts a couple of weeks back?"

Rebecca gasped.

Now she understood why the old woman had come. She had wanted to tell Rebecca they were taking care of someone Rebecca knew.

"I don't believe this. What was she doing in Boston? Did the police catch who did it? This is unbelievable!" she exclaimed, shaking her head from side to side as if trying to negate what she had just heard. "The last time I saw her she was bright and cheery and said she didn't need to talk to me anymore, not that she'd said that much to begin with."

"What can you tell me? What did she come to see you about?"

Rebecca shrugged. "To tell the truth, I'm not really sure. She said she'd had an abortion last summer and that was about it."

"President Woodley said a detective is coming up from Boston this afternoon to talk to people."

"In this weather?" Rebecca asked, skeptically.

"That's the same thing I said. It seems this particular detective went to school in Vermont, likes to ski, and is used to driving in snowstorms."

"So, what do you want me to do?" she asked Brian, pushing aside her shock and sorrow.

"The dean of students is sending out a campuswide e-mail informing everyone of what happened. In it she will indicate that you and I are available if anyone wants to talk. The dean will let me know if a group session is needed in one of the dorms. Probably the best strategy would be for me to stay here and for you to go sit in your booth in The HangOut."

Rebecca nodded. She got up, then sat back down, a pained look on her face. "I'm sorry," she said, plaintively.

"Sorry for what?" Brian asked, having no idea what she was talking about.

"I know it's silly but I feel like I let you down, let Psych Services down. And I certainly let Allison down."

He shook his head. "You don't think you're responsible for what happened to that girl, do you?"

"No. No, I don't, but I can't help feeling that I didn't do my job, that I missed something. There had to have been a sign, some nuance of body language, some change in the timbre of her voice that—"

"That what? Would've told you the child was going to be murdered by some nut in Boston?"

"Is that what happened?"

"What else could it have been?"

"You're right. Like I said, I know I'm being stupid but I can't stop myself. The girl came to me for help and she didn't get it."

"I know you, Rebecca. I hired you, remember? And the reason I hired you was because I knew that any student who came to you for help would get it, as long as the student wanted it. My gut sense about you was that you would never give up on a kid and you haven't done anything in five years to make me think my gut was wrong. If Allison Manchester didn't get any help from you it was because she didn't want it, or thought she didn't need it."

Rebecca smiled weakly. "Thanks," but as she left she wondered if there was something she had failed to notice.

NINE

❧

Even though everyone knew they would die one day, no one really believed it, not even, sometimes, when it was happening. Rebecca remembered a congregant, a tenth-grade math teacher in his forties who had cancer. She was visiting him in the hospital and he had turned to her, a look of astonishment on his face and asked suddenly, "Am I dying?" No sooner were the words uttered than he was dead.

It was especially hard for the young to believe they could die. Why else would they smoke cigarettes, even though they had been raised with more awareness of the dangers than any generation in history? Why else would they drive recklessly fast? Why else would they have sex without using condoms? Allison's murder would not disturb their confidence in their immortality.

A number of students stopped to talk with her as she sat in her booth at The HangOut, but they were more shocked by the fact of the murder than grieved that the victim had been one of them. No one seemed to have known Allison except to say they'd had a class with her or seen her in the library. Even her suitemate didn't know much about her.

"To tell the truth, unless we happened to run into each other in the common room of the suite, I never saw her. I was never even in her room. You know, I might knock on her door to borrow a razor blade or Q-Tip or if I ran out of Tampax, and if she was there, she would stand in the doorway, then close the door, go get whatever it was I'd come for, and hand it to me. I thought at first maybe she had some really good pot or something she didn't want to share but I never smelled anything coming from her room so it wasn't that. No, I have no idea where she might have been any night, or who with. If you want to know the truth, I didn't want to know her problems. I have enough of my own. I guess now it would be sort of convenient if I did know but we just shared a suite, you know, and she stayed in her room and I stayed in mine and sometimes we bumped into each other in the common room and said hi, how's it going and like that but that was it. She was a great person to room with because we never saw each other and we stayed out of each other's lives. The only thing I know about her is that she was quiet and she did all her talking on the computer. I heard that keyboard click-clacking a lot. That's about the only way I knew she even existed."

It was midafternoon when a tall African-American woman wearing a dark green ski jacket and matching ski pants approached Rebecca's booth.

"I'm Detective Pamela Williams, Boston Homicide. You're the rabbi?"

"Yes, but please call me Rebecca."

"Is this an OK time to talk?"

"As good as any. Won't you sit down?"

Detective Williams unzipped her ski jacket and took a small notebook and ballpoint pen from its inside pocket. She flipped the pages until she came to the one she was looking for. "What can you tell me about Allison? How long had she been seeing you? And what brought her to you?"

Rebecca thought that everything the detective wanted to know was covered by privilege but Brian had given no indication that she would be violating anything if she shared what she knew about Allison. And if he had, Rebecca would have argued with him. For her, the principle was not as important as the reality: Allison had been murdered and the murderer had to be caught. So Rebecca answered Detective Williams's questions and was sorry that she knew so little.

"You wouldn't happen to know the whereabouts of her computer, would you?"

"It wasn't in her room?"

"No."

"I'm sorry, I don't."

"Any idea who her boyfriend was?"

Rebecca shook her head. "She never said."

"So you didn't know she was pregnant?" Detective Williams asked quietly.

"Pregnant! I had no idea." Rebecca stopped and then continued. "But now that you mention it, it makes sense, and I should have caught it."

"What's that?"

"The last time I saw her was right here. She seemed very happy. I thought it was because she had decided to ignore whatever was bothering her, which is not unusual, especially with students. But now I think I understand. Why didn't I see it then?"

"See what?"

"That she would try to assuage her guilt over the abortion by getting pregnant as soon as she could."

"And you can't make a wild guess as to who the father was?"

"No. The art of counseling is to wait and let the client tell you what he or she needs to."

Detective Williams smiled. "Just the opposite of being a detective."

"How—how did she die?"

"She was strangled. Whoever killed her pushed her body out of his car onto Storrow Drive thinking that a car would run over the body and quite possibly obliterate the real cause of death. But we got lucky. Seemingly, the driver of the first car that came along afterward saw someone lying in the road and stopped."

"She was such a beautiful girl," Rebecca said softly. "I'm sorry I can't be of more help."

"It's odd but no one seems to know anything about her. She seems to have kept to herself and didn't make any friends. But coming up here was just a formality anyway. Whoever did it is in the Boston area. Maybe a student at one of the colleges there. It certainly looks like a crime of passion." As she got up she reached in her pocket and took out a card holder from which she extracted a business card. "Here. My direct line. If you think of anything, give me a call. Now I think I'll head for Stowe and hopefully a little night skiing and a run or two down the slopes in the morning before I go back. Eighteen inches of fresh powder and it's still snowing! Do you ski?"

Rebecca shook her head. "Have fun."

"Thanks. I will."

When Brian had told her that morning about the detective from Boston who liked to ski, Rebecca had pictured a man, blond, with wraparound sunglasses. Did it make her a racist and a sexist because it would never have crossed her mind that there was a black female police detective who liked to ski? Probably, and she was ashamed of herself. For all Rebecca knew, there were thousands of African American skiers and they were all headed for Stowe at that very moment to chat about ski wax and virgin powder before they pushed off with their ski poles down the slopes. There were probably thousands of Jewish skiers, too, no, hundreds of thousands, no, millions of Jews schussing down slopes and schlepping around ski lodges who needed a rabbi to say a *bracha* for them before they followed the black skiers down the slopes.

But she couldn't imagine herself on skis let alone walking across campus and into The HangOut without limping. She was afraid that if she wasn't visibly a cripple, no one would notice her, not even God, and she wanted Him to see every day what He had done to her, wanted Him to see her and feel her rage at Him, a rage she clung to so God would not forget her.

It was already dark when she left campus at five o'clock but the snow had stopped. Because the plowed roads were bordered on each side now by high banks of snow, it was easy to follow the twists and turns of the narrow roads. She wondered how people endured the darkness of winter in places where it did not snow much. Snow was the light through the darkness.

When she got home she went upstairs, turned on a lamp and davened Mincha and Maariv even though technically it was too late. But she liked saying that she was done with this day and was ready to begin the new one. The Hebrew came from her tongue more rapidly than she could understand the words but it was not the words that mattered but the act of standing there, her body swaying back and forth, repeating the words that had been said by Jews all over the world for almost two thousand years, words whose meaning was as much in their harsh musicality as their definitions.

She had just finished praying when the phone rang.

"Hello?" she answered it, flopping down onto her bed.

"Rabbi. Sorry to disturb you at home."

It was the college president, Maurice Woodley.

"I won't keep you. I was wondering if I could prevail on you to speak Sunday morning at the memorial service for Allison Manchester. The consensus seems to be that the college should do something to publicly acknowledge this horrible tragedy. Evan Green, the student body president, and Emily Dixon, the editor of the campus newspaper, will speak, as will I, but we need something more, a spiritual perspective if you will."

Rebecca wanted to say she had made plans to go skiing in Stowe with a thousand African Americans. But she owed Allison something.

"I'll be glad to say something, sir."

"Thank you. I knew we could depend on you. You'll be speaking last."

She groaned inwardly as Woodley hung up. Why did people assume that the title of rabbi automatically conferred wisdom and insight into the soul's mysteries and that you would know the right words to say for any and every occasion, whether it was blessing a child's teddy bear, which she had done or the funeral of a child who had fallen down steps. Being a rabbi had not made her wiser nor anyone else she knew who bore the title. Some of her rabbinical school classmates hadn't even been very smart, which, however, didn't mean they hadn't become more successful than she had. They had been wise enough to know who among their congregants to flatter, who to schmooze with periodically over lunch, and how to make small talk with everybody. The Rosh Yeshiva had studied Talmud and Torah with her so she would know how Jews understood holiness. Few words of small talk ever passed between them, only words about

God and his creatures, from the gnat who preceded people in creation to Leviathan, the great sea monster with whom God played every day. But American Jews preferred small talk to holiness, gossip to prayer, and rabbis who afforded them the opportunity for vicarious righteousness. But perhaps vicarious righteousness was preferable to none at all.

When Rebecca arrived at the campus auditorium that Sunday morning, it was already half-filled with students and faculty. On the right side of the stage the college string orchestra was tuning their instruments to Oliver Preston's pitch pipe. To the left four folding chairs were arranged in an arc a few feet behind the lectern.

Rebecca made her way slowly down the far side aisle and sat at the end of the first row next to the steps that led to the stage. After a moment the auditorium was filled with the mournful majesty of the Albinoni Adagio in G Minor. Rebecca closed her eyes, half listening and half wondering what words would come out when it came her time to speak. Though she had certainly thought about what she might say, she had always relied on being able to craft sermons and speeches from what she was feeling in herself and from the congregation as she stood before them. Five years had gone by since she had spoken publicly, five years since she had stood before an audience and attempted to put words to their inchoate feelings and unconscious thoughts. She hoped she could still do so.

Funerals and memorial services had always been easy for her (weddings had been the most difficult). The dead needed her in ways the living did not. Today she hoped she could find words to weave a small handkerchief of consolation for whoever needed it, and especially for Allison. Rebecca looked around and was glad to see that the auditorium was almost full. Because so few had known Allison, her death needed to be mourned all the more.

The orchestra came to the end of the Albinoni and the two student speakers and President Woodley walked out from backstage. Rebecca did not recognize the female student, a thin girl in a denim skirt, white Aran sweater and long dark hair that came halfway down her back. She would have been attractive if not for the purple lipstick. Behind her was Evan Green. On a campus where students considered they were dressed up when they put on jeans that weren't ripped at the knees, Evan earned Rebecca's admiration and respect for wearing a three-piece gray pinstriped suit, white shirt, and pearl-gray tie that would have faded into the whiteness of the shirt if not for the deep, dark brown of Evan's face. His black shoes were shined to a high polish, and they were shoes, not loafers. She'd seen so many impeccably dressed men in loafers, an indication to her that their stance in life had not evolved beyond high school.

Rebecca got up and joined the others onstage, taking the last seat. She looked out into the auditorium and was glad the house lights had not been dimmed. The entire campus community seemed to be there, faculty, students and even staff as she saw Martha sitting in the back near Patric. Rebecca remembered that Allison had been one of his students and that the last time she saw her, Allison had sat down for a moment in the booth where Patric was grading papers.

Maurice Woodley cleared his throat, looked over and nodded to Emily Dixon, who went to the lectern. She began by reading an original poem about flowers and how we loved them, not because they lived a long time but for the beauty they gave us during their brief time of blooming. At the poem's end she said, "I had a class with Allison freshman year and I always wanted to say something to her but she was so beautiful that I was kind of intimidated. I didn't think a girl that pretty would want to be friends with someone like me. I was sure she had plenty of friends. But it seems like she didn't. I'm sorry now that I didn't try to make her my friend," she concluded, her voice trembling, and sat down.

Evan Green walked to the podium and stood there as if he could command the audience to do anything he wanted, which was why he had been elected student body president for the past three years, running unopposed.

"I am angry," he said in a soft but deep voice. "I am angry that a member of our community died alone and afraid and none of us knew her well enough to know why she was in Boston and whom she went to see. We pride ourselves on being a community. We spout a lot of rhetoric about John Brown College being a place that cares. People who live in a community are connected to each other. People who live in a community are supposed to know when something is wrong in someone else's life."

He had not raised his voice and yet Rebecca could feel a taut anger in the silences between sentences, in the way his voice trembled as if he was going to scream but he never did. She didn't know if he was sincere or if he was acting and it didn't matter. Who was to say that artifice could not move the emotions as deeply as sincerity? Rebecca listened admiringly as Evan Green continued and put forth a vision of the kind of community John Brown College needed to be.

"In the early years of the civil rights movement in the sixties, people said they were trying to create what they called 'the beloved community.' As I understand it, this was not a geographical place but a way of being in which, in the words of Martin Luther King, Jr., one would be judged not on the basis of the color of his skin but on the

123

content of his character. In a beloved community it would not be imperative that everyone like everyone else. Who you like or dislike is personal. But you don't have to like someone to care about his or her well-being. That's what a beloved community is—a way of living in which each cares for the well-being of the other.

"If we lived in such a community, Allison Manchester would be alive. Perhaps we can learn from her death and create such a community and no one from John Brown College will ever again suffer such a horrible and frightening death."

When Evan Green turned from the podium to return to his seat, Rebecca noticed for the first time that he didn't have any notes in his hand and she hadn't seen him put any in his pockets.

President Woodley spoke next but Rebecca wasn't sure what he said. She supposed college presidents and rabbis were alike in that no one really listened to what they said but how they said it. Woodley had a voice that reminded Rebecca of Pablo Casals playing one of the Bach suites for solo cello, so it didn't matter what he said. Listening to him she understood that the human voice was, at root, a musical instrument and sometimes the words it spoke were merely in service to that music.

When he sat down Rebecca limped slowly to the lectern. She stood there for a moment and was surprised when she heard herself reciting the famous lines from Ecclesiastes:

For everything there is a season, a time for every experience under heaven:
A time to be born and a time to die
A time to plant and a time to uproot what is planted;
A time to tear down and a time to build up;
A time to weep and a time to laugh,

A time to grieve and a time to dance;

A time to throw stones and a time to gather stones,

A time to embrace and a time to refrain from embracing;

A time to seek and a time to lose,

A time to keep and a time to discard;

A time to tear and a time to sew,

A time to keep silence and a time to speak.

(Afterward, several students thanked her effusively for "reciting the words of that Judy Collins song." They hadn't known "it had so many words.")

"Life is not fair," she said softly. "If it were, children would not die; planes would not crash; people would not be killed in tornados, floods, avalanches, and in all the other horrible ways in which people lose their lives.

"Not only is life unfair, sometimes it is cruel and mean and hateful. To die in an accident is unfair but understandable. We call it fate, being in the wrong place at the wrong time. We say, 'Well, her time was up.' And in such thoughts, inadequate as they are, we find solace.

"But life becomes incomprehensible when we must confront the reality of one human being, deliberately, willfully, and with malice, taking the life of another. Who would do such a thing, and why? How completely and totally self-centered one must be to murder another person. Nothing justifies murder. Allison Manchester deserved a long life, not a cruel, lonely, and terrifying death.

"I refuse to stand here this morning and try and make sense of Allison's murder. To do so would be to give the solace of justification to the murderer. I will not do that. Neither will I insult you and say that Allison's murder was part of a divine plan which we as humans cannot understand. I will not accept a God who makes murder part of His divine plan.

"So, let's be honest. People die meaningless deaths every day and one has been dropped on the doorstep of this college. There is no meaning that can be derived from her death and she had not lived long enough to give her life much meaning.

"We are here this morning not only to grieve a life we hardly knew. We are here to grieve the life that will never be. In my religion there is a compendium of religious discourse called the Talmud, and it says that he who kills another destroys a world. And so we come here today to grieve not only the life Allison Manchester was deprived of but to mourn the souls that would have been her children and grandchildren and their children down through the generations to the end of time. A universe of possibilities died when Allison Manchester was murdered.

"But there are those in my religion who believe souls return to the world. I hope that is true because Allison Manchester deserves to come back and have a long and fruitful and happy life. Until that time, I pray that the soul of Allison Manchester will be given peace and that the one who selfishly took her life will not have peace ever again."

Rebecca limped slowly back to her seat where the students and President Woodley all shook her hand warmly. The string orchestra began playing the Barber Adagio for Strings and people made their way slowly out of the auditorium.

"How do you do it?" President Woodley leaned over and whispered.

"Do what?"

He smiled ruefully. "What you said just now certainly went against conventional wisdom, but it was honest and it went to the heart of the kinds of questions the students must have been asking themselves. I suppose these are the kinds of problems you must deal with as a matter of course."

She gave him a sympathetic smile. "You mean the unraveling threads of a heart?"

"What do you mean?"

"During my first year in the rabbinate, a man came to see me whose wife had left him to be with a woman and I saw that the threads which had made up the fabric of his life had unraveled. That was when I understood what I'm supposed to do—look for threads that have come loose and figure out how to help someone weave them back into place, or sometimes weave a new design."

"Well, I appreciate your being here this morning, Rabbi," he said, standing up. "I'm glad I had the good sense to sign the papers when Brian Moon hired you." He shook hands with her, the two student speakers and strode away.

When Rebecca saw Martha walking onto the stage she stood up and the older woman hugged her tightly, then looked at her and said, tears in her eyes, "I feel like I'm at peace for the first time since I learned my boy had been killed in Vietnam. Thanks for talking to us like we had sense." Martha hugged her again and walked away.

"Rabbi?"

Rebecca turned to see Evan Green. "Could I ask you a question?"

"Of course," she responded, sitting back down.

He sat down in the seat Maurice Woodley had occupied. He loosened his tie and undid the top button of his white shirt.

"What's on your mind?" Rebecca wanted to know.

"I'd like to know where God was when Allison Manchester was

killed. My father's a minister of one of the largest African American churches in D.C. and at this very moment he's telling the congregation that God is merciful and that God answers prayer and takes care of the poor and that God loves them. That's what I grew up hearing but I don't understand how my father can say things like that with all that's going on in the world. You know what I mean? That's why I appreciate what you said about not trying to understand what happened to Allison by saying it was all part of God's plan. To be honest with you, if God's plan includes killing little children and people starving to death in Africa and Asia and Latin America and Allison being murdered, then I've got some problems with God. And to be really honest, I don't want anything to do with a God like that." He stopped and chuckled quietly. "My father would kill me if he heard me talking this way but it feels good to say what I really feel."

She nodded. "I agree with you. I've often wondered what happened to the God who entered history and parted the Red Sea. Where is the God who stopped Abraham from sacrificing Isaac?"

"Do you doubt the existence of God?

"Not at all. But I do wonder if He is on the side of the evildoers now. I think God was present at Auschwitz, only against the Jews."

"You're kidding!" Evan was genuinely shocked. "How can you be a rabbi if that's how you feel?"

"Maybe that's why I'm not a rabbi anymore."

He stood up. "Well, I think you are and if you ever have a synagogue near where I'm living, I'm joining." He stood up and shook her hand. "Thanks for making me feel like I'm not crazy."

The next day the life of the campus was back to normal. It was as if Allison Manchester had never lived. Students were beginning to leave for Thanksgiving but a few dropped in to talk. One male student was distraught at having received an e-mail that morning from his girl-friend at home announcing that she didn't want to see him anymore. That was a kind of death, too, and although Rebecca knew he would survive she didn't tell him that. Instead she asked if he had to go home for Thanksgiving. In fact, he didn't. He was supposed to be at his mother's but he didn't get along with his stepfather. He could spend Thanksgiving with his grandmother. That would assuage his mother's guilt for not having her mother for Thanksgiving dinner, would make his stepfather happy, and his grandmother would be surprised and de-lighted not to spend the long weekend alone. And he wouldn't have to worry about running into his girlfriend or sit by the phone hoping she would call. The boy was actually grinning by the time he left her office and thanked her profusely for her help.

Five years ago, Rebecca might have gone home pleased with her day's work. Now she understood that she did nothing more than ap-ply common sense to most of the problems she heard, a common sense she seemed incapable of using in her own life, though she wasn't sure any longer if she could call the activities of her daily exis-tence a "life," not if having a life meant feeling creatively involved in and connected to those with whom she lived. But if she was honest with herself, she had to admit that she had always felt more excited and involved with the rabbis of the Talmud like Hillel and Sham-mai, anyone, it seemed, who was not alive.

TEN

❧

When Rebecca awoke Thanksgiving morning, she glanced at the clock and smiled when she saw it was ten. She closed her eyes again, not to sleep but to enjoy not having to go anywhere or be with anyone. Thanksgiving was not a holiday she'd celebrated until she and Dennis were married. Most Jews did celebrate it, she supposed, and that was fine with her. It was a secular celebration and one that might have been derived from the Jewish holiday of Succoth. But her parents were European and for her father at least, Jews had Thanksgiving every Friday when they observed the Sabbath, a day on which you could not ask God for anything or even complain because Shabbat was a day to praise God and be grateful for His gifts.

She was glad no one in the past two years had invited her for Thanksgiving if for no other reason than not having to make conversation with whichever eligible Jewish man her hosts had invited for her. It had always been someone from Montreal, the nearest large Jewish community, and they had been nice enough, she supposed. She had crossed the border more than once for a follow-up date or two, but when it became clear that sex for her existed only within the sanctity of marriage, men lost interest.

Having sex only if she were married created a problem because Rebecca had no interest in marrying again, which meant she would never have sex again, and she did not think the self-induced orgasms she had in the shower or from a vibrator qualified as sex. She doubted she would ever meet anyone who understood her in the intricate pathways of his cellular structure, who loved her simply because she was. Because she couldn't have children, the sole object of marriage for her had to be intimacy of spirit and she doubted that the man existed who wanted to be intimate with hers. But oh, how eagerly she would take into herself, body and soul, the man who first took her into his soul.

A few years ago, the thought of being alone for the rest of her life would have sent her into the sloth of self-pity but when she bought the house and transformed it into a space just for herself, something changed. She didn't know it until, one Thanksgiving at someone's house, she'd been chatting with a young English professor (Jewish, of course) from McGivens University in Montreal. Tall, lean, with a boyish smile and a touch of gray at the temples, she had found herself starting to think about what it would be like to have him as a husband, but the fantasy stumbled over a question: Where would he fit in her house? He would need space for his books, computer, CD collection, and he probably had paintings and prints he would want to put on the walls and lamps with faux Tiffany shades and couches and chairs and she realized that she had no interest in blending his life with hers or hers with his. She liked coming home and knowing everything in it was her— there was very little furniture because she didn't want anyone to find a comfortable place to sit because then they might want to stay a while and she might not want them to. She had refrained from calling the front room the living room and the middle one the dining room because she didn't want to have preconceived ideas about what activities would take place where. With built-in floor-to-ceiling bookcases on the walls of both rooms, there was no space left for Van Gogh prints of tortured ecstasy or sentimental paintings of bearded Hasidic men dancing.

Except for the books and magazines, her house was empty and the absence of visual noise kept her from being overwhelmed by the cacophony within. If she couldn't find a space for a man in her house, even in a daydream, where was the space for one in her life? Or perhaps it was simply that she had never met the one for whom she would make space, in her body and her home.

She yawned and got out of bed slowly. It was almost hot in the room with the sun coming through the skylight and she narrowed her eyes against the glare off the snow.

"Good morning," she said to Chai Mountain. As always, it did not return her greeting.

She took a long shower, the water so hot it was as if her flesh were being cauterized by hot needles burning away the sorrow, anguish and grief of the past week and she thought of Devorah, the aunt she had never known. Maybe what the world needed was more people to mourn the passing of lives simply because they had been lives and now they were not.

As she got out of the shower, toweled off and slipped into a pair of corduroy pants, chamois shirt and thick wool socks, she noticed how tender her breasts were. Her period was coming. She never understood why some of the women she'd gone to rabbinical school with had insisted that God was female. If God were female, the clitoris would have been in the palms of women's hands, both of them; children would have been born from eggs that men produced and had to sit on; and menstruation, vaginal discharges and odors would have never existed. Indeed, a female god would have seen to it that vaginas were detachable. Since that was the part of a woman men most wanted, a woman could have taken it off, handed it to the man, and said, "Have it back in two hours, and make sure it's been washed and blow-dried." But from what she had heard, most men wouldn't need that much time. Dennis sure hadn't. Obviously God was male because who except a man would try to show how clever he was by coming up with something as ridiculous as vagina, clitoris, uterus, and stick them in the narrow space between a woman's legs where they could not be seen, were hard to find, and then cover them all with hair. But the penis! Hah! The penis was the epitome of simplicity wedded to function. It got hard at the sight of any opening whether vegetable, animal, mineral, or undetermined and with very little friction released its *stuff* and, within a little while, was ready for the next opening. Women had to be put in the right mood, touched with just the right amount of pressure in the exact spot, and then pray that the man didn't move or try something fancy that he'd read in a Chinese lovemaking manual, and after all that a woman could be at the very threshold of an orgasm and then, for no reason that Rebecca had ever been able to discern, the orgasm would dribble away like the stone Sisyphus watched roll down the hillside. Obviously God was male and He probably suffered from premature ejaculations.

As Rebecca put slipper socks on over her woolen ones, she was looking forward to a day rich with cups of black coffee and *Times* crossword puzzles. She had not had time to do a puzzle since Allison's death, but had saved the appropriate sections containing them. Since she never read the rest of the paper, she wondered why she bought it every day when she could have printed the puzzle from the paper's Web site. But there was something about folding the paper and holding its thickness that a puzzle printed on a sheet of typewriter paper or done sitting at the computer could not match. What better way to spend the long Thanksgiving weekend than doing crossword puzzles, noshing and napping.

Rebecca had just reached the bottom of the stairs and was turning toward the kitchen when a beam of light from the front room flashed into her eyes. She frowned and squinted, thinking it must be the sun reflecting off the finials of the Torah scroll. She continued toward the kitchen. The light flashed again, this time so brightly that Rebecca put up a hand to block it from her eyes.

Though she really needed that first cup of coffee, her curiosity led her into the front room. The light was not coming from the Torah scroll but from beside it. As she got closer to the table she saw a rectangular wooden box resting beside the scroll and glowing like a field of buttercups in the summer sun. The box was a little longer and wider than a sheet of paper but deeper than a jewelry box and looked as if it had been sanded and lacquered until it was breathing the light in which it seemed to be resting.

Where had it come from? Rebecca knew it had not been there last night. Somebody had been in the house, but who? And when? Although she didn't lock her doors—no one in Brett did—she would've heard a car coming up the hill or someone entering the house. Living where silence was as loud as a scream, even the raspy conversations of crows caught her attention. But maybe someone *had* sneaked into the house. What if he were still here?

Rebecca listened but heard only the soft hums of the furnace from the basement and the refrigerator from the kitchen. Quietly, she went to the front door, but there was no snow, melted or not, in the entranceway to indicate that someone had come in. She peered through the narrow panes in the door: there were no footprints on her unshoveled front walk and porch. The only other way into the house was through the garage. Quietly Rebecca made her way to the kitchen and opened the door to the garage. There was no sign of forced entry. She wondered what she would have done if she had discovered someone but she had known she wouldn't. The house was like her outermost layer of skin. She knew it had not been entered.

Yet she was frightened. Where had the box come from? She stood in the doorway to the front room and stared at it. The only thing she could think of was that the old woman had put it there, that it was an artifact from the synagogue of Czechowa and belonged with the scroll.

Rebecca limped over to the table and cautiously put out her hand toward the box. As her hand moved forward, the light withdrew until it disappeared into the wood of the box. What was going on? she wondered, her hand suspended above the box. The box was glowing, almost pulsating with muted light. Slowly the light became brighter and emerged sinuously from the box, surrounding Rebecca's hand. Though the light had no substance, she could feel it guiding her hand downward. As her fingertips touched the top lightly, the light retreated into the box.

Rebecca had never felt anything like the wood of the box which was as soft as sunset. After letting her fingers linger over the top for a moment, she began feeling along the recessed front edge. Her hand stopped when it felt a small square of metal. It was a clasp, which seemed to unfasten itself merely at her touch. Slowly, she raised the lid.

The box was lined with thick, plush, dark red velvet. In the center sat what looked to be a manuscript. *Kelaf*, she thought. The manuscript was held together by three neatly tied leather thongs. In the

center of the top page, in the most beautiful Hebrew calligraphy she
had ever seen, was written

חיי

My Life, she translated. The construction was formal, even Biblical. Someone was playing a joke on her. An elaborate one, certainly,
but a joke nonetheless. Who would put such effort into playing a joke
on her? There was no one who cared about her that much.

She touched the cover. The parchment was far smoother than that
of any Torah scroll she had ever touched. The punch line of this far-
fetched joke had to be in the manuscript itself. She lifted it from the
box, set it gently on the table, and opening it, turning, sat down and
began reading.

בראשית בראתי את השמים ואת הארץ

Rebecca stopped and read the sentence again, this time aloud.

"Breisheet baratee et hashamayim v' et haaretz."

She couldn't believe what she had just read and read it yet again,
this time translating it into English.

"In the beginning I created heaven and earth."

That was supposed to be funny, she imagined, but she was not
amused. In fact, she was annoyed. She put the manuscript back in the
box, closed the lid and went to the kitchen, where she put water on to
boil and spooned coffee into the paper filter of the Pyrex coffeemaker.
As she waited for the water to boil she paced nervously.

"So, nu?"

Rebecca stopped and looked around. The old woman!

"He wants to know why you read only the first sentence?"

"What are you talking about?" Rebecca asked, annoyed. The last thing she wanted right now was to carry on a conversation with a dead woman.

"Don't get upset with me. I'm just the messenger. But if He gave *me* something of His to read, something He wrote in His own hand, I wouldn't have left it sitting on the table, even if I can't read."

Rebecca blinked hard, then gulped. "I beg your pardon."

"He said you read the first sentence and put it down."

"Who said?" she asked warily, not sure she was hearing what she was hearing.

"Him. Who do you think?"

"You don't mean—" Rebecca's voice faded into disbelieving silence.

"Who else could write 'In the beginning I created the heaven and the earth'?"

The water was boiling now and if there'd ever been a time in Rebecca's life when she needed a cup of coffee, this was it. She poured the water over the coffee and waited impatiently for it to drip.

"The little short angel gave me the box," the voice continued. "He's colored. You know, I never saw a colored person until I came on this side. And a colored Jew! Who would've thought there could ever be such? Anyway, he's God's beadle or something of the sort. By the way, did you know angels don't have wings? Oy, was I glad of that! I don't think I'd enjoy flying. Anyway, he, the colored angel—why can't I remember his name?—told me to put it on the table and that's what I did."

Rebecca wanted to tell the old woman about the black Jew who led Rosh Hashanah and Yom Kippur services at the little synagogue in Saint Johnsbury where she went for the holidays and who sang the prayers as if he believed God cared. But this was no time to get distracted. "Are you telling me that book was written by God Himself?"

Although Rebecca couldn't see her, she heard the old woman shrug as she said, "You aren't going to be like all the others, are you?"

"What do you mean?"

"Well, it seems like He has written this—what do you call it?— auto-something—"

"Autobiography?"

"Yes! That's it! Autobiography! From what I hear, and don't get me wrong, I'm not one who gossips, but the word is He's been trying to get somebody to read this autobiography for a long time. Centuries. Millennia! All He wants is for somebody to read it and tell Him what they think. But everybody thinks it's a joke and they either throw it away or burn it up. He's given it to some really important people like Rabbi Akiba, Thomas Aquinas and Augustine—and you should hear the two of them arguing all the time. Maimonides said the very idea of God writing an autobiography was an affront to reason, whereas somebody named Martin Luther put nails in his copy. Nobody has ever read it to the end, not even any of the popes and He wrote the copies for them in the most beautiful Latin calligraphy you can't imagine."

"Why doesn't anybody finish it? What's in it?"

"How should I know? He hasn't given me a copy and I can't read anyway. All I know is what the colored angel told me. People read the first page or two and get so angry they burn it. A few read about half before they throw it away. And He goes to a lot of trouble to do it, too. He rewrites it each time special for the person He's going to

139

give it to, but no one has ever read it to the end. Maybe He's not that good a writer."

"Stop! Wait a minute!" Rebecca exclaimed, exasperated. "You really expect me to believe that on the table in the front room of my house is a manuscript written by God? About His life?" she asked, knowing she was repeating herself but unable to do otherwise.

"Why is that so hard to believe?"

Rebecca laughed dryly. "You know? You're right. I don't know why that is any harder to believe than the fact that I'm standing here talking to a Jewish woman who has been dead for fifty years. If I can believe that this woman and all the Jews of her town are living in my house, why is it so hard for me to believe that God has given me His autobiography to read?"

"Exactly. The angel—Hymie! That's his name! Hymie Brown! Nice young man!—anyway, Hymie told me to tell you that if you finish reading it, He would love to talk to you about it."

Rebecca laughed loudly but the sound was devoid of mirth. "You mean God will come and talk to me, face to face, if I finish reading His autobiography?"

"That's what Hymie said."

"That's some incentive!" Rebecca exclaimed sarcastically. "What makes Him so sure that I want to talk to Him face to face? What's He like?"

Rebecca heard another shrug. "Never had the pleasure. You think anybody can just go and have a conversation with Him? That's not how it works over here. I asked Hymie what He looked like and even he didn't know. He said God leaves notes telling him what He wants him to do. Hymie writes notes back and leaves them someplace and then comes back later and gets God's answer. You must be somebody really special if God says He wants your opinion."

The coffee was finally ready and Rebecca lifted the coffeemaker by its neck, but her hand was trembling so much that she put it down. She took a deep breath and this time managed to pour coffee into her cup.

"What if I'm like the rest? What if I decide I don't want to read it. Can I throw it away? Can I burn it?"

"Everybody else did. Why not you?"

And with that the old woman was gone.

Rebecca stood in the kitchen for a long time, leaning against the counter. She drank one cup of coffee, poured a second, then went back to the front room. She sat at the table and stared at the box. She sipped slowly and when the cup was empty, she went back into the kitchen and poured herself another one. Suddenly, she realized how hungry she was. While the bagel was toasting, she cut two thin slices of onion and a slice of tomato. She put several pieces of lox on the bagel, then the onion and tomato, put them on a plate and the plate and cup of coffee on a tray, and returned to the front room. She took the manuscript from the box and began reading.

ELEVEN

❧

In the beginning I created heaven and earth.

Except that is not how it happened.

I did not create heaven and earth. I wouldn't have minded, but to be honest, the idea never crossed my mind. Why would it have? I existed in and with Darkness. Indeed, since there was no light, I did not even know the darkness was Darkness, or that I was I.

I do not know what happened. One minute, Darkness, and the next there was an incredible explosion. I suspect Darkness conspired against me, though I don't know how or with whom. We have never talked of it. I never had an easy relationship with Her. I craved Her but also feared Her. I longed to get away from Her but She was all there was. Perhaps the gasses that combined to create the explosion emanated from the friction between us. Or perhaps it was just the opposite. Perhaps Darkness opened Herself to my longing to be at one with Her, and we knew each other and the explosion was the climactic simultaneity of our intimate knowing, a knowing so profound that everything became new, including us, in an explosion of energy that will never cease.

So, I cannot say that I created heaven and earth, not if by create you mean that I did so with intent and prior knowledge of what I was doing. All I know is that something happened and I watched, fascinated, as gasses commingled and created colors I have never seen the likes of since. This went on for millions of what you call years until finally the gasses cooled and suns and planets coalesced. Millions of years more passed as these bodies collided to create moons and asteroids, each jostling to find its place amid Darkness until finally there emerged one orb that was a beautiful melding of blues and greens and whites and, most remarkably, seemed to have a life of its own.

All the other orbs were either places of a heat so intense that they were little more than masses of boiling liquid or they were so cold that they were merely accretions of ice from surface to core. But earth, because that is what the unique orb was, earth was alive, a being of never-ending gestation, spontaneously giving birth without pausing to scream—plants, animals, reptiles, insects, fish. On and on and on life came forth from it! I was amazed. I still am!

I watched. I saw animals giving birth and mothers nursing their young. After watching these, dare I say, miracles for some time, I began to wonder: Where was my mother? Where was my father? How had I come to be? Had I drawn milk from a woman's nippled breast? I thought about it a lot but as far back as I could remember there had always and only been me and Darkness. Was Darkness my mother? I did not think so but how could I be sure? Darkness has never broken Her silence to speak to me.

I observed the life forms on earth organize themselves into groups and families and societies. Even small creatures like bees and ants had an intricate structure in which they lived out their lives. It seemed that every being had a companion, someone like it. Everything in the entire universe had something or someone—except me.

Is there any terror greater than not having your essence recognized and loved by another? How could I know myself if I remained unknown by others? I pondered what I should do. I noticed that animals and humans had a great need for water, and every morning and evening the animals would gather at rivers, while humans went when animals did not. So one morning I decided to stand at the edge of a river to see what would happen.

No sooner was I there than the animals at the stream saw me. Creatures came from every direction. Birds circled around me, each singing its particular song, lions roared, tigers growled, deer danced, and it was so wonderful. I laughed and laughed and laughed, something I had never done in all the foreverness of my existence.

But as happy as I was, one creature was absent. Humans, the ones I desired to be known by the most. But they would not come to the stream until the animals departed, so I left and the animals returned to slaking their thirsts. Once they did and went on their ways, humans came to the river. I returned and stood in the same place as I had for the animals. To my surprise, the humans were completely unaware of my presence. They did not even glance in my direction. I moved and stood directly in front of a small group. One among them even looked up, looked directly into my eyes but, as I looked into hers, it was obvious she did not see me. How disappointing. Apparently humans were not as intelligent as the other creatures.

I decided a more direct approach might be required. The next day when they came to the river I stood directly before each one and said, "I am God." They acted as if they did not see me. Each morning I came to the river and each morning they acted as if I was not there. Baffled, I did not know what to do.

Then one afternoon a young man came, knelt down, and stared into the stream. Curious as to what he was seeing, I looked into the water. There, looking back at him, was an image of himself! He moved his hands slowly over his dark hair, and his image in the stream did the same. He smiled, seemingly pleased by what he saw.

When he left I was so excited I could scarcely stand it. I had never thought about what I looked like, had never conceived that I looked like anything. So I knelt by the river as the man had done and peered in. There was no visage starting back at me. I looked and saw only water and the reflection of the sky. Why wasn't I able to see myself? Could it be that—no. I did not want to contemplate that, but nothing else made sense. I did not have a face. I did not have a body. I did not exist! Except I did.

Much time passed before I understood: I existed, but I was without form. Can you imagine what it is like not to have a form? Everything, even the gnat, occupies a finite space. "Mine! This centimeter of earth belongs to me and no one else!" Even an evanescent dandelion seed had corporeality. But I was infinite and without form. I could not occupy a finite space because I was the infinite space being occupied.

Reluctantly, I gave up hope of being seen. At least by humans. The animals and trees, grasses and water and even stones knew me well. Incidentally, stones are very intelligent and have incredible memories. They have seen it all! Think about that! Dinosaurs? Been there. Ice Age? Lived through it. And they have strong feelings, too. There's one stone that was pissed on by George Washington at Valley Forge and, well, if you'll excuse me, it's still pissed. I've never understood why this particular stone is still upset about it while all the other stones at Valley Forge considered getting pissed on as part of what life is like if you're a stone.

Forgive me. I digress, but this is why I needed to write an autobiography. Most humans do not know how alive everything is, even though humans have a breadth and depth of experience, a complexity of rich emotion and thought that not even a redwood tree can match. (Ah! the redwoods! Such poetry you've never heard.) Despite my closeness to everything else in creation, I believed that it was only in a relationship with humans that I could know my own breadth, depth and complexity simply because, in all of creation, no other being exhibited the humans' range of activity. They

146

possessed the power to conceive something in their minds and with their hands, make it reality—tools, weapons, shelter, clothing, art. Not to mention music and dance and, their most extraordinary creation of all—language. I knew that it was only in a relationship with them that I would have the opportunity to know myself.

I did not know what to do. I went to live by the river where, at the least, I could enjoy the companionship of the animals, and I could observe humans. Obviously there was something I did not understand about them. So I watched and waited. I saw children grow to become women and men and then they had children who grew, and on it went for many generations. Day after day, generation after generation, they came to the river and did not see me.

Then one day a young woman came to the river alone. She walked slowly, her head down. She was young but her body sagged as if a weight were pressing down on her, though she was not carrying anything, not even a container in which to put water. I thought I knew that invisible weight because I had lived with it for millennia. Is there any weight in all the universe heavier than loneliness?

She went to the edge of the water and stared at it. I could see that she was not gazing at her image. Her eyes were not seeing anything because they were dimmed by the despair of her singularity in creation. She began walking into the water. Deeper and deeper into the river she walked and, just as the water came to her neck, a rage came over me as I understood what she was about to do. I refused to let her die.

I still do not understand precisely what happened, but she stopped. Her mouth opened and her eyes widened. She was looking at me and then she started screaming but not in terror or pain but in shrieks of happiness as tears flowed down her face. Instead of going deeper into the river, she turned and ran out of the water and onto the path that led to her village.

I was afraid to move. I waited anxiously to see what was going to happen next. Almost immediately she came running back and stood at the edge of the water, staring at me. It was as if she needed to make sure I was real. Satisfied, she ran off again. I was glad she had returned because I needed to be sure that she was real, that she had seen me, that she had stared directly into my—and then I stopped. Did I now have form?

Hardly any time passed at all before she returned, but this time she brought three older women with her. She pointed at me and the other women saw something. They dropped to their knees and prostrated themselves on the ground at the river's edge. Over the course of the afternoon everyone from the village came to the river and when they saw me, their eyes grew large and their knees bent and they fell to the ground and prostrated themselves.

I did not understand. Why were they lying on the ground like that? What did they see when they looked at me? I looked into the water. I saw only water. What was it they saw and thought was me? Or perhaps they saw nothing and sensed my presence instead. It was as if something in them was awakening, a new perception of who they were and what their possibilities were. Gradually, over centuries, I watched as humans learned that they were spirit as well as material, and they saw me as the source of that spirit. In every language they were ascribing names to me—Legba, Elohim, Shaddai, Zeus, Brahman, Atman, Juno, Athena, Zarathustra, and on and on. They created rituals to link their spirit with mine; some fell to the ground while others knelt and still others bowed from the waist. Some said I resided in the sky while others said my home was in the east and still others said my home was in the west and there were yet others who said I was everywhere. Wherever I resided for them they ascribed powers to me far beyond any I was aware of possessing. If I believed them I was responsible for the air they breathed. I could open the heavens and unleash flooding waters, or cause the very earth to open and swallow them if I was angry with them. There was nothing I could not do and would not do to them if they displeased me.

It took me many years of your time, even centuries perhaps, but eventually I understood why they approached me in terror and obeisance. When the finite touches the infinite, divinity is born. From the terror emanating from this encounter with infinity, God, gods and goddesses are created. Divinity is the way humans make peace with the terror, the way they ascribe meaning to that which is beyond meaning. To them I became The All, That which Is Beyond, The Everywhere, All-Time and No-Time, without Beginning and End.

I was simultaneously embarrassed and horrified! I had wanted to be known, had wanted release from aloneness. But the humans' exaggerations of who I was and what I could do left me more alone than ever. They killed sheep and oxen, burned them on pyres as offerings to propitiate me. What use did I have for a charred slab of animal meat and why did they think I wanted to do them harm? Some humans were so terrified they thought it would please me more if they killed children and virgins and offered them to me.

I was sickened and ashamed. I had been unwilling to bear my loneliness and had indulged my desire to be known by them and to have them know me. Disgusted with myself and them, I retreated into Darkness. Then something happened and everything changed, but in a way I could not have predicted and for which I was not prepared.

High on a mountain a naked young woman was tied to a stone slab to be killed. The holy men, as they called themselves, chanted praises to me. I had heard it many times before and would not have paid attention if not for the look on the face of the young woman who was about to be sacrificed. I expected to see that look of terror and pleading and desperation I had seen so many times before, that look imploring me to intervene and stop her from being killed. Why they thought I had the desire or power to intervene in human affairs was a mystery to me.

But this young woman did not struggle against the thongs that bound her. She did not scream until her throat was raw; no tears flowed from her eyes. She stared up into the sky with a look of adoration. I had never seen such love on anyone's face. I wondered if the holy men had given her something to drink—a hallucinogen of some kind—as they often did to those they were going to kill in my name. But as I was to learn, that was not the case this time.

Even at the moment the holy man raised his arm, his hand gripping a large blade-shaped stone that would crush her skull, the expression on her face did not change. If anything, the look of adoration intensified as she watched the stone descend. At the instant the stone smashed into her skull, a foglike wisp rose from her body and ascended. Up, up, and up it came until it stood before me.

I realize you must be confused. After all, if I am infinite, then why do I describe what happened as if she needed to come to a specific place to find me? Couldn't she have found me anywhere? That is true—for the living. For the dead it is different.

To tell the truth, I am not fond of the dead and I don't often make myself available to them. They come with their stories about their lives and want me to tell them that they had done well, that I forgave them for the wrongs they'd done and the good they had not done. Quite frankly, I was not interested. Hymie Brown enjoys them and their stories, however. If he hears any stories he thinks I might enjoy, he brings them to me. That is how I heard about you.

But I digress again. Where was I? Oh, yes. The young woman who was sacrificed.

"This is not You," her voice came from the wisp of fog.

I had no idea what she was talking about.

"This is not You," she repeated.

"What do you mean?" I wanted to know. She was frightening me.

"The other one, the one who enjoyed my dying. He loved that I gave Him my body and soul. You do not love me. Where is the one who loves me?"

I did not know what she was talking about.

She began crying. "Where is the one who loves me?" she asked over and over.

Her anguished tears were unbearable for me, and my inability to withstand her pleas forced me to relinquish the tight control I had unconsciously been exercising. Suddenly I heard a voice say, "I am here, beautiful one."

I had never heard a voice like that. It was deep and seemed inordinately proud of itself.

"Yes, that is You. You are here!" she said adoringly.

It took a moment before I realized, shocked: The voice was coming from me! I may not have had form, but humans had perceived my presence. Only it was a presence of which I was unaware, or, more honestly, a presence of which I had kept myself unaware. Now that presence was making itself known to me. With horror I had to accept that because I am infinite, a part of me enjoyed having children and virgins sacrificed in my name, sacrificed to propitiate my wrath, a wrath which was very real.

I was so ashamed. How could I have been so ignorant of myself? Being aware that I was infinite did not mean, apparently, that I knew every sinew of my infinitude. It appeared that humans knew me better than I knew myself.

The inner turmoil was almost unbearable. I refused to accept that there was a part of me that enjoyed having children and women sacrificed in my name. So when I saw a man on another mountain about to murder his son because he thought I had told him that doing so would prove his love for me, I stopped him and gave him a sheep to sacrifice instead. I thrust myself more and more into human affairs in an attempt to stop them from doing evil in my name. All of this was, of course, an acting out of my inner struggle; I was trying to find a way to live with my own evil. However, nothing I did assuaged evil.

Humans were timid when it came to doing good, but how they came to life when they committed evil. Their acts of goodness were not filled with lust, but their acts of evil sent the blood roaring through their bodies. Humans could not escape their evil as long as I did not escape my own. I had to do something and I had what I thought was a brilliant idea. I would become flesh. I would walk among them as one of them and tell them that I was Love.

And so I did. "God is Love!" I preached. "God is Love!"

They understood and applauded my words, but it was strange. In the main, their behavior did not change. They continued to revel in evil, killing each other with swords and with malicious words.

But perhaps they did not understand how profound Love is. There had to be something I could do that would convince them. But what? How could I convince them beyond the shadow of a doubt of my love for them? Then it came to me. They put the highest value on their lives and had no qualms about taking the lives of others. What would happen if I offered myself to be killed? Could there be any greater demonstration of my love for them than allowing myself to be sacrificed? What if I told them to give their evil to me? Would I be freed of my own evil if I willingly took on theirs? I didn't know, but it was a risk I was willing to take.

Only after I put this drama in action did I understand. By then it was too late. By proclaiming myself to be Love and saying they could give their evil to me, humans did something I had not anticipated. They separated me, the embodiment of Love, from evil. Evil became a separate entity, something outside themselves and separate from me. They even gave the evil part of me a name—the Devil, Satan, the Evil One. By projecting their evil and mine onto a fictitious demon, many humans recast themselves as warriors in an eternal battle against evil, and those who did not join them in that battle were themselves deemed to be evil. Thus, evil became not actions but people who did not believe as they did. In the name of goodness, evil flourished and became wealthy.

Seeing people murdered in the name of God and Love made me lonelier than I had ever been. The holy men had sacrificed virgins because they were afraid. After I assumed flesh humans no longer feared me because now they claimed to know me, to know who I was and what I wanted, and they murdered in my name and from love of me.

Evil triumphed in the name of Love. Evil ruled in the name of God's goodness. Oh, I know all the philosophical arguments about the glory of Michelangelo's Sistine Chapel murals and Bach's Mass in B Minor and all the great works of literature, et cetera, et cetera, et cetera, and how these counterbalance the human genius for evil and prove the glory of the human enterprise.

That's a rationalization. The great works of art exemplified the best in the human spirit and were the result of years of sacrifice by individuals who committed their souls to their genius. Goodness also requires time and effort and sacrifice. There are very few Michelangelos of goodness and compassion in the world. But evil. Evil is available to everyone and, best of all, evil does not requires effort. You can do evil by doing nothing. The world abounds in Michelangelos of evil.

That young woman whose pleas allowed me to see my evil was also the inspiration for my attempts at autobiography. Writing is a bridge from one solitude to another, and that was what I craved—to be relieved of the burden of my aloneness and share the truth of who I was with another. I wrote the first autobiography on the wall of a cave. Well, it wasn't writing, per se, but pictures. Ah! Such pictures! There was one person who understood and she drew pictures on another wall of the cave. Her kinsmen were so frightened that she could create likenesses of the animals they hunted that they killed her.

So I made no more attempts at autobiography until humans developed writing. Then I wrote stories of my life and left them for the holy men and holy women to read. They would read one or two pages and then burn them.

I didn't understand. Maybe they were poorly written, I thought. Even though I know every word of every language, I will be the first to admit I'm no Shakespeare. I spent more time on each draft until I felt the language conveyed music as well as narrative and meaning.

I thought those who did all the writing about me would be the ones who would most enjoy reading what I had to say—Moses, King David, Matthew, Mark, Luke and John, Saint Augustine, Rabbi Judah the Prince, the popes, people like that. I thought they would be thrilled to have my autobiography. I have to admit that it was daunting to think King David would be reading something I wrote. Now there was a man who could write! I was so eager for his opinion. But I made the mistake of putting the manuscript on his night table while he was carrying on with that Bathsheba woman. I don't think he ever realized it was there.

Only one person read my autobiography in its entirety to that time. And he understood and he wrote his understanding in language plain enough for everyone else to understand.

> I am the Lord, and there is none else, I form the light, and
> create darkness:
> I make peace and create evil; I, the Lord, do all these
> things.

Look it up in that Torah of yours—Isaiah 45:7. It can't be stated any more clearly than that. But no one wants to know me as I really am. They prefer their fantasies of divinity to the bare reality. I have only myself to blame for the moral confusion. When I took on flesh to embody love and goodness, morality became too one-sided. Finally I saw that I had no choice. The only hope I had of correcting the imbalance was to go to the other side.

So I took on flesh as evil. When I did I was surprised. I no longer felt alone. I had never been loved with such passion. When I embodied goodness, people went to their respective places of worship and talked and sang about my goodness, but when they left, they did so little good. But when I took on flesh as evil, people did evil with more devotion than ever, now that I was on their side. They cheated and lied, stole and murdered. Men raped women and abused their daughters, and those who committed none of these acts pretended not to see, especially those who extolled my goodness on their respective sabbaths. In some ways they were better at evil because they knew what goodness was.

I had never been loved with such dedication and ardor, and I was afraid that I would become enamored of my evil. Indeed. It was more than fear. I was certain I would eventually succumb to the delicious power evil conferred. I needed help but whom could I, God, turn to for help? The answer was obvious: the only ones who could save me were those who wrote so knowingly about me and those who spoke with so much emotion about my goodness.

So, in desperation, I write and rewrite my autobiography, tailoring each writing to the person I give it to in the vain hope that someone will answer my plea for help, that someone would retrieve me from evil.

If you have read this far, perhaps you are that person, Rivka. Do you have the courage to help me save myself?

The manuscript ended there. Rebecca stared at the last page but without seeing it. She was chilly but turning up the thermostat would not make her warmer. Finally, she closed the manuscript and returned it gently to the box.

It certainly made sense that no one had finished reading His autobiography. Who would want this God? And did anybody really want to meet God face to face? People thought they wanted to see God but given the chance, how many would decide they preferred mystery? And if God could be seen face to face, He could not be God. Or could He? Maybe God could not be God until someone sat with him, face to face.

Rebecca ate her bagel, cold and hard now, and when she finished, took the dirty plate and empty cup into the kitchen. She made a fresh pot of coffee, returned to the front room and sat down again at the table. She took the manuscript out of the box and turned the pages, reading sentences and phrases at random to reassure herself it was real. If it had been written in English she would have been convinced it was a hoax. But biblical Hebrew? With its smaller vocabulary and complex grammar, no one had written in biblical Hebrew for more than two thousand years.

It was real. God's autobiography. She fantasized about contacting the *New York Times*. They would call in the world's leading scholars to analyze the calligraphy, the grammar, syntax, vocabulary, while scientists tested the ink and parchment for age. Even if the manuscript were pronounced authentic, Rebecca wondered if the newspaper would publish it. Or even if it should. Panic and anger would sweep much of the world if *this* autobiography were published. But the panic would be quickly replaced by anger and denial. Yet maybe there were others like her for whom this was the only God they could accept.

the AUTOBIOGRAPHY of GOD

As darkness seeped into the house and shrouded her in stillness, tears came into her eyes in gratitude for God's acknowledgment that He had willed the taxi to hit her (though He had not said so directly, she knew). Perhaps He had wanted her to read His autobiography because she had known since she was eight years old that evil flowed from God in at least as great abundance as mercy and compassion. Was she the only one who knew God enjoyed evil more?

Since the Holocaust, some Jewish thinkers had been in despair because of God's seeming indifference to His people. Others sought refuge in the "unknowability" of God, holding blindly to their faith that everything was a part of God's plan which we were incapable of understanding because everything God did was for the good. Some Hasidic rebbes dared whisper that the Holocaust had been God's punishment of the Jewish people for abandoning His ways. No one dared write what she thought was obvious: If God intervened to save His people at the Red Sea, and had not intervened at Auschwitz, it could mean only one thing: God had switched sides.

She wiped her face of tears, grateful that, at long last, she did not feel alone with what she had known since childhood.

Even before brushing her teeth the next morning, Rebecca went downstairs and immediately into the front room. The box was there next to the Torah scroll and she opened it to be sure the manuscript was still inside. It was. She took it out and glanced at a few pages to reassure herself that what she had read the previous day had not been an invention of her loneliness.

Just as Rebecca put the manuscript back in the box and was closing the lid, the voice said, "So, *nu*? You finished it!"

"Yes. I did," Rebecca responded, with pride.

"There was a lot of betting as to whether you would."

"Oh? Betting? You mean, actual gambling?"

"That's what betting is. The odds were a million-to-one that you wouldn't."

"Did anybody win?"

"That girl. The new one. She was the only one."

"You mean Allison?"

"Her. That's the one."

"What did she win?"

"Nothing. There's no money over here or anything like that. When you win something, everybody knows you're the winner and that's enough. And anyway, it's just something to do to pass the time since we have so much of it. I never knew how much time there was until I got here and found out that when you're dead you don't sleep."

"I beg your pardon?" Rebecca was horrified. "The only thing that has kept me from not being afraid of death is thinking that one day I'd sleep forever."

"That's not how it is. Most people are just here a short time before they get new bodies and go right back. But people like us who died in that place and people who were murdered or died in some horrible way, we can choose to go back or not. And the people who are really righteous. They can choose. Those of us who stay become spirits and once you're a spirit, you're never tired."

Rebecca sighed. "Well, what about those of us whose souls are tired and we don't have any desire to come back? Do we get a choice about whether to stay and become spirits?"

"Well, there're people like me who go back and forth between this side and the other side. It's funny but when I lived on this side where you are, I spent a lot of time on this side where I am now. Now that

I'm dead I'm doing the same thing. When I was alive, I thought I might be dead. Now that I'm dead, I wonder if I'm not still alive."

Rebecca frowned. What the old woman said reminded her of something, but what? Then it came to her. "Are you Devorah?"

There was a long pause.

"How did you know?" the voice asked finally, in a whisper.

"My mother told me about you."

"Ah! And what did she say?"

"That you went to all the Jewish funerals and cried like it was your job."

Devorah sighed. "It is true. Someone had to feel the pain others didn't want to feel. I don't know why it was me but it was. It was awful! When people die they leave behind all the pain from the sins they committed or the sins committed against them, the pain from their unfulfilled dreams and the pain from not being the person they were meant to be. That's the biggest sin of all, not being yourself. My job was to be like sand at the edge of the ocean and soak up as much of the pain as I could so it was not left to wander around and attack people. That's why I cried so much. I could not believe how much pain there was. Oy! Sometimes I would walk past a cemetery and almost faint because of all the pain, especially that from the Christian ones. I went out of my way to avoid walking past Christian cemeteries. Not even I could withstand the pain that came from those graves."

Rebecca thought about Rebbe Nachman who, in his last year, lived next to a cemetery in which lay the bodies of Jews killed in a pogrom, so he could pray for their souls. "They say people hear you crying at Auschwitz."

"Aiiiii! The only reason the pain from that place hasn't killed me is because I'm already dead."

"I wonder if I'm not a lot like you."

"No. You are better. I was just a helpless woman who stood with one foot in the world of the living and one in the world of the dead. But you? You have learning. A rabbi, no less. And you're a . . . a . . . what's the word?"

"Therapist?" Rebecca answered, using the English word because she couldn't find a Yiddish equivalent.

"Yes. That's it. Therapist. You can understand the pain. I felt it but understood so little. Which reminds me. We have a rabbinical kind of problem."

Rebecca smiled. "What is it?"

"Well, there is this man whose wife died in that place. After he was liberated he went to London and married a beautiful girl. They were married for many years, had three beautiful children, and she died. So he married a third time. They were married a while and then she died. He just died and what he wants to know is: Which wife should he live with now? The three wives all say he was a wonderful husband, very loving, and each of them wants him to herself. He doesn't know what to do. He loved all three and doesn't want to hurt anyone's feelings. So which one should he choose?"

Rebecca laughed aloud. "Why don't you ask King Solomon? He's smarter than I am."

"We did, but he didn't understand the problem. He has seven hundred wives and three hundred concubines."

Rebecca laughed again. "Of course. How could I have forgotten?" She thought for a moment. "Well, tell him to go with the wife who knew him."

"And what does that mean? They all knew him."

Rebecca shook her head. "They all lived with him. He should be

160

with the one with whom his heart felt safe. The wives know which of them that is. And he does, too."

"I hope what you said makes more sense to him than it does me."

Rebecca sensed that Devorah was about to leave. "Wait. I have a question for you."

"Nu?"

"When . . . when is God coming?"

"Ah! That's what I came to tell you. He said tonight."

"Are you serious?" she answered. "Tonight?" Rebecca didn't know what to do. Should she straighten up, vacuum and dust? Put a bottle of white wine in the refrigerator? Prepare cheese and crackers and stuffed celery? But wait a minute! This was God! She should kill a fatted calf or a lamb without blemish, build a fire, and roast it so as to create a pleasing odor. Except He'd written that He didn't like meat.

"He said, tonight."

"Did he say what time?"

"No."

"What should I wear, Devorah? And how do I act? Do I curtsy, prostrate myself? And how do I address Him? Adonai? Elohim? Melech? El Shaddai? What? What?"

"Just be yourself. He says He gets all the pomp and circumstance in churches and synagogues and mosques. But I think He's kind of nervous about coming to see you."

"Me? Why? I'm nobody!"

"You're the only one, besides Isaiah, who ever read his autobiography all the way through. I think He cares about your opinion."

"Are you kidding me?"

"No. He said Isaiah was a little disappointed in him after reading it but you weren't. He said He trusts you."

Rebecca didn't know if she liked the sound of that. If He trusted her, was He going to ask her to do something ridiculous like sacrifice her only son, even though she didn't have one, or get pregnant without having sex? She wouldn't agree to that, either. If she was going to have a baby, she definitely wanted the sex.

"What should I do, Devorah?"

"How should I know? God has never come to see *me.*" And she was gone.

Rebecca sank down into the rocking chair, her hand resting idly on the box that held God's autobiography. What would she and God talk about? She assumed He was not affected by the snow or how cold it was, so that took care of the weather for a conversation starter. She didn't have a television, and she didn't read the newspaper, so that left out current events, sports, movies, and practically everything else. She could discuss Torah and Talmud, but He didn't seem to much care for religion. Even so, maybe she could ask Him all the things that had been bothering her, like how did He part the Red Sea and what was manna and why had He stopped sending it? But, according to Him, He hadn't done any of those things. Obviously God should be talking to Maimonides or Rashi or somebody who, unlike her, had sense enough to ask an intelligent question.

Rebecca spent the afternoon trying on every dress, skirt, blouse, and pair of slacks she owned. She felt like she was getting ready for a date. A date! Had God ever been on a date? Probably not. So He might be as nervous as she was. But, no, it wasn't a date because she wasn't going to be trying to seduce Him into liking her, which was the minimal objective of a date. However, it wouldn't be bad for God to like her. In fact, it could come in handy. But when you went on a date you showed a little cleavage, even if the date was with someone you didn't like but wanted them to like you because it was good for your ego to know that you could seduce someone you wouldn't want to help you across the street if you were blind, but no way was she going to show cleavage to God! But then again, being God He had probably seen her cleavage, and more, which was also upsetting. Maybe He had chosen not to look. She wasn't going to ask.

Rebecca finally decided that she wanted to feel comfortable, or as comfortable as one could be meeting God face to face, so she put on a pair of jeans and a bulky knit sweater. The next decision was where would they talk—in the front room, the kitchen or up in her bedroom? She was a little uncomfortable with the thought of having God in her bedroom, but it was also her living space, which just happened to have a bed in it. If she was going to be comfortable, then she had to be in the room where she felt most like herself and that was upstairs. So she settled on the bed and picked up a *Times* crossword puzzle from the stack on the floor. One-Across: Russia and Idaho. She scanned the puzzle quickly to see if it had a theme. At least six times the clue read, Russia and some state. Obviously, it must means towns with the same names. Moscow was in Russia and Idaho and it fit One-Across.

But she couldn't concentrate for wondering how God was going to appear—in a flash of lightning, a cloud of smoke, a burning bush? Every time she heard a noise, she looked up, but no one was there. Sometimes she wondered if she had heard anything at all.

The evening went slowly. Rebecca had to go to the bathroom but was afraid to move from the bed. What if God came while she was sitting on the toilet? But He was God. He would know she was sitting on the toilet. But would He? The God whose autobiography she had read didn't seem to know much of anything.

Finally, unable to hold it any longer, she made a quick run to the bathroom and hurried back without flushing. But God had not come and slowly she began to wonder if He would. Maybe something important had come up, like a war somewhere or maybe a little kid was dying who needed Him, but she stopped herself. None of that sounded like the God she'd read about. It seemed that she'd been stood up by God, but maybe it was her fault. He probably looked down and saw her in a pair of jeans and a sweater and thought she was being disrespectful. Obviously, she'd done something wrong and if she hadn't been so tired and depressed, she would have cried. She looked at the clock. One A.M. In two hours it would be time to say Kaddish. She pulled back the covers and without bothering to undress, crawled under and was asleep immediately.

"I apologize for being late."

Although the voice was soft, almost shy, Rebecca awoke immediately and sat up in bed, looking around. She supposed she hadn't been sleeping deeply. Rebecca didn't know what she had expected God to sound like. Well, that wasn't true. Everyone knew God had a deep voice. It was impossible to imagine the high-pitched, light voice she had just heard saying "Let there be light," and get any more of a response than a giant cosmic yawn. But at least He was speaking English. She'd been afraid He would speak biblical Hebrew. She reached over to turn on the lamp next to her bed but the voice said, "Please. Not yet."

As her eyes adjusted to the darkness Rebecca could make out a form sitting in her rocking chair at the far end of the room by the windows.

"What did you think of my autobiography?"

Rebecca was glad God was going to carry the conversation. "I was surprised You told the truth," she said bluntly.

The figured nodded. "So you're not disappointed in me?"

"No. Not really. I mean, I wish You were more like the God we would like You to be, but that's not Your problem."

"I can't tell you how happy it makes me to hear you say that. I hate disappointing people."

"What is it like knowing people would be disappointed if they knew the real You?" Rebecca asked gently, suddenly aware she was speaking to God as if He were a client.

There was a long silence. Then Rebecca heard the soft sound of weeping. Instinctively she reached for a box of tissue, but stopped, not knowing if God blew His nose or if He even had one.

"Are you OK?" she asked, finally.

"I'm fine," the answer came. "No one ever asked what it's like being me. Perhaps I could let you see my face now."

"I would like that. I don't like talking to the darkness."

There was another long silence. "I'm a little nervous, you understand. I suspect it is like when a man and a woman make love for the first time and she's worried that he will notice that her breasts droop and one is larger than the other and he is worried that she will think his penis too small. So I am about to expose myself to you—no pun intended—and I am apprehensive."

"I'm sure it'll be fine," Rebecca reassured Him.

"Very well. You may turn on the light."

With nervous eagerness Rebecca did but she saw little more of God than she had before as He was sitting outside the arc of light. "You have to come closer."

God inched the rocking chair more toward the bed.

"Closer," Rebecca said firmly. "I still can't see you. Come closer. It'll be all right. I promise."

God picked up the chair, but he walked backward until he came to the foot of the bed and into the light. But He didn't turn the chair or Himself around.

"What're you so afraid of?" Rebecca wanted to know, getting impatient. "Turn around."

God sighed and turned around slowly until He was face to face with Rebecca. She looked at Him, gasped, and then screamed as she scurried out of bed and flattened her body against the wall beside the door. She stood there for a moment, her eyes shut tight, afraid to open them. After a moment she took a deep breath and let it out slowly, hoping that when she opened her eyes she would not see who she thought she had seen. Slowly, she unclenched her eyelids. The figure sitting in the rocking chair and looking down at his lap was who she'd thought He was.

His dark hair was brushed away from a part on the right side of his head and downward at an angle over the left side of his forehead. The eyes were dark and the lips thin. There, between his nose and upper lip was the unmistakable and telltale mustache, thick and square like the bristles of an artist's brush. He had on an ill-fitting brown suit, white shirt and black tie. She kept staring at Him and no matter how hard she tried to see someone else, there was no mistake: God looked like Adolf Hitler.

"I'm sorry," He apologized. "I—"

"Who are you?" Rebecca interrupted, shouting. "Are you Hitler? Am I to believe that God is Adolf Hitler?"

"Please. Come back to your bed. It is chilly. I will explain. Please."

Rebecca realized she was shivering, though whether it was from cold or fear she was not certain. Warily, she returned to bed, sat with her back against the headboard, and pulled the covers tight around her. She stared at Him angrily but His head was lowered as if He could not meet her eyes. Finally He looked up, His eyes pleading with her.

"I'm sorry."

"Stop with the self-pity!" Rebecca responded angrily. "Answer my question! Am I supposed to believe that You took on flesh and came to earth as Adolf Hitler?"

He sighed. "Why is that so hard to believe? If I am given credit for the beauty of the sunsets and the majesty of the cedars of Lebanon and the wondrous fish of the deep, then am I not also responsible for tornados and avalanches and hurricanes? If I am the author of Life, am I not also the author of Death? If I am responsible for good, am I not also responsible for evil? You read My autobiography. I thought you understood."

Rebecca thought she had also, but the God she was staring at far exceeded anything she would have imagined. "Maimonides said because God is all good, there can be no evil in Him."

God shook his head and smiled wryly. "I had the hardest time understanding him. He was far too rational for me. Why did he assume I was all good? *You* never assumed that."

Rebecca felt herself becoming calm as God's words returned her to the truth of her experience. "No. Not after you had the taxi hit me."

"I suppose I should apologize for that, but then again, can you imagine your life without what happened that Sunday afternoon?"

She shook her head. "Not really."

"Without that accident you would be an entirely different person, wouldn't you?"

She nodded.

"So, what should I apologize for? Providing you with the opportunity to become someone you could not have become otherwise?"

"So I should thank You for Auschwitz because without it my parents would not have met and I would not exist?"

"And why not?" God answered. "Every day people thank me for their good fortune, which often comes at the expense of someone else's ill fortune. There is a car accident and six people are killed and two survive. What do the survivors say? 'Thank God, it wasn't me!' They might as well be honest and say, 'Thank God, He killed the others.' But if you want an apology, I'll give it to you."

Rebecca thought about accepting an apology from Adolf Hitler and shook her head. "That's all right. I'll pass."

"Good. I would have been disappointed in you otherwise. Now, back to Maimonides and all the others who proclaimed me to be all good. They should have known better but they didn't understand their own scriptures. Think about what's written in your Torah. It's right there in Genesis."

Rebecca went through the opening chapters of Genesis, seeing the Hebrew text in her mind, and when she came to the lines she thought God was referring to, she stopped and said them aloud:

"*Va'yivra Elohim et hadam b'tzalmo, btzelem Elohim bara oto zachar u'n'keiva bara otam.* And Elohim created man in His image, in His image God created him, male and female He created them."

God chuckled. "Precisely."

"So, if we are created in Your image," Rebecca continued, "and we have the capacity for evil as well as good, then so do You."

"Yes!" he exclaimed. "What a relief to hear that finally said aloud. As long as humans avoid their own evil, I am left looking like this."

"Which means we can make You into someone better," Rebecca said simply.

"I hope so," God responded softly, and as suddenly as He had appeared, He was gone.

For a long time Rebecca did not move. She stared at the rocking chair where God/Hitler, had sat and talked to her. As hard as she tried to remember every detail, she knew that some had already slipped away and that, in time, her mind would try to convince her she had dreamed it all because part of the mind's job was to cast doubt on what the heart knew to be true, and the heart, because it had no words, often lost the argument.

When another gray dawn began bringing light into the room, she awoke, unable to remember if she had said Kaddish with her congregation or if they had not come. However, her mind was preoccupied with God's visit and their conversation. She got out of bed and went downstairs to make coffee. When it was ready, she poured a cup, then sat at the table in the front room and wrote down as much of the conversation as she remembered. She wrote in Hebrew, both because it seemed appropriate and, if she died suddenly, she was afraid of what others might think if they came across handwritten notes in English of a conversation with God. But seeing something in Hebrew, they might not even bother to have it translated, and just as well.

Rebecca touched the box that held God's autobiography. Thomas Aquinas, Augustine, Martin Luther, the Baal Shem Tov, Rabbi Judah the Prince, and many others had rejected the opportunity to talk to God face to face. She hadn't. Why? She could have burned the manuscript but she hadn't. Was it because she was a woman? Pandora had opened the box; Eve had eaten the fruit of the tree; and though both myths concluded that the world would be a paradise if these women had minded their business, stasis was not the ideal condition. Maybe women preferred the truth, regardless of the consequences. She hated herself for sounding like her feminist classmates from rabbinical school, but Adam hadn't been the one who had wanted to see. Eve had listened to the serpent because she had a sense that the life she had been given was not as rich as the life she could have— if she ate the fruit.

Maybe that was why, Rebecca thought, she'd read the manuscript. What had Devorah said? The biggest sin of all was not being the person you were meant to be. Rebecca didn't know who she was meant to be. She knew only that she wasn't that person yet. Maybe Maimonides and all the others didn't read the manuscript because they were being who they were meant to be. Maybe they'd had no need to read it. Whereas she? What had her need been? To know that God knew His own evil.

And now she knew and knowing, she was not who she had been. She had no idea who she would become. All she knew now was that God needed her. When she knew what to do about that, perhaps she would be who she was meant to be.

The next day was Shabbat and Rebecca did not expect Him to come, at least not until after sunset. So instead of that Saturday being the day of rest she had known all her life, a day when she stopped doing and allowed herself to merely be, she fretted and worried if He would come that night. But God hadn't promised, hadn't promised anything. Yet there she was, sitting on her bed, staring at the empty rocking chair.

Rebecca picked up the same *Times* crossword puzzle she had been saving since the day after Allison's murder. (*Russia and Texas. Odessa.*

Russia and Nebraska. Hmmmm.) She put the paper down. Why hadn't He come back? Maybe she'd said something wrong. Or maybe there was something she should have said and hadn't. Maybe she should have put on makeup which she never wore anyway, but a little blush wouldn't have hurt.

"Stop it!" she said aloud, disgusted with herself for obsessing over a nonexistent relationship with a God who looked like Adolf Hitler. If only there was someone to whom she could talk, who wouldn't laugh at her or think she was losing her mind.

But there wasn't. Everyone from rabbis, ministers and priests to the person who went to synagogue or church only on the major holidays was sure they knew that God was good, merciful, compassionate, All-Knowing, All-Powerful, and Always Present. Where was the evidence for such confident assertions? Surely not in a world where poverty, the sexual abuse of women and children, famine and murder were as ordinary as dirt.

"You're right," came a light, high-pitched voice from the rocking chair.

Rebecca looked up quickly and it was him—Him, she meant. She was disappointed to see that He still looked like Hitler, but a tired and depressed one. This time He was wearing the black uniform of the dreaded SS, but it was wrinkled. The white shirt was yellow around the collar and the knot of the black tie did not hide the collar button. He reached in His pocket and pulled out a pack of cigarettes.

"Would you mind not smoking in here?" Rebecca said sharply.

God slowly returned the cigarettes to the side coat pocket from which he'd taken them.

"I'm sorry," she said, realizing that she had just told God Himself not to do something. "I didn't mean to speak so harshly."

171

He shrugged. "Don't worry about it. It's refreshing to hear some- one speak to me as if they aren't afraid."

Rebecca didn't know that she wasn't. She had spoken without thinking, forgetting who He was. But looking at Him sitting in her rocking chair He didn't look fearsome. Merely lonely and—dare she think it?—afraid.

"You said I was right. Right about what?" she asked God in an ef- fort to start a conversation.

He sighed. "Well, I am ashamed to admit it, but I am as susceptible as any human to the good opinions of others. And yet, unlike humans perhaps, I have come to find those opinions confining, burdensome. How can I be myself if I am afraid that self will not be accepted? It is humans who want to be good, merciful, and loving and compassion- ate. At least they think this is how they want to be. Obviously, they don't or they would be. So they want me to be what they think they ought to be. This is simultaneously flattering and oppressive."

"I know what you mean," Rebecca said quietly. "When I limp by in a Ralph Lauren skirt, people can't give me the pity they would like to."

"I always admired that about you," God said.

"I beg your pardon?"

"You never limped. Just your body."

Tears rushed into her eyes at the first words of recognition she'd ever heard, at the first words acknowledging how difficult it had been to resist the comforting seduction of expecting less of herself because her body was not whole. But by wearing fashionable clothes she had asserted and affirmed her body's wholeness, different though it was.

"Thank you," she said.

"No. It is I who should thank you."

And He was gone.

TWELVE

❧

The Monday after Thanksgiving, Rebecca had scarcely gotten settled at her office desk when there was a soft knock on her door.

"Yes?" she said.

The door opened slowly and she was surprised to see Evan Green. "I apologize for not making an appointment," he said, standing in the doorway.

She hadn't seen him since the Sunday morning they had spoken at the memorial service for Allison. Rebecca was glad to see him and reassured him that it was fine that he had not made an appointment.

"Please. Come in. If you want, you can put your coat on the coat tree in the corner."

After he did so she gestured toward another and larger room off her office space where there was a couch with a coffee table before it, comfortable stuffed chairs, and a rocking chair.

"I'm not disturbing you, am I?" Evan wanted to know.

"Not at all."

He sat down at the end of the couch closest to the rocking chair. Rebecca shifted the chair so she could look directly at him and he, her.

Not until that moment did Rebecca realize that in her five years at the college no black students—the few there were—had ever come for counseling. She was ashamed not to have recognized this long before. There had to have been some African American students in need of psychological counseling in the past five years. Ralph Ellison was right: blacks were invisible to whites. She remembered how frightened she had been of the black students at Columbia, most of whom had walked around looking angry all the time. Maybe that was the only way they could make themselves visible to people like her who probably would not have noticed them otherwise. They had nurtured a limp, also. Rebecca had never had a black person for a friend. When she'd gone back to school for her MSW, she'd been friendly with blacks in her classes but it had never occurred to her to share with them something of who she was away from school. Would they have been interested in going to a Friday night service, a Passover seder, or in having her teach a page of Talmud? She wanted to say probably not, but that would be a judgment that preserved her unintentional, unconscious, but very real racism. The simple but painful truth was she had failed to give them the opportunity to say yes or no, and thereby failed herself.

Evan was smiling shyly at her as if he were not sure what he had come to say, or even why he had come and if what he *thought* he wanted to say was worth anyone hearing, so Rebecca relieved him of the burden of beginning and said, "I was very impressed by your speech at Allison Manchester's memorial service. There aren't many who could speak that well extemporaneously. When we talked afterward you said your father is a minister. Are you thinking about becoming one yourself?"

"I think about it," he said solemnly, "but I'm not sure I could stand up and tell people that God is good and that God is always right when I'm not sure."

"Maybe you're supposed to be the one who stands up and says maybe God isn't good sometimes. Maybe He isn't always right."

Evan laughed uneasily and shook his head slowly several times. "I don't know if I could do that." He stopped. Rebecca did not ask anything. She didn't want the conversation to veer into a discussion about theodicy.

Evan was looking down at his hands, which were clasped one inside the other. "Thanks for what you said about my speech," he said quietly, "but I felt like I was spouting rhetoric. I meant everything I said, but there was so much I didn't say."

"Like what?" Rebecca prodded gently.

"I guess that's what I wanted to talk to you about. Have you heard anything? Have the Boston police caught anybody?"

It took her a moment to realize he was referring to Allison's murder. She also noticed that he hadn't answered her question but she answered his. "If they have, I haven't heard. I would think they would have told us if they had."

Evan's head went down toward the hands again. He started rubbing his right fist against the left palm. Rebecca noticed tension lines come into his forehead and though curious as to this sudden change of mood, she waited. Finally, he looked up at her and said quietly, "I was with her in Boston that afternoon."

"I beg your pardon?" This was the last thing Rebecca had expected to hear.

"I was with Allison the day she was killed."

Tears came into his eyes and he blinked rapidly and when that didn't hold them back he wiped his eyes, then let out a heavy sigh. Rebecca was so taken aback she didn't know what to say. So she waited.

Evan was looking down at his hands, the right fist still rubbing against the palm of the left hand. Finally he continued. "We were in love. We met during first-year student orientation last year. As student body president I was involved in helping them get settled. I saw her the first night of orientation. She was in my group and I saw her sitting by herself in the back of the room. As group facilitator I knew I was supposed to ask her to join the group but something told me to let her be. After I got the group playing a game to help them open up and talk about where they were from and what they were thinking about majoring in and things like that, I went back to her and asked if she was all right. She said she was."

Evan smiled sadly. "I had thought she might be very shy but when I looked into her face I saw a sadness as if she had been mourning for someone or something almost since the day she was born. After I got to know her, I understood. She had been beaten down by the unwanted attentions of boys *and* quite a few men. I can't imagine what it must be like to be desired as if you're nothing more than a cream-filled pastry. The only way she knew to protect herself was to retreat into a corner, literally and psychologically, yearning to be a part of the social life around her but knowing worse might happen if she joined. That night, though, all I knew was that she was the saddest person I'd ever met. So I told her she could go to her room if she wanted, or she could stay where she was. To my surprise, she stayed.

"When the session ended Allison was the first to leave. Everyone else headed for The HangOut where there were doughnuts, hot chocolate and cider. I was tired and went to my room. About a half hour later there was a knock on my door. I opened it and it was her. My room number was in the orientation packet. She wanted to know why I hadn't tried to get her to join the group. I said I respected her wish not to. I'll never forget what she said: 'You're the first boy who has ever respected anything I wanted.' She came in and we talked almost until the sun came up. She told me things she'd never told anyone."

He stopped as if he wasn't sure he wanted to go on. Rebecca waited patiently. When he turned back to her his eyes were once again filled with tears but this time he did not bother to wipe them away.

"I loved her so much," he said, his voice breaking. "And she loved me. No one knew and that was how we wanted it. We didn't want to be a topic of conversation. So we kept our relationship secret. One of the perks of being student body president is that I get a suite to myself and last year she would come there to study almost every evening. I was out at meetings a lot and when I *was* there, people were always knocking on my door with a problem of some kind. Being student body president sounds important but I'm just somebody to dump problems on. She stayed in the bedroom so no one ever knew she was there, but we didn't actually get to have that much time together. So we hit upon the idea of driving to Boston every couple of weeks so we could be together. Sometimes we went to the aquarium but most often, we went to the Museum of Fine Arts."

Evan shook his head sadly. "Allison said I was the first boy she *wanted* to touch her and she didn't understood why I wouldn't. She would touch my shoulder or grab my arm or reach to hold my hand and I would freeze. She began to wonder if there was something wrong with her, began to wonder if I wasn't attracted to her, if I didn't think she was beautiful.

"Finally I had to tell her the truth, a truth I was having a hard time dealing with. I loved her like I had never loved anyone but there was one problem: she was white. My mother had given me firm

177

instructions: 'You can go to that white school in white Vermont but if you fall in love with a white girl, don't bother coming home because you won't be my son any more.' And there I was in love with a very blond, very blue-eyed, and very white girl. I didn't know what to do. So I told her that her being white was a problem. She was hurt and angry. She wanted to know if I had been playing with her emotions and would have dumped her when an attractive black girl came along. She really got to me when she wanted to know how my mother was different from some redneck in the Ku Klux Klan who wouldn't want *his* daughter to be in love with *me*. I didn't have an answer. Until that moment I had always thought only white people could be racist.

"She broke up with me at the end of first semester last year. I have never been so depressed in my life. I guess it wasn't easy for her either, because a few weeks after we got back from winter break I got an e-mail from her asking if we could be friends. E-mail was better than nothing. As it turned out e-mail brought us closer because I was able to pour out my soul to her and tell her what it felt like to be black and she told me what it was like being the object of almost every man's sexual desire. After a couple of months of e-mailing it was obvious to me that I would be a fool to let my mother decide who I could and couldn't love.

"So one night I went to Allison's suite and told her that I loved her, that I didn't care what my mother thought but that I wanted to be with her, maybe forever. I expected her to leap into my arms. Instead she started crying and told me she was seeing someone else. I thought I was going to die right then and there. She said she had been wanting to tell me but she was afraid she'd lose me. I asked her to break it off with this other person. She said she wanted to, but he was very possessive, very jealous, and she was afraid of what he might do. I asked her who it was and all she said was that it wasn't anybody on campus. I asked her if she loved him more than me. She said she didn't, but this person loved her and she didn't want to hurt his feelings.

"She begged me to remain her friend. I figured I stood a better chance of getting her back if I stayed her friend than if I went into a funk of self-pity and walked off, which is what I wanted to do. So we continued e-mailing each other, more than ever, it seemed. Three, four times a day we sent long e-mails back and forth. I was like her living diary. She could tell me anything and that's how I knew she still loved me because the person you love is the person you tell everything to.

"She even told me about my rival, whom she referred to only as Agathon, though that wasn't his real name. I recognized the name from Plato's dialogues and assumed he was a graduate student in philosophy at Columbia or NYU, because every weekend it seemed she was going to New York and he would take her to concerts, the ballet, fine restaurants. It was obvious he had more money than I did and I couldn't compete with that.

"The semester ended and she went home to New York and I went to D.C. I hadn't been home more than a week when she called. My mother answered the phone and gave me this odd look as she handed it to me. Allison started crying the instant she heard my voice. When she stopped crying enough to talk she said she had to see me, that she needed me and there wasn't anybody else she could talk to and could I come to New York."

He stopped and looked earnestly at Rebecca. "You probably know all about this, but it was my first time."

"What do you mean?" she asked.

"It was the first time I knew that whatever decision I made would affect my life forever. I felt like the whole world and everyone and everything in it stopped breathing. I had to make a choice. My mother's a lawyer and she had arranged for me to have a summer internship on the Hill with an African American congressman. However, I knew that if I told Allison I couldn't come, I would lose her forever, that I would not even have her friendship. This was the first time in my life when I had to make a decision as to what I valued the most, and whichever decision I made, there would be consequences that might be painful. But it was obvious. I told her I would be there the next day.

"When I got off the phone my mother wanted to know if 'that girl on the phone' was white. I said, 'Her name is Allison. She has blond hair and blue eyes. She lives in New York and I have to go see her.'" Evan smiled. "My mother surprised me. I expected her to start screaming and yelling and telling me to pack my stuff and get out. There was a long silence and then she said, 'Since you know how I feel about black men and white women, and since I've also made it very clear that I wouldn't tolerate you falling in love with a white girl, I can only conclude that Allison must be very special for you to so blatantly disobey me.' I said, 'She is.' And that was all that was said.

"A lot of John Brown students live in New York and so I didn't have a problem finding a place to stay. I called Allison as soon as I got in the next day and we met at the marina on Seventy-ninth Street. That's when she told me she was pregnant, and this guy she was seeing didn't want her to have the child. Allison didn't want his child either, but having an abortion was the worst thing she could think of. She was raised Catholic and I don't think she knew how Catholic she was until then. She wanted to know what I thought she should do. I said the most ridiculous and the most courageous thing I'll probably say in my life." He smiled. "I told her that I loved her and if she wanted to have the baby and keep it, if she wanted to put it up for adoption, or if she decided to have an abortion, I would be with her, that whatever she decided she wouldn't be alone. I don't know what I would've done if she'd decided to have the child and keep it. I was in no way ready to support her and a child, but at that moment I felt like I could have.

"I think all she needed to hear was that she wouldn't be alone with her decision because her immediate response was that she wanted an abortion. She didn't think it was right to bring a child into the world she would hate because the child would remind her of someone who had used her.

"A few days later I went to the abortion clinic with her. After that everything changed." He stopped and looked down into his hands which were still now.

"What do you mean?" Rebecca prompted.

"A few days after the abortion she said she wanted to go up to the Cloisters. For the rest of that summer we went there several times a week. She said she felt at peace when she was there. I came to like it there, too, with the Gregorian chants playing as we made our way slowly through the various galleries. She spent a lot of time looking at statues and paintings of the Virgin Mary. Afterward we would go and sit on rocks and look out over the Hudson River and she would cry about the baby she said she killed. I didn't say anything. I just held her.

"In August her parents left for the place they rented in the Hamptons every summer. Allison didn't want to go and she asked me to come stay with her. One afternoon when she was crying and I was

181

holding her, it happened. We made love. And that was practically all we did the rest of the month.

"I knew what she was doing. I knew she wasn't using any kind of birth control and I wasn't. I knew and I didn't care. Was she using me? I don't know. Maybe. But I don't think so. I wasn't just some guy who happened to come along. We knew each other's souls. She loved me and I loved her. That was all that mattered.

"The day she was killed we drove to Boston to go to the MFA and it was there, before a painting of the Virgin Mary, she told me she was pregnant. I was very happy. I wasn't surprised. As often as we made love I knew she was going to get pregnant, or my semen had no sperm. I was very happy. Then she told me she had a date with Agathon. I was pretty upset. I didn't know she was still seeing him. She said she wasn't but he had been calling and e-mailing, that he wanted to see her. She said she knew he would leave her alone when she told him God had forgiven her and had made her clean by allowing her to be pregnant again. I didn't want her to see him and told her so. She said I had no reason to be jealous.

"We went outside and she gave me a big hug and the most wonderful kiss. That was around five o'clock. We agreed she would meet me in Harvard Square at eight. Then she hurried down the steps and into a car. I didn't pay any attention to the car, plus it was already dark. I wandered around bookstores in Cambridge until it was time to meet her. I waited in the square until midnight. All I could think was that they had gotten back together and I drove back here, crying all the way."

Tears rolled down his face now but no sound came from his lips. Rebecca handed him the box of tissues from the coffee table. He took the box but did not avail himself of a tissue. She understood.

Sometimes it was comforting to feel the wetness of grief's tears on your face.

Eventually he took tissues and began drying his face and eyes.

"Will it ever stop hurting?" he asked softly.

Rebecca shook her head. "No. This is your wound. As time passes, the wound will hurt less but the hurt won't disappear. And, at times, the pain might even intensify. But your wound will also become your teacher—if you let it."

"What will it teach me?"

"That is not for me to know."

"Thanks for being honest with me."

"You're welcome," she returned. "Evan? You need to talk to the Boston police."

He shook his head vigorously. "I can't do that."

Rebecca was surprised at how quickly his mood changed. One instant his face had been filled with sorrow. Now anger and suspicion flashed from his eyes.

"Why not?"

"Because I'll become their one and only suspect. They'll say I made the whole story up. What if none of the guards at the MFA remember seeing us that day? It was dark when she left me and got in the car. I couldn't tell the color or the make. They'll say there never was another guy, that I got her pregnant the first time and was angry because she got pregnant again. Allison was the epitome of white beauty who didn't get her blondness from a bottle nor her blue eyes from contact lenses. No white cop is going to believe she was in love with me. And if he does, he's going to hate me even more."

"The detective in charge of the case—Detective Williams—is a black woman."

Evan laughed harshly. "That might be just as bad, if not worse. You aren't going to tell her anything I've told you, are you?"

"Of course not," Rebecca said immediately. "Everything you've told me stays between us. But if you remember any little detail that might help the Boston police, would you get in touch with them? They have a special number for tips on this case."

"If I remember anything I'll do that."

As soon as Evan left, Rebecca hurried to her desk and looked up Saul's number in the campus directory. She dialed it quickly hoping he was there. The phone rang and rang and she was just about to hang up when he answered.

"Saul? Rebecca."

"Rebecca!" he exclaimed. "To what do I owe the honor?"

"I need your help. Are you going to be in your office for a while?"

"I have a class at two. What's going on?"

She looked at the clock on her desk. Damn! Someone was coming in a half hour but Rebecca would be done by noon. "I'll be there shortly after twelve."

THIRTEEN

❧

As Saul hung up the phone he wondered what had led Rebecca to call him. There had been a time when he had hoped to hear her voice at the other end of the phone any time it rang. Now that he had, he wasn't foolish enough to think she had awoken that morning to find herself madly in love with him. And, much to his relief, that was not what he desired any longer.

So much had happened since that awful New Year's Day at Patric Marsh's house. Saul and Rebecca had talked about it on the phone, each trying to help the other understand the anger toward Jews they had felt at the table, even from those who had said nothing in the face of Patric's outburst.

"Where did so much anger come from?" he had asked Rebecca. As the words came from his mouth, for some reason he heard them as being not about Patric Marsh, Roger Crawford, or the other gentiles at that table. No. He heard the question as being directed at himself. But he had never thought of himself as angry. Even as a child he had been little chubby Saul, who always had a smile on his face and something funny to say. Or so he had thought until he saw his face as it really was.

Saul swung his chair around and stared out the window at the snow-laden landscape. Reb Yitzchak. He hadn't thought about him in decades until that afternoon on the phone with Rebecca when his face came floating up from memory like a body from a wrecked and sunken vessel. Saul was eight when Reb Yitzchak had come to speak to his Hebrew school class about how to write a Torah scroll. He was a thin man in a rumpled black suit; a white shirt stained brown with remnants of food, buttoned all the way to the top though he did not have on a tie; and a black hat on his head. Over the top of his belt dangled strings, the ritual fringes of the small prayer shawl he wore next to his skin. He had a red mustache joined to a scraggly beard hanging from his chin like a bib, except it came to a point and gave his thin face a demonic cast. This effect was exaggerated by the large spaces between the front teeth and the tightness and open hostility in the eyes.

There had been a moment when Reb Yitzchak had looked at Saul who was sitting on the front row and Saul had stared back at him and it was as if they knew each other, the neglected, abused and hurt parts, the parts that would have cried had they known how and been given the opportunity, but having been cheated of both self-knowledge and opportunity, the face of the one became demonic and the body of the other had already begun expanding in order to house the pain of its soul. In that moment Saul felt something he had never felt for anyone in his young life, not even his parents, and that was unconditional love.

Ten years Saul studied with Reb Yitzchak and learned the intricacies of how to write a Torah scroll, traveling from his suburban home on Long Island to the small basement apartment in Williamsburg until the Sunday morning he had found Reb Yitzchak kneeling on the floor of his tiny apartment, his head in the oven, the gas on. Atop the stove was a note on which he had written in beautiful calligraphy, "Another Jew for Hitler." Saul had put the note in his pocket, not wanting the police or anyone to see it.

Twenty years had passed since that Sunday, twenty years in which even passing thoughts of that morning had been thrust so deeply into memory that recollections of it could not have been retrieved even if he had tried to dredge them up, which he never would have. But there they were, unwanted and unbidden, and all because he had asked a question more to keep Rebecca on the phone a little longer than because he expected or wanted an answer to it.

Since then he thought he had spent more time in memory than in the present. There, at the center of memory's core, was the unwavering stare of Reb Yitzchak, a stare whose hostility had never relented in all the years Saul had been his student, and Saul returned the stare and saw himself in it, saw that, like Reb Yitzchak, living well was beyond him, no matter how much effort and good intent he put into it, no matter how fervently he prayed, and there was nothing to be gained from pretending otherwise, and with that mere hint of self-acceptance came the realization of what happened when you permitted pain to become anger and anger to become self-hatred and self-hatred to become self-pity. That was when suicide became the last desperate attempt to make yourself lovable, and Saul understood Reb Yitzchak's suicide as an act of love designed to show him who he would become if he didn't take possession of his soul.

Saul wasn't sure he had as yet accomplished that monumental feat but having shed a hundred pounds that year was surely a down payment.

When Rebecca reached Saul's office the door was open and she saw him sitting in the chair behind his desk, staring out the window. She wondered for a moment if she was at the wrong office because the man in the chair was thinner than she'd ever seen Saul. But when she looked at the nameplate on the door, it read "Saul Greenberg." She knocked lightly.

Saul turned around in the chair. "I'm sorry. Have you been standing there long?"

"Only a moment," she responded, walking into his office. "You've lost weight! You look wonderful."

He blushed slightly. "Thank you. I've been working out all year, changed my diet, and some other things."

"Well, it is certainly working. Don't stop."

"I won't. I'm starting to like the person I see staring from the mirror."

Rebecca smiled. "I'm very happy for you."

"Thank you. Now, enough about me. Your phone call piqued my curiosity."

"Is it all right if I close the door?"

"Please."

Rebecca did so.

"Let me take your coat," Saul offered, getting up from behind his desk and coming to help Rebecca remove her coat. "So what's going on?"

"I need your computer expertise. Can you access a student's e-mail?"

His dark eyes narrowed. "Sure, but that's against college regulations. I could get fired."

"You remember Allison Manchester, the student who was murdered?"

"Of course."

"Well, I had a conversation with someone this morning that made me wonder if it might not be important to take a look at Allison's e-mail correspondence."

"Wouldn't it be easier just to check her computer?"

"Yes, but her computer is missing."

"I think I'd feel better if you got in touch with the police. They could get a subpoena."

Rebecca shook her head. "Can you imagine the uproar on a campus like this if the police showed up with a subpoena to access a student's e-mail? Our students are always looking for a cause they can support and I can't imagine anything that would get them demonstrating more quickly than finding out the police could pry into their e-mail."

"Good point."

Saul went over to the table where his computer sat. "All computer files are backed up on the college's server each night and they remain on the server for at least a month, and sometimes longer, depending on whether someone remembers to erase them. We're a small school but we have a huge server, so generally the backup is erased at the end of each semester. Let's see what we can find. I put in the server so I certainly know how to get into it without leaving any evidence behind."

Rebecca was surprised at how rapidly and surely his fingers moved over the computer keyboard. He typed for a few moments, humming quietly to himself. She smiled when she recognized that Saul was humming the somewhat mournful trope to which a haftorah was chanted in synagogue. This was the first time she'd been to his office and, looking at the books on the shelves beside the door, she was surprised to see more volumes in Hebrew than the computer science books she'd expected. She'd had no idea he read Hebrew that well. The books were primarily Torah commentaries, books she had on her shelves though she hadn't opened one since the end of Shabbat morning services at her house.

"Almost there," Saul muttered under his breath before returning to his aimless humming of trope.

Rebecca's eyes continued around the room and in the two cases on the wall to the right of his desk were the books and journals about computer science she'd expected to see. She turned back toward the computer where Saul sat still typing rapidly, and that was when she saw the framed drawing hanging on the wall above the computer. It was a portrait of a man with a dark, scraggly beard and eyes that burned fiercely as if by the gaze alone he could eradicate all evil.

"Done!" Saul announced.

Rebecca, still entranced by the drawing, said, "That's a remarkable piece of art. Wherever did you get it?"

Saul blushed. "That's Reb Yitzchak. He taught me how to write a Torah scroll."

She looked at him, surprised. "You never told me you had studied to be a sofer." When he looked away, embarrassed, she asked, "Who drew the portrait? It's quite remarkable."

"I did. A couple of nights ago."

"Saul! What're you doing playing around with computers when you have talent like that?"

Instead of answering he got up from the table and offered Rebecca the chair in front of the computer. "I think this is Allison Manchester's e-mail account."

Rebecca sat down, her attention focusing quickly on the screen and the directory of Allison's e-mails. She scrolled down, skipping the ones from "EG," whom she assumed was Evan Green. She supposed she should look at those just to verify that Evan had been telling her the truth, but his tears and his grief were truth enough. But, who was "77446th043?" This was obviously someone who wanted to keep his identity hidden. Rebecca highlighted the e-mail and the message appeared in the pane below.

I don't understand why you won't even have a cup of coffee with me at The HangOut. What would be the harm in that? You don't think you can avoid me on a campus this small, do you? And I know you think of me as much as I think of you.

Agathon

This was it! Agathon! Rebecca read the message again and this time she noticed Agathon's reference to The HangOut. Agathon was someone on campus!

Quickly Rebecca went to the next e-mail from "77446th043":

I don't understand why you're ignoring me, why you won't even respond to one of my e-mails. I need you. You are the very breath of my being. I would even settle just for the chance to look out across the room and see you in class like I did last semester. Why can't you understand that aborting the baby was best for both of us. And it wasn't even a baby. When you had the abortion it was so small it couldn't be seen without a microscope. I know you believe it was a life but it wasn't. It could not have lived outside your body and life begins when you are able to sustain it on your own. You know as well as I do that if you had had the baby it would have sapped your life and energy. You would have become a prisoner of motherhood and there's no reason for you to do that in this day and age. I offer you a life with me, a life of travel to exotic places, fine restaurants, and

almost anything your heart desires. I don't understand how you
can refuse all I have to offer. I don't understand. Please help
me understand.

Agathon

Rebecca read the e-mail again. She needed to make sure. Yes,
there it was. "I would even settle just for the chance to look out across
the room and see you in class like I did last semester." She wanted to
believe the e-mail had come from a student but a student would have
written "look across the room." Only someone standing at the front
of the room would be looking "out across." And although many students at John Brown came from well-to-do and even wealthy families, would any of them have thought to offer a female student "a life
of travel to exotic places, fine restaurants, and almost anything your
heart desires"?

With the next e-mail the tone changed.

Allison. I don't understand why you won't at least answer me. I
need you. I haven't felt like this since I was a teenager. It's
ridiculous. I know. Why would you want someone my age? All I
have to offer you is a love unlike any you could ever know.
There is a world of feelings, of subtle, exquisite emotions only
given to someone who has lived as long and as deeply as I have,
a world you might never have another chance to know. You said
yes to that world once. I do not understand why you are refus-
ing that world now.

Agathon

Why didn't you tell me about these e-mails? Rebecca asked Allison silently. Why didn't you tell me, dammit? But she knew why. Allison was being stalked and didn't know it. Stalkers followed women around, showed up at places where you didn't expect them. But stalking by e-mail? Rebecca didn't know if there was even a law that covered such. But the new reality of women's lives was that sexual harassment now came as easily through words on a computer screen as an unwanted hand on a breast.

The next e-mail continued in the vein of the previous one.

My love for you consumes me. I can think of little else but you. I need you back in my life because you are my life. Do you understand that? And I understand that I may not be as important to you as you are to me, and that's O.K. I don't mind. We need not love each other with the same intensity as long as our love for each other is real and genuine, and I know it is. Please write me.

Agathon

Rebecca hated herself for not knowing the difference between waiting for a student to open up and talk, and asking questions and trying to make that student talk. If she had been less accepting of Allison's silence, the girl might still be alive. But if she was going to be honest with herself, she had to admit something. She hadn't taken Allison as seriously as she might have—and could have and should have. And why? Was it because Allison looked like everything Rebecca would never be, regardless of the wardrobe in her closet? Long, straight blond hair, blue eyes, expensive makeup applied so skillfully that most were not aware she had makeup on. Allison Manchester had been the epitome of a shiksa, the derogatory Yiddish word Jews used for non-Jewish women. Everything about Allison had been perfect. Each long strand of her blond hair lay straight from her head to the middle of her back. If her hair had split ends, Rebecca had no doubt they repaired themselves without any effort on Allison's part. Her clothes fit her slim but perfectly proportioned small body as if they were sewn on. Rebecca had not taken Allison's tears seriously, not really. Yes, she had wanted to create a ritual for her and her aborted fetus but Rebecca had been motivated by her own need to feel she was making a difference in somebody's life. She could not say that she had given a thought to what Allison might have needed. And with a shame as deep and cutting as any she'd ever felt she realized that she had judged Allison negatively for her physical perfection as people had judged her negatively for her physical imperfection.

Professionally, Rebecca had been blind to her countertransference, the unconscious projection of positive or negative attributes from the therapist to the client. And it had cost the child her life. Rebecca could hear a voice telling her she was being melodramatic, that she was taking too much responsibility, that she hadn't put her hands around Allison's throat and strangled her, and that was true, but the effects of some truths were merely to rationalize away deeper ones. By not taking Allison seriously, by equating her soul with the sheen of her blond hair and her pale white skin, Rebecca had pushed the child away, pushed her, literally, into the hands that had squeezed the life from her. Because she had callously refused to care for Allison Manchester's soul when it existed on this side, she was determined to care for it now.

Rebecca's attention returned to the computer screen where she saw that the icon for the last message had an arrow beside it indicating Allison had written the sender back. She navigated to the Sent folder, opened it and found the message:

> I have some exciting news I want to share with you. Can you meet me tomorrow evening in Boston? I'll be out front on the steps of the MFA at five.

Rebecca opened the reply:

> I'll pick you up at five. I miss you terribly.
>
> Agathon

"Saul?"

He came over.

"Can you find out who this person is?" she said pointing to Agathon's e-mail address.

Saul studied it for a moment. "I'm afraid not. My hunch is that his messages went to a server in Europe which strips his real e-mail address off and substitutes the one you see there. This is how a lot of child pornographers keep from getting caught."

It didn't matter. Rebecca thought she knew who Agathon was. "Thanks, Saul," she said, getting up. "Could you copy all of Allison's e-mails onto a disk or CD for me?"

"Sure."

"Thanks."

When Rebecca got back to her office she looked at her file from her sessions with Roger Crawford from the fall semester of last year. She remembered one session during which he had described the student he said he was in love with. She went through her notes quickly until she found what she was looking for. She read Roger's description of the student again. It fit Allison Manchester like her well-made clothes.

That evening Rebecca sat in the middle of her bed, not sure how to do what she knew she had to do. She had to talk to Roger. But what could she say? Her therapy sessions with him had not been a success, though the longer she worked as a therapist the more confused she became about how to define success. Roger had come to her because he was enamored of a student. At least that was what he said and some days he seemed genuinely interested in resolving his transference while other times he seemed to want to goad Rebecca into approving, not only his emotions but his acting on them. Outwardly she had remained neutral but he probably felt her moral disapproval and that was why he'd abruptly and angrily ended therapy.

She had failed Roger. She had failed Allison. The stance of objectivity required of her as a therapist conflicted with how she would have responded as a rabbi. A rabbi would not have hesitated to question Allison (or her Jewish equivalent), to probe until the girl had told her who the father of her aborted child was. Rebecca would have done so because the enormous energy required to keep a secret from others also kept you walled off from yourself. If she ever saw Dennis again hurrying along a narrow street in Jerusalem she would ask him to forgive her for never sharing with him why she limped, to forgive her for not inviting him into her wound. How can two truly be married if each clings to his and her respective wounds as if they were milk-filled breasts? Judaism forbids one to mourn excessively, even for oneself.

As a rabbi she would not have hesitated to tell Roger his emotions for Allison reflected the emotional maturity of an eighteen-year-old. Had he considered what the consequences of his infatuation might be? In Judaism there was no escaping the consequences of one's missteps. Even Moses, the man God chose to lead His people out of slavery, had not escaped the consequences of his. (At least that was how the version she knew went. She didn't want to imagine God's.) Moses did everything God asked of him—returned to Egypt, led the Israelites through the Red Sea, and then wandered in the desert with them for forty years. (She couldn't imagine spending forty years anywhere with her former congregants.) Yet God didn't allow him to enter the Promised Land for one of two reasons:

When he fled Egypt and went to Midian, the daughters of Jethro, the high priest, introduced him to their father as an "Egyptian" because of how he was dressed. Moses did not correct them and say he was an Israelite. Because he denied who he was, God denied him entry to the Promised Land.

The other reason was just as ridiculous. All the years the Israelites wandered in the desert Miriam's well followed them and supplied water. When Miriam died, the well vanished and they didn't have water. God told Moses to speak to a rock and the rock would produce water. Instead, Moses hit the rock twice. Water came forth, but because he had disobeyed God's instructions, God did not allow him to enter the Promised Land.

"Of course I was angry," came the soft, high-pitched voice from the rocking chair.

Rebecca looked at Him, startled. "I wish you wouldn't do that," she said. "Can't you knock, clear your throat, or something? And I would appreciate it if you respected my privacy and didn't listen to my thoughts."

"Forgive me," God said. "I thought you knew that I am always present, just not visible. And I'm sorry, but it is impossible for me to distinguish thought from speech because thoughts are speech to Me."

Rebecca noticed that God's tone of voice was colder and more forbidding than she had heard it previously, and his black SS uniform was ironed and had sharp creases, and He was wearing the hat with the Death's Head on it. What was going on? Why had He changed? She had almost reached the point of being able to at least tolerate the pitiful-looking Hitler who had sat there previously, but this one? This was Evil Incarnate.

He reached in his pocket and pulled out a pack of cigarettes.

"I thought I asked You not to smoke in here."

God took a cigarette from the pack, snapped his thumb and forefinger, and a small flame was produced. He lit the cigarette and inhaled deeply, then exhaled. "Yes. You asked." He inhaled again, looking at her with eyes devoid of compassion. "Now. Moses. You want me to be more understanding, to realize how much stress he was under after killing the Egyptian and having to run away from everything familiar. He was having an identity crisis and probably didn't know at that time whether he was Egyptian or Jew. You think I am harsh because I did not simply chastise him for hitting the rock instead of denying him the one thing he had been longing for those forty years."

God had not taken His eyes from her face and she, determined not to be intimidated, held His gaze, though she wanted nothing more than to look away.

God took another deep drag on the cigarette. "You want me to be a therapist, don't you? Therapists understand. Therapists forgive. That is not what I do. Actions have consequences and the consequences must be lived."

"Even if you don't know the consequence in advance? Why didn't you tell Moses what would happen if he hit the rock? He didn't know!"

God took another drag on the cigarette and put it out on the arm of the rocking chair.

"I can't believe You did that!" Rebecca exclaimed, almost bursting into tears. "I love that chair!"

"How can you love something that cannot love you in return? Love is a blending of mutualities."

"And how would You know?" she shot back.

God smiled. "Very good, Rabbi. Very good. I like your spirit. But, back to Moses. Why didn't I tell him what would happen if he disobeyed me? Because it never occurred to me that he wouldn't do as I said. For almost forty years I'd told him to do this and that and he had done it without question. I tested him mercilessly by asking him to do ridiculous things like sacrifice two doves or a calf, a lamb, whatever. There's a whole section of your Torah filled with the most outrageous sacrifices, but Moses, without question, wrote them out and did them. So why wouldn't I expect him to do as I asked this time? 'Moses? Speak to the rock.' Now, Rabbi, I ask you. How hard is it to speak to a rock? I was so looking forward to it. I'd been practicing for days making water come from the rock after Moses spoke to it. It was going to be almost as awesome as parting the Red Sea. But what did Moses do? He hit the damn rock, not once but twice.

"I was stunned! I thought I knew him but it seemed I did not know him at all. I was disappointed that he, even he, would allow himself to

199

be taken over by a momentary gust of emotion. He broke my heart. So I broke his and would not permit him to take even one step into the land he had been journeying toward for forty years. Moses broke my heart!" And just as suddenly as He had come, He was gone.

Rebecca sat on the edge of the bed for a moment, then got up and walked fearfully over to her rocking chair to see how bad the cigarette burn was. But there was no cigarette burn in the chair's arm nor stub of cigarette nor cigarette ashes, and the chair gleamed as it never had when she polished it.

Why had God come to visit at just that moment? Was He afraid she was going to break His heart? And if so, how? What could she do that would break the heart of the Almighty? Or had His heart been broken already by how callously she had responded to Allison? She would talk to Roger tomorrow but as a rabbi, as the representative of a fractious relationship with a God who, because of one or two transgressions, would judge as worthless a lifetime of obedience and service.

Early the next morning, after Rebecca had said Kaddish with the Jews of Czechowa, the phone rang. It was Brian Moon again. This time it was Patric Marsh who was dead.

FOURTEEN

Rebecca waited at the counter for Mr. Applewhite to get the mail that had accumulated over the past three days. She glanced at her watch and saw that it was two o'clock. In New York City, Patric's funeral was starting. The college had officially closed for the day and chartered a fleet of buses so all who wanted to attend could go. Rebecca wondered if she was the only one who had not boarded one of those buses at dawn.

Maurice Woodley had not understood her refusal, especially since she didn't bother to explain. Both he and Patric's family had implored her to speak at the funeral. Rebecca did not know his family and was surprised when his sister, Ellen, called and said "Patric spoke of you often and fondly. He had enormous respect for you. It would mean so much to me, Patric's brother, and our eighty-seven-year-old mother, if someone as close to Patric as you obviously were would give one of the eulogies. He told me how moved he was by what you said at the memorial service for that poor student who was killed last month."

Rebecca wished she could have said Jewish law forbade her from participating in a Christian funeral, but it didn't. She could have said that because it was a Friday and the sun set so early this time of year she doubted she would be able to get from the funeral to her parent's place in Brooklyn before Shabbat began. While that was true, there were many Fridays she had come home from the college well after sunset. She tried to think of a believable excuse but all she could say was, "I'm sorry. I can't."

"Well, that'll be our loss, but I think I understand," Ellen offered. "We are all overcome with grief and certainly you must be since you knew him so well. I hope we get to meet sometime. I'm sure you could tell me many things about my brother. You probably knew him better than we did."

Since last New Year's, Rebecca wasn't certain she had known Patric at all, but that didn't matter now. He was dead and yes, there was certainly grief and no little guilt. Patric had been her friend almost since her first day at the college. Yet she had destroyed that friendship because of one anti-Semitic remark made while he was half-drunk. She hadn't treated him any better than God had Moses. Now he was dead. The least she could have done was go to his funeral. Attending the dead was the purest mitzvah because the dead could not thank you.

So why had she left the dorm where she'd slept last night and gone to her office instead of boarding one of the buses? At the time she thought she needed to be away from the paralyzing fog of mass sorrow. Every night she and Brian Moon had met with students in small groups for grief counseling, and that was after talking with many individually throughout the day. But Rebecca doubted she and Brian would have been able to do as much as they had if not for Evan Green, who had called for a prayer service that first night. At seven o'clock practically every student on campus went to the auditorium where Evan Green led them in prayer and song for an hour. Rebecca had never heard any songs quite like the ones he sang. She was surprised that someone so slender had a voice that could fill an auditorium without using a microphone. "Guide my feet while I run this race," he sang in a mournful melody. "Guide my feet while I run this race. Guide my feet while I run this race, because I don't want to run this race in vain." And soon, the auditorium of mainly white students, most of them too sophisticated to believe in a Supreme Being, and too arrogant to ever acknowledge their need of a guiding presence in their lives, was singing along with him: "Hold my hand while I run this race . . ."

Rebecca had not had the chance to thank Evan, but after that night, there was less hysteria among some students. Allison's death had been little more than a curiosity for most of them, but everybody knew Patric. He was the most popular professor on campus. Many students had never been stunned by the death of someone important to their emotional lives and their grief tended to be exaggerated as they did not know what they were supposed to feel and how they were supposed to react. Rebecca had spent each night in a different dormitory, staying up almost until dawn talking with grieving students. The prospect of being on a bus filled with tearful melodramas for the seven-hour trip to New York and back was more than she could do. But Brian had not slept very much either for the past three days, and he had done his duty and boarded a bus that morning. Rebecca had gone to her office and typed her notes into the computer on those students whose grief for Patric had seemed to unearth unexpressed grief having nothing to do with him. Even Roger had come to see her. So pervasive was his grief she wondered how she could have ever thought he killed Allison, especially after what he told her.

"I have an older brother who works on Wall Street, if you can imagine that, but even though we share blood, he is less a brother to me than Patric was. I can't believe I won't be able to pick up the phone and call him with a question about some arcane religious practice and have him give me the answer without having to consult a book. And his friendship. No one could be a friend like he could. Last fall when I thought I was going mad because of that ridiculous fantasy about that student whom I'm sure you figured out was Allison Manchester, may God rest her soul, Patric was the one who suggested I talk about it with you and I guess I owe you an apology for stopping so abruptly. Quite frankly, I had become so ashamed of myself I couldn't bear to contemplate what you must have thought of me, and while I'm apologizing I suppose I should also apologize for baiting you as I did at Patric's on New Year's. Quite frankly, I was a mess last year. Male menopause or something of the sort. And now, just as I was beginning to feel like I could stand to look at myself in the mirror again, this happens. I honestly don't know how I'm going to fill the void Patric's death has created."

"Here you are, Rabbi," Mr. Applewhite said, giving her the mail. "This time of year it's mostly catalogs. Of course that wouldn't have anything to do with you, since it's Christmas catalogs."

She hadn't known, being unmindful of when the Christian holiday came.

"If you don't mind my saying, I've seen you looking better," he continued.

Rebecca smiled weakly. "It's been a long three days."

Mr. Applewhite nodded sympathetically. "Well, what with that girl getting murdered last month and now Professor Marsh getting killed in that terrible car accident, I would imagine it's been rough for you people up at the college."

"It's been difficult," she agreed.

"I've lived in this area all my life. Sixty-nine years. And if there's one thing I've learned, it's not to take the roads for granted, no matter how many times you've driven them. Professor Marsh had been here a good ten years. I would've thought he would have had better sense than to try and drive somewhere in that sports car of his on a night like Monday night. We got at least an inch of sleet and freezing rain and then seven inches of heavy snow on top of that. Even I wouldn't have been out on a night like that. What I don't understand is if he had to go somewheres why he didn't take his four-wheel drive SUV? Why do you think he was out so late on a night like that anyway?"

"I don't know," Rebecca mumbled.

Mr. Applewhite shook his head again. "It's a pity."

Rebecca hadn't had time to think about it but as she drove away she, too, wondered: Where had Patric been going? Especially in the Porsche, a car he drove only in the summer. It had been found fifty feet down the side of a mountain by a snowplow driver. It appeared the car had come around a curve too fast or perhaps skidded on the ice. Whatever the reason, the car had gone into the air, landed on its roof and slid down the mountain until it came to rest against a stand of birch trees. The driver's license and credit cards in the dead man's wallet identified the crushed body as that of Patric Marsh.

The more Rebecca tried to imagine why Patric had been out, the more puzzled she became. He was not a man who acted recklessly, especially with the Porsche. He was one of those Vermonters who had two vehicles: one they didn't mind exposing to the rigors of winter which included road salt that ate away at the undercarriage of cars if not washed off quickly; the other car, however, the one they loved, was reserved for that brief but exhilarating span of time between the last snow, which some years didn't come until the middle of May, and the first, which might come as early as mid-October.

As Rebecca approached Pulpit Road she shifted into second and gunned the motor. The SUV bounced up the steep hill, the motor whining loudly, until it reached the top where Rebecca eased her foot off the accelerator and simultaneously released the breath she had been holding in. The icy road continued level for another mile and she smiled when she saw her gray, two-story house just before the road ended.

Home. It had been three days since she'd been there, three days since she'd lived anything resembling her own life—no crossword puzzles, no davening Mincha and Maariv, no reciting Kaddish at 3:00 a.m., no conversations with Devorah, and certainly no word from God. She pulled into the driveway, pressed the automatic garage door opener she kept on the seat beside her, and pulled into the garage, pressing the remote, closing the door behind her.

Once inside, she put the mail on the table in the front room next to the Torah scroll and the box that held God's autobiography and went upstairs and began to run hot water in the tub. Undressing quickly, leaving her clothes and undergarments on the floor where she stepped out of them, she poured bath salts into the tub and then sank slowly into the warm water. She adjusted the faucets until the water ran so hot it almost scalded her. But she needed to burn away the grief, manufactured and real, she'd witnessed over the past three days. There had not been a moment to know her own sorrow and now, finally, tears came into her eyes and she understood why she had not boarded one of the buses that morning, why she had not wanted to wear the public mantle of rabbi and speak at Patric's funeral. The tears ran freely down her face now.

"You hurt me so much!" she howled aloud. "You hurt me so much!" And Rebecca sobbed until her throat was raw.

Finally, exhausted, the bath water almost cold, she got slowly out of the tub and wrapped herself in a large, fluffy salmon-colored towel and then put on a green Bill Blass terry cloth bathrobe. After pulling on a thick pair of woolen socks, she went downstairs and took a pair of silver candlesticks and candles from one of the kitchen cabinets. She carried them into the front room and, after putting the candles in their holders, set them on either side of the box that held God's autobiography. She lit the candles, moved her hands in a circle around each candle three times, then covered her eyes and sang the blessing: "Baruch ata Adonai Eloheinu Melech Haolam asher kidshanu b'mitzvotav v'tzivanu l'hadlik ner shel Shabbat"—Blessed are You, O Lord our God, Ruler of the universe whose mitzvot add holiness to our lives and who gave us the mitzvah to kindle the light of Shabbat.

Rebecca stood for a moment looking at the small flames and the soft light they created. Having read God's autobiography, she wondered why she bothered to light the candles and say the blessing anymore. The answer came quickly and it was simple: Because that was what Jewish women did in their homes on Friday evenings. She could not imagine her life without that moment of lighting the candles every Friday evening. On normal Fridays she did it eighteen or so minutes before sunset as she was supposed to, but even on Fridays like this one, she did it when she could. She felt calmer afterward, the two still flames a portal through which she walked into the presence of all the Jewish women around the world, past, present and future, who lit candles.

If this had been an ordinary Shabbat evening, her meals for that night and Saturday would have been cooking in the oven. But nothing had been ordinary since Allison's death. Rebecca was too tired to cook now. All she wanted to do was have some tea and go to bed. She went into the kitchen and ran water in the electric kettle, and turned it on.

Despite herself, her mind returned to Patric. Why had he gone out and why had he taken the Porsche? He loved that car. "Since I never had children, I got a Porsche instead," he liked to joke. Where could he have been going? But perhaps that was the wrong question. Maybe the question was, what had compelled him to go out? Had he received a phone call? Maybe there was something at his office—a book, a paper, a scholarly journal—that he had to have that night because of a lecture he was preparing. But no. Those might have been plausible reasons if he had not driven the Porsche. There was only one explanation, though it didn't make sense, either. Patric had not been in his "right" mind.

Rebecca had just reached for a box of tea from the rack when she stopped. Hadn't Roger said something similar about his infatuation with Allison? Except he had used the word "mad," she thought. Was it possible that Patric had— She shook her head. That was impossible. Not Patric, she told herself. She recalled seeing him sitting in the back of the auditorium at the memorial service for Allison but she hadn't paid any attention to him, focused as she had been on what she was going to say. Her mind went back to the last time she'd spoken with him, which was the afternoon in The HangOut, and the box of tea she had just grasped dropped onto the countertop just as the kettle of water started whistling.

"Oh, my God!" she exclaimed. "Oh, my God!"

The kettle whistled louder now but Rebecca did not hear it as she saw again Allison walk over to the booth where Patric sat. Rebecca had noticed it at the time but had not paid attention. Allison had sat down opposite Patric without breaking stride. She had sat down as if she knew him so well she didn't need to ask his permission to sit.

Rebecca started when she finally heard the loudly whistling kettle and unplugged it. As if in a daze she poured the boiling water over the tea bags lying in the bottom of the gray stoneware pot she used only on Shabbat. So what if Allison had sat down across from Patric without asking or being invited? What did that mean, especially at a place like John Brown College, where students called professors by their first names? Rebecca was ashamed for thinking that Patric had been involved with Allison. Three nights sleeping on thin, narrow mattresses in dormitories where, when one loud CD player was turned off, another seemed to automatically take its place, had not only put knots in muscles Rebecca didn't know she had, but fatigue was making her delusional if she thought how a student sat down in a booth across from a professor meant anything.

When the tea had steeped sufficiently, Rebecca filled the gray tea bowl and carried it into the front room where she sat down at the desk and began going through the mail. Most of it was, as Mr. Applewhite had said, catalogs for everything from lingerie to Jewish books to computer software to garden supplies. Consumer pornography for the middle class and because she was so susceptible to that kind of foreplay she didn't look at the catalogs but put them aside to take to the recycling center. Except the ones for clothes and lingerie. The rest of the mail was magazines, newspapers, bills and appeals for funds from various Jewish charities. At the very bottom was a manila envelope with no return address and "$.77 Postage Due" written on it. Mr. Applewhite had forgotten to get the money from her. The address was handwritten but she didn't recognize it.

She opened it. Inside were two thick, sealed envelopes. Rebecca took them out. One was addressed "To Whom It May Concern." The other was addressed simply, "Rabbi." She looked at it as if an intense enough stare would tell her what was inside so she could lay it aside as easily as she had the catalogs, because something told her she didn't want to open the envelope. But she did and took out five single-spaced, typed pages.

```
Dear Rabbi,

It has taken me a while to decide if I want to address you as
Rebecca or Rabbi. And perhaps that was part of the problem all
along. I wanted to separate the two.
```

There was only one person she knew who would begin a letter like that. Yet it was still a shock when she hurriedly went to the last page of the sheaf of papers and saw Patric's signature. Trembling, she resumed reading.

```
I suppose I never accepted the extent to which you cared, re-
ally and truly cared, about how God wanted you to live your
life. You believed God cared if you ate a cheeseburger. I
wanted so much to believe with such naivete. That's why I
wanted to sleep with you, though you never noticed. Sleeping
with you was the only way I knew to get close to being like
```

you. In Plato's Symposium Agathon says to Socrates: "If I touch you, I may get a bit of the wisdom that came to you."

"Oh, Patric, no!" Rebecca cried in an anguished whisper.

I thought that if I slept with you I might become closer to God.

If you are reading this it means I am dead. At least I hope I am not lying comatose in some hospital, doomed to awake and have to live. The weather forecast is for sleet, freezing rain, and snow, the perfect conditions for a car to spin out of control and go down the side of a mountain. It is my prayer that God will be merciful and I will die instantly.

In the other envelope is a notarized document, my confession to the murder of Allison Manchester. Also in that envelope are two keys. One is to my office and the other is to a filing cabinet in my office. In the bottom drawer of the filing cabinet is Allison's laptop computer. On it is all of our e-mail correspondence. I took the key to her suite from her purse after I killed her and took the computer from her room. But, vanity of vanities, I could not bring myself to delete words I'd written. I hope you will go to my office, get the computer and destroy the files, which is also what I hope you will do with this letter and the confession. Once I explain you will understand.

Last fall, a young woman walked into my class and, for the first time in my life, I felt God's presence, the experience

of oneness with all, of the "peace that passeth all understanding." When I saw Allison I knew that joining with her
would give me that experience of the Divine for which I had
yearned all my life.

At the end of the semester she told me she wanted to do an in-
dependent study on mysticism with me. If that was not a sign
from God I don't know what was. Mysticism, the experience of
union with the Divine. I have put the details of how the relationship unfolded in my confession. Suffice it to say here that
the relationship with her was more than I had ever imagined a
relationship could be. She was my soul. I was disappointed that
she was passive in bed but that was due to inexperience, and
anyway, I had enough passion for us both. I was prepared to
love her for eternity.

However, at the end of the spring semester, she said she
didn't want to see me anymore, that she had never wanted to
sleep with me, but because I was her professor she had been
afraid not to. I was devastated, shattered. A week or so later
I got an e-mail from her telling me she was pregnant. I didn't
understand. I thought all young women in this day and age took
birth control pills, that the pills came with the boxes of ce-
real or glasses of orange juice they had every morning. I told
her to have an abortion and I was relieved when she e-mailed
to say that she had. But she went on to add that she never
wanted to see me again, that she had come to me as a student
who admired a professor and I had taken advantage of her, had
used her, that God hated us both for what we had done.

212

I e-mailed her throughout the summer begging her to change her
mind, to at least have dinner with me. She never answered.
That day I saw you in The HangOut was the first time I'd seen
her since the end of school last spring. When I saw her talking to you my heart was beating so fast and hard I thought
I was having a heart attack. When she came over to me and sat
down as if that was where she belonged I was convinced my season in hell was ending but she didn't even say hello. "I'm seeing someone, someone who loves me for me, and someone I love.
Please don't e-mail anymore." And she got up and left.

But I knew she needed me as much I needed her, so I continued
e-mailing her, trying to bring her to her senses. Finally, one
day she e-mailed back and said she had wonderful news and to
pick her up outside the Museum of Fine Arts in Boston. I
thought she wanted to reconcile. I was happier than I'd ever
been in my entire life.

When I drove up I saw her on the steps of the MFA. I saw her
kiss some boy as she had never kissed me. It was too dark to
see who she kissed but I knew she wasn't coming back to me.

When she got in my car I looked at her. I don't know what happened. I looked at her and I saw this rather ordinary-looking
girl. It was warm in the car and she undid the top buttons of
her coat to reveal a black turtleneck sweater, a gold cross on
a chain between the rise of her breasts. Her hair was dull and
stringy and when I looked into her eyes all I saw was the
eager excitement typical of girls in their late teens who

think no one has ever experienced what they are experiencing.
I couldn't believe this was the one to whom I had pledged
eternal love, the one I thought I needed like I need oxygen
and water. The girl I had loved had a numinous aura about her
and her blond hair glowed and her blue eyes danced. The girl
I had loved had the innocent look of the Madonna. The girl
sitting in my car was as plain as a bowl of cold oatmeal. I
couldn't believe she was the same person. What kind of trick-
ery had she practiced on me? What had she done to make me
think she was my pathway to the Divine?

That was when I knew I had to kill her. I couldn't permit her
to remain in the world and entice and deceive other men as she
had done me. I knew killing her was the right thing to do when
she told me God had made her clean again and permitted her to
get pregnant and she was going to marry the father of her
child, Evan Green. Needless to say, I was stunned. She had
left me for Evan Green? I asked her if she was prepared to
live with all the attention she would get being married to an
African-American and I reminded her that she had to think
about how difficult it would be for their children. I told her
that I doubted Evan Green could support her in the manner she
deserved. That was when she laughed at me. She said she had a
trust fund that would take care of them for the rest of their
lives and all Evan had to do was love her.

I was stunned. I hadn't known her at all! She must have been
laughing inside herself the times I told her all that my money
could give her. She didn't need my money. She didn't need

anything I had to offer. What happened next is in the other envelope.

What happens now is in your hands. Does one act of insanity on my part negate all the good I've done? Does this aberrant act outweigh all the good my books and lectures have done? Imagine how shattered and disillusioned all those who believe in me will be if they learn I had a sexual relationship with one of my students and killed her? And please, Rabbi, consider this: Knowing America as I do, I have no doubt that my "tragic" death will spur a sharp increase in the sale of my books and CDs. In my will I have designated that my estate and the future proceeds of my writings, etc., be divided between the college and medical research. What would be gained by your giving my confession to the police and it being made public? Finally, I would ask you to consider the impact of my confession on the future of John Brown College. If it were revealed that one of its founders and its most prominent faculty member was a murderer, I have no doubt that parents, alumni, and benefactors would desert the school.

Even though I will be dead when you read this, I will continue to live for many, many years in the souls of all the people whose lives have been changed because of my words. I know you will protect that life and those people.

I love you, Rebecca.
Patric

"You lousy bastard!" Rebecca said aloud as she flung the pages of the letter onto the floor. "You lousy bastard!"

Suddenly, He was sitting on the couch at the other end of the room. Rebecca gave a momentary start. God was dressed in a dark suit, white shirt and dark tie held in place with a tie clip emblazoned with the Nazi swastika.

"So now you know who killed Allison," He said coldly. "What does it matter if the world knows Patric Marsh was the murderer? This was a good man. He doesn't deserve to have his reputation destroyed, and what are we except our reputations?" He laughed. "Look at mine!" He laughed again, louder, then became serious again. "Patric's confession will leave people with no choice but to believe he was a murderer. However they will hate you for taking from them their image of this man in whom they invested their souls. Think about all those people. They need to believe in Patric Marsh more than they need the truth. A lie can be as sustaining as truth as long as no one knows it's a lie. Leave them the comfort of their untruth. What's it to you? The well-being of all those people is more important than truth."

He stared at her, his eyes without expression. Rebecca wondered if this had been the expression on his face when He told Avraham He was going to destroy Sodom and Gomorrah. Had Avraham stared back, or had he dropped his eyes and looked down, wondering who was he to argue with God? Or had Avraham's compassion for humans been so immediate and overwhelming that he spoke up without hesitating and began pleading for the lives of some of the most sinful people the world had ever seen?

Rebecca stared back at Him, and suddenly she wanted to laugh. He looked silly with that ridiculous square of hair beneath His

216

nostrils. Why had so many Europeans let themselves be led by a man who looked so silly? Maybe it hadn't been the man who entranced them but the story he'd told, a story that had exalted them heavenward not because of anything they'd done but merely because they had blond hair, blue eyes, and pale white skin (which ironically he did not). Hitler had been the consummate storyteller of the twentieth century because he wove a tale so many wanted to believe was true, a perfect tale because it had a villain whom Western civilization had been seeking to immortalize as Evil Incarnate throughout its history, the damned Jews who were no more than lice to be burned like the vermin they were, and burn they did, 6 million of them and not one nation even whispered a polite "No." Maybe it wasn't compassion for the people of Sodom and Gomorrah that led Avraham to argue with God but merely displeasure with the story God told about who the people of Sodom and Gomorrah were. Maybe Avraham wanted them to have the chance to tell God that their story was not the one He thought it was. Maybe compassion lay in listening to someone else's story, even God's.

"The Talmud says one person is equal to the whole of creation," Rebecca said to God, finally.

God laughed harshly. "You want Me to believe that nineteen-year-old Allison Manchester was equal to all of creation?"

"Yes."

"Nonsense! Compared to Patric March, what did she contribute to the betterment of humanity? Justify the good that will come from your telling the world the truth about him."

Rebecca didn't know what to say. Logically He was right but she remembered what she had told so many students over the last five years, especially the women—*The heart has reasons for which the mind does not have words.* Maybe that had been Avraham's mistake. He had bargained with God instead of listening to the reasons pulsating deep within the heart.

"I won't give You a reason," she answered, finally. "You'll just argue with me."

God laughed dryly. "That's a weak excuse."

Rebecca smiled. "Only to a man."

This time His laugh was loud and uproarious and He vanished, seemingly into the laugh itself.

Rebecca looked at her cup of tea from which she had not sipped even once. It was cold now. She went to the kitchen, poured the cold tea into a another cup and put it in the microwave for sixty seconds. Her hands were shaking slightly when she removed the cup from the microwave and she didn't know if more from exhaustion, Patric's letter, or God's visit.

She went back to the front room and picked up the pages of Patric's letter from the floor, folded the pages, and put them back in its envelope. She looked at the one addressed "To Whom It May Concern" and slipped it back into the brown manila envelope. Holding both envelopes, she took her cup of tea and sat in her rocking chair, closed her eyes and moved the chair back and forth in a slow, gentle motion. She thought about Patric's plea and God's argument that her responsibility was to protect all the people whose lives Patric had affected for the good. He wanted her to believe she had the power to determine whether Patric would be remembered as a good man or a murderer.

Perhaps she did. But at what price to herself? Was she supposed to live the rest of her life protecting Patric's reputation, a reputation he could have preserved by not imposing himself on Allison Manchester, or by not writing a confession, or by not choosing Rebecca as his confessor? He had to have known what she would do. And perhaps that explained everything. He wanted her to do what he had lacked the honesty to do.

She sipped the tea slowly, relaxing as its warmth spread slowly through her body. When the cup was empty, she left it on the table next to the candles which had almost burned down and went slowly upstairs. God had been right to punish Moses for not saying he was a Jew, for striking the rock instead of speaking to it. Goodness was not a trait you acquired; it was a value you practiced when you were on the verge of doing evil. Did Patric's murder of Allison negate all the words he had spoken and written, words that had undoubtedly changed many lives for the better? Words came easily to people like Patric and like her, but goodness, unlike evil, had to be struggled for repeatedly. Judaism spoke of good and evil not as qualities which defined people but as energies—the *yetzer hatov* and the *yetzer hara*—the impulse to do good and the impulse to do evil—energies people possessed and could choose to use or not. Unfortunately it was not always clear which was which. Just because Patric murdered Allison, did it nullify the impact his words had on others?

She entered her bedroom and turned on the lamp. She was going to have to call President Woodley. Rebecca hoped he was back from the funeral in New York. He would not be happy to hear what she had to tell him. But there was someone else she had to call first. She looked in her wallet for the card with Detective Williams's phone number, picked up the phone, and began punching in the numbers.

FIFTEEN

❧

Even though it was Shabbat, Rebecca met Detective Williams and Maurice Woodley in the latter's office at eight o'clock that Saturday morning. She told them that Patric had murdered Allison and gave the detective the still-sealed letter containing Patric's confession. When Rebecca finished speaking, President Woodley looked not only tired from the funeral and the travel back and forth to New York but as if he had also aged twenty years.

"I . . . I don't know what to say," Woodley began wearily when Rebecca finished speaking. "I find all this hard to believe. Quite frankly, I don't want to believe it. Patric Marsh? Murder?" He looked at the detective. "Is this true?"

Detective Williams had been sitting on the leather sofa in the corner of the president's office, holding the pages of Patric's confession with latex gloves as she read it. She had just finished when Woodley addressed her.

"There are details in here only the murderer would know. I need to get this back to the lab and have the saliva on the seal of the envelope checked for DNA, see if we can lift fingerprints from the envelopes and letter, as well as retrieve Allison Manchester's computer. But I think all that will simply put the dot over the *i*. This confession, and it's notarized, is enough."

221

Maurice Woodley shook his head. "My God! The murder of that girl was enough for this college to go through. You have no idea how much time I've spent on the phone with parents, reassuring them their children are safe here. How can I reassure them about their children's safety when our most prominent faculty member murdered one of them?" He looked up at Rebecca. "You realize this spells the end of John Brown College."

"It doesn't have to," she responded quietly.

"I'm all ears, Rabbi."

"Well, sir, I think you should release the news instead of waiting for the Boston police to do so."

Woodley looked at her sharply, hope returning color to his face. "What do you mean?"

"I think you should call a campuswide meeting tomorrow morning and announce that the college uncovered information that Professor Marsh had been involved in a personal relationship with Allison Manchester and killed her, and, immediately on receiving this information, you called the Boston police. Then you go on to talk about how shocked and upset you were, et cetera."

He thought for a moment, then smiled, nodding his head. "A brilliant idea. If we get our version out first, the media will follow our lead instead of us having to defend ourselves from them."

"Yes, sir."

"I like it! I like it! There's just one little detail missing."

"What's that?" Rebecca wanted to know.

"You."

"Me?"

"You. I need you to be on that stage tomorrow and help the students make sense of all this. Quite frankly, I can't. I don't understand why a man of Patric's standing and reputation would risk everything over an adolescent. Oh, I know there's the occasional faculty member who sleeps with a student and when I have proof, I fire him or her, but, if I understand you correctly, he was willing to give up everything for her. And then, murder! Murder! Rabbi, *I* need you to help *me* understand, to help me come to terms with this. I thought I knew him. Frankly, I feel a sense of personal betrayal. I thought I was a good judge of character. Obviously I'm not. Rabbi, we need you to help us."

Rebecca shook her head. "Sir, I don't understand any more than you do."

"We need you to help us," Woodley repeated softly.

She nodded. "Yes, sir," she whispered.

Rebecca turned to leave when Detective Williams stopped her.

"Excuse me, Rabbi. I'm going to need to see the other letter, the one Professor Marsh addressed to you."

Rebecca hadn't thought to bring the letter with her. "There's nothing in it pertinent to his confession," she said.

"I'm the only one who can say what's pertinent to the case," Detective Williams shot back.

Rebecca wondered why people assumed they could push her around and she would accede. Was it her limp? Did they really think she was weaker because one leg was slightly shorter than the other? Didn't they know that a limp could make a person stronger than steel? Or maybe Detective Williams saw this as a black-Jewish thing. Rebecca had enough stress in her life right now without taking the cover off that particular basket.

"Detective Williams, it is not your authority that is at issue here. It's mine. I am an ordained rabbi. I am under no obligation to show you his letter or even his confession. In his letter to me, he gave me the option of handing over his letter but explicitly expressed the hope that I would not do so and thus protect his reputation. I decided to violate his confidence and give his confession to you. If his confession leaves something unanswered, then perhaps that would be the time to discuss the contents of his letter to me."

The detective stared at her angrily and Rebecca looked back, then sensing she shouldn't get into a staring contest with a police detective, regardless of gender or race, she averted her eyes and that seemed to break the tension.

"Weren't you curious to read his confession?" Detective Williams asked.

Rebecca shook her head. "Not in the least. In his letter to me he admitted killing Allison. I didn't need to know the details. And his confession wasn't addressed to me personally. It wasn't mine to read."

Detective Williams nodded. "If I need to see the other letter, can I reach you at home?"

"It's the Sabbath, but I'll leave my phone on."

It was only ten when Rebecca returned to her house. There was still time to daven the Shabbat morning service. She went in the front room where her siddur and tallit were and as she always did, looked at the Torah scroll and the box, except the box was gone! The box with God's autobiography. It was gone!

"So, *nu?*" came a familiar voice.

"Devorah? The box! The one you brought. It's gone!"

"I know. He said I should come and get it back. Not Him Him, but Hymie Brown. I'm beginning to wonder if maybe Hymie Brown is really Him. He sure seems to know what Him wants. I asked Hymie if he was Him but he said he wasn't."

"Did Hymie say why God wanted it back?"

"He said God wanted to write the next chapter."

Rebecca couldn't help wondering if it was another chapter for her to read or a chapter about her for someone else to read—if he or she dared. "I see," she said aloud, disappointment in her voice.

"I came to tell you good-bye," Devorah went on.

"Good-bye? Where're you going?" Rebecca wanted to know.

"Nowhere. Hymie Brown told me I can stop going back and forth between there and here. I couldn't believe it when he told me, so, to be sure, I said, 'Does that also mean I don't have to go back to that place anymore?' He wanted to know what place, and then he remembered. 'Oh, *that* place. No. You don't have to go there anymore either.' It's a good thing. I had just about run out of tears. So, I came to say thank you for saying Kaddish with us and for being our rabbi."

"You mean you don't need me anymore?" Rebecca asked, wistfully.

"One of us is going to be our rabbi now. He doesn't have a name, or if he does, I don't know what it is. I like him because he doesn't let you fool yourself. Everybody calls him Rosh Yeshiva."

Rebecca gulped but didn't say anything more.

"I might get in trouble for telling you this, but I thought you'd want to know."

"Tell me what?"

"That girl? The one who got killed?"

"Allison! What about her?"

"She won't have anything to do with him."

"With who?"

"The one who killed her. Who else?"

"What do you mean?"

"He came and wanted to see her but she doesn't want to be with him. Anyway, she has the spirit of her baby that wasn't born to take care of. Don't tell anybody I told you."

Rebecca almost laughed, wondering whom she could tell.

"Oh, yes. Hymie Brown told me to tell you not to worry about what to say tomorrow. He said it's all taken care of."

"I beg your pardon?"

But Devorah was gone.

Rebecca went over to the table and touched the spot where the box had been. She wondered why God had taken it. However, on reflection, she understood that the box wasn't hers. And yet, God's autobiography was hers because she was part of it—a page, a paragraph, a sentence, maybe just a word or a syllable or even the space between two words. God's story of His infinity was comprised of everyone's autobiography. God's well-being is dependent on the stories we create with our lives, she thought. But who was willing to consciously assume such a responsibility?

She thought Rebbe Nachman had done so during the last year of his life when he lived next to the cemetery and prayed for the souls of the dead and Rebecca thought about how close she felt to William Fein who had built her house, to Devorah, the Jews of Czechowa, how much she had enjoyed walking through the cemetery with her former congregants and listening to them talk about their dead, and how much more comfortable she had felt officiating at funerals and yizkor services than weddings. She wondered if she had failed as a rabbi because her true congregation was comprised of the dead and the grieving. With the dead everything was elevated to essence. To touch the souls of the living one all too often had to fight through defenses, wade through neuroses, fears as strong as vines choking a tree, and pride swarming like hornets. But in death the soul sparkled like wildflowers in a meadow of tall grasses. She loved the dead in ways she could never imagine loving the living. Was she going to end up like Devorah, weeping at the funerals of strangers?

Would that be so bad?

It was early evening when the phone rang. It was Detective Williams.

"I hope I didn't spoil your Sabbath. I tried to wait until after sundown to call you."

"That was very thoughtful. Thank you."

"I won't be needing your letter. The girl's computer was where he said it would be. I've read enough of the e-mails and they certainly prove he was obsessed with that girl, insanely so, I would say. It's very sad, because I also found on her computer e-mails between her and someone named Evan. Patric Marsh destroyed more than one life when he killed that girl. He destroyed a marriage of souls between two young people. Anyway, thank you for your cooperation, Rabbi. My apologies for throwing my weight around this morning. And my condolences. This all must be very difficult."

"It is," Rebecca said simply.

That Sunday morning Rebecca got to the auditorium before anyone arrived and sat in the front row as she had before the memorial service for Allison. She still did not know what she was going to say but she paid no attention to the thoughts and images going through her mind and let them pass like schools of fish being pushed by an unseen but cold current until finally when no more words and images floated past a verse from Psalm 97, part of the Kabbalat Shabbat section of the Shabbat evening liturgy, came to her, not in an image but in a voice, a man's voice that was as light as new love and wise as death: *Ohavei Adonai. Sinu ra.* Love God. Hate evil. Rebecca smiled and said silently, *Toda raba, Hymie Brown. Shalom.*

Toda, Rivka. Shalom, he answered and she heard him smile.

President Woodley had sent out an e-mail saying there would be a collegewide convocation at which he would give them news regarding the death of Allison Manchester. A notice like that was guaranteed to fill the auditorium and at five minutes to eleven, there wasn't an empty seat anywhere. People were standing at the back of the auditorium and along the sides.

Promptly at eleven Maurice Woodley walked out from behind the stage and stood in the pool of light made by a single spot on the lectern as the house lights were lowered.

"This is the second time in the past month we have had to grieve one of our own. It is unusual for a college to lose two of its members in so short a period of time and in such tragic ways. If there was anyone on campus who was a star, it was Professor Marsh. He had been here since the beginning, participating in those early conversations with me and others about what kind of a college we would have if we could start from nothing. But Patric realized immediately that we were not talking about an institution as much as we were talking about a vision of what a human being could be. He said he could only be part of an institution that dedicated itself to the creativity and spirituality that lay at the nexus of the soul. And certainly he had the ability to bring that creativity and spirituality out in almost every student and person he encountered, whether in the classroom or his books and lectures."

Woodley paused and Rebecca noticed that he opened his mouth and then closed it again and she knew the moment of truth had arrived.

"And that makes it difficult to understand what I am about to tell you. Yesterday morning information came into my hands regarding the unfortunate death of Allison Manchester." The silence in the auditorium seemed to become deeper.

"That information was turned over to the Boston police who last night confirmed what I still find hard to believe. Rather than have you see it on the evening news or read about it over the Internet, you deserve to know first.

"Among Professor Marsh's papers was found a document. In that document he confessed to having been involved in an intimate relationship with Allison Manchester."

There was a moment of stunned silence before the auditorium burst into a cacophony of excited conversation, gasps, exclamations of "Oh my God!" and "Holy shit!" The noise continued until slowly people realized that Woodley had not moved and was, in fact, waiting for them to once again be quiet.

"It was a relationship Allison Manchester did not seek or encourage. But Professor Marsh was obsessed with her. Unfortunately, he was able to keep his obsession hidden, because if I had known I would have dismissed him. If I had been able to do that, Allison Manchester might be alive today. But I did not know. The evidence is clear that Allison broke off the relationship with Professor Marsh and entered a relationship with a fellow student, someone whom she loved deeply. However, Professor March continued to stalk her." Woodley stopped and nervously licked at his lips. He took a deep breath, and with a tremor in his voice, said quietly, "Finally, he murdered her."

The noise in the auditorium was almost overwhelming as people shrieked, burst into loud sobbing, and everyone talked at once as if needing to confirm what they had just heard by having it repeated by someone else. Woodley did not try to restore order but waited patiently as people absorbed the shock and then, after a few minutes, quieted and he continued.

"In the document Patric Marsh left, he also confessed that his accident was an act of suicide which he contrived to make look like an accident."

Once again the auditorium was filled with the sounds of people shocked to the core of their beings.

Fearful he might lose control of the audience, Woodley continued speaking in a louder and more commanding voice and the audience quieted immediately. "I share your shock and consternation. I do not know what happened that made Patric Marsh feel there was no other resolution than murder and suicide. Like you, I will struggle for quite some time, maybe the rest of my life, to make sense of all this. As the initial step in that endeavor I have asked Rabbi Nachman if she would speak to us and help us as she so ably did when we gathered to memorialize Allison Manchester. Rabbi?"

The auditorium was quiet, almost deathly quiet, as Rebecca got up from her seat at the end of the first row and limped across the stage to the lectern. She looked out into the blackness of the darkened room, a spotlight on her. "Please turn up the house lights."

There was a long pause while someone was found who knew which switch to pull but everyone remained almost perfectly quiet and when the house lights came up, Rebecca sensed an almost audible sigh from the audience.

"Patric was my friend," she began quietly. "When I came here five years ago, he was the first person to invite me to his home. I was surprised he had taken the time to get a copy of and read the senior thesis I'd done at Columbia, as well as my rabbinical school thesis.

"Patric was my friend and he has not stopped being my friend. I hope you will let him remain yours. It would be easy for me to stand here and utter words of condemnation for what he did. But this is not a television talk show where hapless people are seated on a stage for an audience to ridicule. It is always easy to feel self-righteous at someone else's expense.

"Our task is a complex one. We knew Patric as a warm, friendly, outgoing, and, above all, loving person. He cared about his students; he cared about his friends; he cared about the world. And don't let anything you might read or hear about him rob you of knowing that you mattered to him.

"Yet he murdered a beautiful and vibrant young woman. Why? Maybe the answer lies buried somewhere in his childhood, but no. Many people have had traumatic childhoods, and I daresay most of us in this auditorium come from dysfunctional families. I know I do." There was the warm sound of soft laughter. "As a therapist I'm sure I could come up with a psychological explanation as to what prevented Patric from controlling his passion (and I think it was his passion for everything that made us love him so), but whatever reason I could give you would be wrong if it diminished your shock, your horror and your anger at the fact that he killed Allison Manchester.

"Patric Marsh was able to articulate a vision of what it means to be human but he was unable to live it. He was not as good as his words. None of us are. But most of us manage to live in a way that our words and our deeds remain in closer contact than they did with Patric.

"So what do we do? How do we reconcile the man we knew and

loved with the man who murdered? What are we to think of this man who managed to captivate our hearts and, by his action, break them, too? If we are to be honest with ourselves—and if we are not honest with ourselves we cannot be honest with anyone—then we must learn to live with our love for him as well as our outrage at his betrayal of us, his ideals and his presumption that Allison Manchester's life was his to do with as he pleased.

"There is a line in a psalm from the Sabbath evening liturgy which says: Love God. Hate evil. The first is dependent on the latter. And the latter is dependent on the first. I know many would disagree and say that love is the answer to everything, even hatred. Only if we understand that our love of Patric does not exonerate him, that our love of Patric also includes our fierce hatred of his evil action.

"I cannot forgive Patric for what he did. In Judaism, only the person wronged can offer forgiveness to the person who committed the wrong. Even though I am deeply hurt by what Patric did, Allison Manchester was the person wronged. Only she can forgive him and she is dead.

"So I will not presume to forgive him in her stead. No. My task is far more difficult. I will remember all the wonderful times we had together; I will remember his warmth, his love, his caring, and I will be grateful that I had the opportunity to know him. And I grieve with deep sorrow and abiding anger for Allison Manchester who was murdered by a man none of us knew as well as we thought we did."

Rebecca turned and limped slowly off the stage and back to her seat. There was no applause and she did not want it. She did not even care if they liked what she had said because she had been talking as much to herself as them. She had resumed her seat at the end of the first row when it became apparent that President Woodley was not going to return to the podium and nothing else was planned. Slowly, people began leaving, the noise level rising.

Rebecca remained where she was. She didn't want to see anyone. The students especially would feel that they had to say something to her, like "Great speech, Rabbi," and "Cool talk you gave," as if everyone needed to have their egos stroked. She didn't. At least not about what she had just said.

Maurice Woodley walked from behind the stage and down the steps to where she was sitting.

"May I sit for a moment?" he asked, politely.

"Of course."

"There's something I've been thinking about since the memorial service for Allison Manchester. This campus needs some kind of formal religious life. Nothing sectarian, of course, but lectures, discussions, films that address the eternal questions and would present students with a variety of ways to think about those questions. And with the death of Patric, we will need to fill a faculty position and we are desperately in need of someone to offer a course on Judaism. I know someone eager to endow a chair in Jewish studies and I think that same person would be interested in funding a position for a campus director of religious affairs. Would you consider taking on such a position and teaching a course on Judaism?"

"I beg your pardon?" Rebecca managed to stammer.

"Don't say anything now. Will you think about it? And, of course, your salary would be adjusted accordingly. Whatever you need, it's yours. This morning I think you found a way to help our students retain their idealism at a moment when their sense of betrayal would have made them lose it forever." Woodley got up. "Will you consider it?"

Rebecca nodded. "Yes. Yes, I will."

Woodley left her alone and Rebecca waited until she thought the auditorium had emptied, but when she got up to leave she saw Evan Green waiting in the back.

"I'm glad to see you," she greeted him after she'd made her way to where he stood. "I didn't get a chance to thank you for all you did last week and for the prayer service. Your father would be proud of you."

Evan managed a smile. "I was surprised I had so much of him in me."

"How are you?"

He shrugged. "I don't know how to answer that, especially after this morning. I had no idea it was Professor Marsh she was seeing. I'm going to call her parents and tell them, if the Boston police haven't told them already. I wouldn't want them to hear about it on the news tonight or see it in the *Times* tomorrow."

"The Boston police agreed to hold off saying anything until we'd had a chance to tell the campus community. You're in touch with Allison's parents?"

He nodded. "After Allison was murdered and the news came out about her being pregnant, I didn't want them wondering who would have been the father of their grandchild or about Allison's morals or anything like that, so I went to New York and just showed up at their apartment one evening. It was important that they know how much I loved their daughter." He smiled. "Maybe America is changing. They didn't blink an eye when I walked in. Allison had told them about me, about us. You know what's really interesting?"

"What's that?"

"My mother sent them a letter after Allison died. They told me. My mother didn't. But she sent them a letter saying she regretted never having met Allison but saying what a fine person she must have been if she had captured the heart of her son. Over Christmas my parents are coming up from D.C. to meet her parents."

Tears came into Rebecca's eyes. "Evan, that's wonderful."

"I don't know if any of this would have happened if not for you."

"I beg your pardon?"

"I can't explain it. I don't know if it's the things you say or maybe it's just you. Like today. You condemned what Professor Marsh did but you didn't take him away from us. Loving someone and condemning them at the same time isn't easy but that's the only way sometimes. I've been thinking about what you told me about my wound, that it wouldn't ever go away. And I understand a little now why that's so. The wound is my love for Allison and it was that which led me to go knock on her parents' door. So I just want to thank you for all you've given me."

Rebecca didn't think she had given him anything but that wasn't important. He believed she had and she was gracious enough to receive the respect, admiration and affection he was offering her. "You're welcome, Evan."

They were silent for a moment, then Rebecca asked, "So, are you going to follow in your father's footsteps?"

"I think so, but in my own way. I've been thinking that I might want to teach religion. I'm not sure I'm cut out for a congregation. I want to be able to question the Holy Trinity, for example, and not have people get upset with me. I'm applying to University of Chicago School of Religion, Harvard Divinity, and some others. We'll see what happens."

"If you need any recommendations, I'd be proud to write them for you."

"Thank you so much, Rabbi. I'll take you up on that."

"Please stay in touch, Evan. Things are going to be changing around here. Next year at this time the campus may have a director of religious life. Who knows? About the time you graduate from divinity school I might need an assistant."

SIXTEEN

꙳

The next morning Rebecca called President Woodley and told him she accepted his offer but she wanted to have the spring semester to prepare her class for the fall and to visit other campuses and learn how they carried out their religious life programs. She added that she would like to take Evan Green with her on those trips, his schedule and studies permitting. Woodley's only response was to say he would instruct his secretary to give her a college credit card and to tell her her salary would be doubled immediately.

When Rebecca told Brian, her boss at Psych Services of Woodley's offer and her acceptance, tears came to his eyes. "This is what I should be doing, Brian. I'm a rabbi, a spiritual teacher. It just never occurred to me that my congregation would be filled with non-Jews." And dead ones, she added silently.

"I can't pretend to understand. All I know is that I'll miss knowing you're down the hall." And he turned away so she wouldn't see the tears in his eyes.

It took Rebecca the rest of the week to get her files in order for whomever Brian was going to hire to take her place, and to clean out her office. There were three other matters she had to take care of as she began her life anew as part of God's autobiography.

She called Saul and invited him for coffee that Saturday evening after Shabbat ended. When he arrived, Rebecca noticed he was carrying what looked to be a large sketch pad under his arm.

They sat at the table in the middle room where she served coffee and sponge cake.

"So how are you?" Saul wanted to know. "It has been quite a semester for you."

He doesn't know the half of it, she thought. "I think I'm all right," she responded. "I'm a little tired, physically and spiritually, but it's all right. And I never thanked you for your help."

He shrugged. "I didn't do anything. But if it helped, then you're welcome."

"It did. I think if Patric hadn't written me, I still would have alerted Detective Williams to Allison's computer files."

"So that's how the college found out. Patric Marsh wrote a letter to you?"

"No one's supposed to know."

"You're the one who broke the case wide open but Woodley gets up and takes all the credit?"

"That's not how it was," Rebecca protested. "I insisted that he take the credit. I didn't want the publicity, the attention, and I think his taking the credit is what got him and the college that laudatory editorial in the *Times*."

Saul nodded, though reluctantly. "I suppose you're right. Still, I would have liked to have seen you get some recognition."

"My ego doesn't need that kind of recognition."

Saul chuckled. "You sound like you've become a Buddhist or something. Whoever heard of a rabbi without an ego?"

Rebecca laughed.

Saul reached down beside his chair and got the sketch pad he'd brought with him. "I wanted to show you something," he said softly. He opened the pad to another drawing of Reb Yitzchak. In this one the eyes were even more maniacal in their intensity than in the drawing she'd seen over the computer in Saul's office. These eyes reminded her of the tone of Patric's letter.

Saul told her the story about the little boy who apprenticed himself to the sofer, of the ten years of Sunday mornings, of one particular Sunday morning when he presented Reb Yitzchak with a drawing he had done of the one room in which Reb Yitzchak lived, a drawing Saul had worked on all week, proud that he could remember and visualize every inch of the room, could see the angles at which books leaned against each other on the shelves, could see the exact spacing between the bars on the basement window, could see the dust on the radiator cover. How incredible that he could see things in his mind as if looking at a photograph but Reb Yitzchak had quoted the Holy Torah about not making images, screamed, yelled, struck Saul once, twice, three times across the cheeks and then taken his hands and beat them with a ruler and ripped the drawing and set it afire in the kitchen sink. Saul had been a chubby kid of seventeen when that happened and then the next year brought the body protruding from the oven.

"I put away the nuts from which I made ink, the feathers, and the razor blades, everything I'd used in learning to write the words of the Torah. Even worse, I put away myself."

Rebecca looked into Saul's face and saw a serenity she had never seen there, and then she looked back at his portrait of Reb Yitzchak and she heard the echoes from Patric's letter and she knew the demon which had swallowed them both was emptiness, that void in which they had searched in vain for God, never realizing that God was the void seeking to know Itself, the void that was defined in relationship with a human soul.

"What do you mean when you say you put away yourself?" She asked gently.

Saul looked at her sadly. "I mean I squandered the twenty-three years of my life from then until January of this year." Then he smiled and looked at his portrait of Reb Yitzchak. "He was meant to be an artist. That was why he got so angry at me for my drawing of his apartment. And I was too young or too afraid to realize that God resided in my soul's love. And so I ate to fill the emptiness within. For twenty-three years I ate—until last New Year's Day."

"At Patric's?"

"At Patric's." Saul sighed. "I was so ashamed of myself."

"For what? I was glad you were there and proud of you for taking the pressure off me and the way you quoted Talmud."

"I'm glad if that's what you remember."

"Have I forgotten something?"

"I ate the quail. Patric made a point of using my eating the quail to chastise you for not eating it. He held me up as an example of a 'modern Jew,' someone who would not let ancient practices take precedence over pleasure in food and drink."

Rebecca chuckled. "Saul, I have no recollection of that," and she didn't.

"I'm glad but it wouldn't matter if you did. As I drove away from there that night I made a vow that no one would ever use me to shame my heritage."

The next morning he had awakened with an image of the *aron hakodesh*—the ark which housed the Torah scrolls—and in that haze between being asleep and awake, that haze before the tyranny of reason resumed its despotic throne, there came an instant of intuitive understanding which Saul believed came from God and his life was clarified and transformed: He, Saul Greenberg, was an *aron hakodesh*, a place in which the word of God lived. He had gotten up and gone to the fitness center in the basement of the college gym, and had continued to do so five days a week, twice a day, ever since.

They sat in silence for a long while. Rebecca resisted telling him how proud she was and saying all the other things she would have said as a therapist. Finally, she stood up, took his hands and gently pulled him up. Then she hugged him warmly and he returned the hug and in that embrace she could feel there was no longer neediness in him nor even desire for what would not be between them, which meant a relationship was now possible.

"I have something for you," Rebecca said softly. She stepped out of his arms. "It's the reason I asked you to come over." She led him into the front room where the Torah scroll rested on the table. "Do you remember the Torah you wanted me to get from the repository in England?"

"It came?" he asked, incredulous.

"This fall. I was thinking about sending it back, but I want you to have it."

"I couldn't accept this," he protested.

"Why not? You were trained as a sofer and I don't know if this scroll is kosher. You could at least look at it and see what needs to be done and if it's just a matter of redrawing some of the letters, well, you could do that, couldn't you?"

Saul undressed the scroll and stared at it. "I don't know what to say," he finally whispered. "Do you think it would be all right to restore it? I mean, this is a piece of history."

Rebecca smiled. "I think the Jews of Czechowa would be pleased to have their scroll restored."

"Perhaps you can find a place for it on campus now that you're going to be director of religious life."

"That's a wonderful idea, Saul. Thank you."

A short while later, he left hugging the Torah scroll to him like the child he would never have.

Rebecca was surprised at how sorry she was not to have the scroll resting at the center of the table any longer. She couldn't justify keeping it, especially after she'd heard Saul's story but she would eventually have it back. Maybe she'd ask Saul to design an *aron hakodesh* for it and she'd get one of those Jewish craftsmen to stop making wooden spoons and cutting boards to sell at shops in Stowe and have him make the ark Saul designed.

She looked through some magazines and catalogs she kept in a large basket in the front room and found the one in which she'd seen an ad for fashionable orthopedic shoes. She would stop at the store in New York on her way back. Then she picked up the phone and made her plane reservation.

Three days later Rebecca was getting into a taxi in Kraków, Poland. She had been surprised how easy it had been to make arrangements to go to Auschwitz. One phone call and twenty minutes later she had a plane ticket from New York to Warsaw, Warsaw to Kraków, where the taxi driver's expression did not change when she said wanted to go to Oswiecim, as it was known to the Poles. It shouldn't be so easy, she thought.

But it was and now she sat in the backseat of the taxi speeding down a road that paralleled railroad tracks. Were those the same tracks that had held the train which had carried her parents? She wished they were there to tell her if she was seeing what they had seen fifty years ago but they probably had not seen anything from inside the cattle cars. They wouldn't have known if the farmhouses and churches had been there then. She could have asked the taxi driver but she didn't want to know the answer, didn't want to know that there were people living in those houses and praying in those churches who had heard the cattle cars going by filled with Jews, didn't want to know if those people had smelled the stench and thought it was cattle being transported or smelled the stench and known it was Jews. She didn't even want to know what her driver had known and not known, though he did not look old enough to have been alive then. But looking at the Polish countryside shrouded in the black soot rising from chimneys, she didn't think the landscape had changed from what it had been fifty years before and she wondered how anyone could live there with the memories that weighted the air.

When the driver stopped in front of a building, she knew this was not where she needed to be. There were two camps—Auschwitz and Birkenau—Auschwitz I and Auschwitz II. The buildings of Auschwitz I were now a museum that housed exhibits, rooms, each filled with shoes, hair, eyeglasses, luggage. It was here, too, that a gas chamber and crematorium had been reconstructed after the war. "The other one," she told the driver in Polish.

Without a word he exited and continued up the road a short way and stopped before a wall and a large, arched opening through which there were railroad tracks. She paid him.

"You want I should wait?" he asked in English.

"I may be here a long time."

"I wait."

243

It was a cold, gray day and she was the only one there. The moment she walked through the arched gateway the evil was so palpable that she stumbled. She had never thought of evil as having muscles and fists but it did. At least here.

To her right was the tower from which the guards had surveyed the camp. She made her way up the steps and looked out. All the buildings had been torn down after the war by Poles who used the wood to heat their homes. To her right were a few buildings that had been reconstructed to give a semblance of what the camp had looked like. Elsewhere what remained were the foundations where buildings had been. She had studied maps of Auschwitz many times and she could pick out where the women's camp had been, the men's, the gypsys', and that strange area called "Canada," where the possessions of prisoners were sorted.

She walked down from the tower and along the railroad tracks until she came to the place where the trains must have stopped and Mengele decided in less time than it took for the heart to beat who would live and who would die with a wave of his hand to the right or the left. She tried to imagine what it must have been like—the sounds of the train, how the doors of the cattle cars sounded as they were slid open, the noise and confusion as Jews leaped and were pulled from the cars, and Mengele gesturing which way they were to go. She had read the books and seen the films but now that she was here the physical reality of what had been escaped her. Now, it was quiet, almost peaceful. The stillness of a cemetery pervaded everything except for a man coming through the entranceway on a bicycle. He paid her no attention but she watched as he cycled slowly past and exited at the far end as if he came this way every day which, it occurred to her, he did. He was going to work. For some, Auschwitz was nothing more than a shortcut.

She walked slowly along the tracks to the far end of the camp where she found the remains of a crematorium. Huge slabs of stone lay atop each other like ossified bodies and beneath them, still visible, were the steps that had led down to the gas chamber. Atop the ruin of stones a sign in Polish, English, French, German, and Russian read: IT IS DANGEROUS TO WALK ON THE RUINS.

Rebecca sat down on a slab and tears rushed into her eyes. They were not only for the Jews who had died in this place where evil still had power but also for the young Germans who had died in the snows of Russia and whose blood was now a part of the soil of almost every European country where they had sought to make their story the one story for all people, and she cried for all those including Patric who had believed their blood was redder than someone else's and she cried for all the dead understanding that she Rebecca who was Rivka was now chosen to be the one to love God and hate evil and mourn for all those who had not done either. But unlike Devorah who could only weep, Rebecca would also teach the young to mourn and to weep and through her tears she saw a figure walking down the railroad tracks. As he got closer she saw that it was Him in his black uniform and pants with death-sharp creases. The swastikas on his jacket burned crimson like a dying sun. He walked over to her, sat down and lay His head in her lap. As she slowly stroked His hair, He began to cry. His tears glistened like jewels.

ACKNOWLEDGMENTS

In the mid-1980s I was a member of the Religion Committee of the Jewish Community of Amherst, Massachusetts. One evening at a meeting Mrs. Sarah Berger, then president of the congregation, announced that the Holocaust Torah scroll had arrived and that it was lying on the bed in her guest room where she had wrapped it in a blanket. Immediately I wondered: did the spirits of the Jews of that synagogue come to be with their Torah? Thus this novel was born.

I am indebted to my friend, Rabbi Philip Graubart, for his reading of an early draft. I am especially indebted to Michael Denneny for his extraordinarily careful reading of the last three drafts and for his many helpful suggestions. My wife, Milan, is the first person to read my manuscripts. She read and commented on more drafts of this one than she probably cares to remember. I was often exasperated by her fierce attention to details. Most of all, though, I am grateful for all she gives me, even when I am exasperated.

READING GROUP GUIDE

1. What importance does Rebecca's crippled leg have in her life? Why does she choose not to conceal her limp? How does she come to terms with her situation and why?

2. Rebecca decries accusations of vanity: "She took the time to take what God had given her and transform it into a vessel of beauty. Was that any different than taking wheat and transforming it into flour and the flour into challah braided like the hair of the Sabbath Queen?" (page 26). How does Rebecca's care for herself—a quality easily perceived as vanity—juxtapose with her religious inclinations? What other internal struggles does she face?

3. The narrator tells us, "In Judaism the object of learning was not to build a better mouse-trap but to ask a better question. The questions you asked indicated just how closely you were attending to Him" (page 31). What does Rebecca's relationship with her teacher, the Rosh Yeshiva of her old congregation, reveal about the nature of Judaism?

4. Is the old woman who speaks to Rebecca an actual spirit, or a figment of Rebecca's imagination? The novel implies that there are realities beyond our five senses that are just as real. What do you think?

5. The novel presents a God who is neither omnipotent nor omniscient. How do you feel about such a God? If such a God came to you and asked for your help, as He does of Rebecca, what would be your response?

6. Rebecca wonders why God came to visit her and then thinks, "Maybe women preferred the truth, regardless of the consequences" (page 170). Do you think this is true? Why do you think God came to visit a woman?

7. Rebecca realizes that "goodness, unlike evil, has to be struggled for repeatedly" (page 219). When God argues against turning over Patric's confession to the police, is he acting out of evilness? Does he have a point? What do you think of Rebecca's response?

8. Many would call parts of the novel, or the novel as a whole, religious blasphemy. On the other hand, others might call it a deeply religious and devotedly Jewish attempt to explore God. How does Lester challenge religious convention in both small details and with broader themes? How do you feel about the risks he takes with his literal portrayal of God?

For more reading group suggestions visit
www.stmartins.com/smp/rgg.html